# SUCH GOOD FRIENDS

# SUCH GOOD FRIENDS

*Lois Gould*

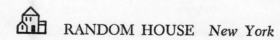

RANDOM HOUSE   *New York*

*For Bobby*

Well, I have lost you, and I lost you fairly,
In my own way and with my full consent.
Say what you will, kings in a tumbrel rarely
Went to their deaths more proud than this one went.
Some nights of apprehension and hot weeping
I will confess; but that's permitted me;
Day dried my eyes; I was not one for keeping
Rubbed in a cage a wing that would be free.
If I had loved you less or played you slyly
I might have held you for a summer more,
But at the cost of words I value highly,
And no such summer as the one before.
Should I outlive this anguish—and men do—
I shall have only good to say of you.

*Fatal Interview* XLVII
Edna St. Vincent Millay

# SUCH GOOD FRIENDS

There were two waiting rooms for the visitors, so at least we weren't cluttering up their nice clean corridor outside the Intensive Care Unit. Bad enough that we brought in barbecued spareribs and stayed there eating and talking and oh God laughing from eight every morning until the last shift of night nurses came rustling in at eleven. As if we were stuck at some disaster of a surprise party waiting for the birthday boy to show up and say *Gee*.

The desperately ill patients behind the swinging double doors could be seen only by appointment, like newborns in the maternity ward, every hour on the half-hour. On the first afternoon of Richard's coma, Danny Mack got past the nurses at two-fifteen by impersonating a doctor. All he did was clip four ballpoint pens on his vest pocket and march in looking preoccupied. ("Did he really? That's hilarious, Julie—you've got to write this whole thing down to tell Richard.") After the first day, though, nobody went in to look at Richard except me.

And nobody ever mentioned what we were waiting for. Just for it to be over, was all. Just for him to see what a fuss we were making, and to be kidded about it, and to laugh too. Meanwhile, there we were, surrounded by strange gray-faced clumps of old people in bulky coats who kept shuffling awkwardly around us, me and my cute friends in their pants suits. The old men were careful not to make noise with their *Daily News,* and the old ladies just sat wadding their Kleenexes (Kleen*ices,* Richard would say) into ever smaller, grubbier balls. All of them knew, by instinct or experience, that waiting in there was different, and I kept wanting them to stop looking at me as if I belonged. The family of/Richard Messinger/thanks you for/your kind expression.

The Intensive Care Unit at Mount Carmel Hospital had fifteen beds. Patients were frequently wheeled in straight from operating or recovery rooms, having developed "complications." Sometimes they improved and then were wheeled triumphantly out to a convalescent ward or private room. Others, like Richard, were bundled hastily out of their rooms at odd hours of the night, due to a seizure, heart attack, fire, earthquake or other act of God for which the company assumes no liability. In the morning their nexts of kin were notified and their rumpled beds made up for new patients. Someone repacked their suitcases and tucked them away in a locked storage closet. In Intensive Care, nobody would be needing his toilet kit, fresh pajamas, new porno paperbacks or dry-roasted mixed nuts for guests. Richard never went anywhere overnight without a small bottle of Kaopectate and two boxes of Mallomars. Mount Carmel dutifully locked these up among his effects; somehow it was nice to know they were waiting too.

If someone died while being Intensively Cared for, he automatically set off a siren that screamed all over the building. The system was attached to each bed and wired ingeniously to the patient's vital organs, so that he had absolutely no way of dying peacefully in his sleep. All departures were piercingly announced in the lobby, elevators, ladies' rooms, staff cafeteria and gift shoppe. Every doctor in the house came for the send-off. One squeak of that signal and they were hurtling through the halls like a pack of dissident white mice taking over Pavlov's maze. And then, from behind the swinging doors, you could hear this anvil chorus of bare fists thwacking on a bare chest. Whoever it was wasn't dead until the fists stopped.

Finally the old relatives in the waiting room would sigh and fold up their papers. They never left anything to remember them by; they emptied the ashtrays, stuffed the fruit and candy into their pocketbooks, took all the get-well cards and picked over the flowers for six carnations that might last another day with fresh water. At the door, one or two would stop and glance back uncomfortably, trying to decide whether to say anything to me. (Well, uh, nice meeting you.)

The larger waiting room had three Naugahyde sofas and four armchairs, light tan or dark brown, neat, sturdy and basically uncomfy. The nurses in Intensive Care were the same, as if somebody went around freshening their smiles with a damp sponge too. A special bunch, those ladies, with special advanced training in button pushing. Doctors trusted them to make *decisions*, even. And discreet? Just try asking if Uncle Ben is better today. His condition is *satisfactory*. You're calling from Detroit, long distance? It's your sister? Her condition is *satisfactory*. Nobody feels good, bad, better, worse. Intensive Care has no critical list, because everyone in there is satisfactory unless you hear the siren to the contrary.

For comfort, try the stack of thoughtfully provided Mount Carmel spiritual paperbooks. Yes, God is definitely alive, though not at all well, in the Intensive Care waiting room. Just riffle through *Heaven's Healthy Climate*, fix you right up. Or how about *Tell HIM Where It Hurts*. Miss M. Detweiler, the nurse who first ushered me in there, allowed herself a creased eyebrow of disapproval when I murmured "Oh God," and turned on her chunky rubber heel. But I hadn't really offended her; she came right back to water the gladioli. There must have been fifty dollars' worth of funeral-parlor pink arrangements there, all standing around dying horribly in cut-plastic vases. Why is it that everybody sends "glads" to the dead or dying? And had Miss M. Detweiler done all she could to save them? Not bloody likely.

I decided to try the smaller waiting room, from which you could watch the swinging doors and doctors going in and out on their errands of mercy. The doors had small glass portholes set so close together that they looked slightly cross-eyed. I could just see the foot of Richard's bed, the small white peak of his neatly covered, motionless toes. They had a swell word for his condition: decerebrate. What they didn't have was an explanation. "De/ce/re/brate: away from, out of, below or under the state in which one experiences brain action." Anyway, a coma. They'd had to cup his hands gracefully around two fat rolls of cotton, they said, to keep them from turning into rigid, grotesque claws. A classic symptom of decerebration, you know. When I first arrived at the hospital, a nurse presented me with Richard's wedding band (*14K, J to R, For Keeps*, thirty cents per block letter, thirty-five for script). She was sorry, she explained; Mr. Messinger's fingers were swollen from his condition. "Oh, that's perfectly okay," I replied inanely. I wanted *her* to feel better. "He

really hates wearing it . . ." (Listen to me, will you just?)
"I mean . . ."

"You may see him now if you wish," said the nurse, kindly
ignoring my apologies. And then she unveiled him.

Tubes had been attached to every one of his orifices, including three new ones they'd found it necessary to drill for
him since he'd started decerebrating. The night nurse
thought he was sleeping too deeply; she had called his
name, clapped her hands in his ear, shook him, then pushed
the appropriate panic buttons. Now Miss B. Wachtel pulled
the sheet down gently to check Richard's attachments. I
stared, horrified, fascinated, at the delicate hollow plastic
ribbon fitted to his penis. "That's a catheter to draw urine,"
Miss B. W. said, watching me. I squirmed. Richard's voice
echoed somewhere in my head: "I'm sorry we don't screw
more often." "*You're* sorry," my voice echoed back. I couldn't
see anything but his immobile, catheterized prick. We'd said
our last sorrys-about-that two months ago, the last time we
had made love. He had whispered it hoarsely into the back of
my hair as he pulled me down off the bed onto my knees,
like a child reciting prayers. Now you lay me down to sleep.
"Face down. There, like that. But lean up on your elbows a
little. Yeah. Now . . . ahh. Ahhh."

Or maybe it was three months ago. I'd lost track again.
Never mind; it hadn't set any records. Richard had been
"Christ, I'm tired" for over a year now. Or sometimes "No,
not really sick, just feeling like shit . . . I don't *know* why."
Occasionally there was all this goddamn *work* to do. "*Your*
goddamn bright idea I should spend my nights illustrating
a fucking children's book. I'm the only art director in New
York who has to break his balls free-lancing to pay the rent

—pardon me, *main*tenance. You wanted a co-op? You gotta co-op. I got *Melancholy Melinda and the Magic Melon Patch*, pictures by Richard Messinger. So why don't you just mosey on to bed, okay?"

Melinda had picked her last melon and gone to press finally, but I was still moseying on to bed. Okay. After that he was tense and restless: "Going out to get some air . . . No, don't wait up; you know you'll fall asleep with all the lights and Johnny Carson on."

The third time out he'd confessed that the air he needed was the kind supplied by Bessie's, one of those grubby Third Avenue bars that had become so stylish that Bessie, a twittery old auntie-hippie, whose sandals gave her bunions and who couldn't keep a drink order straight, but who shared her best pot with her worst customers, had no qualms about charging $3.75 for a burger with seven French fries. Bessie's was always packed at midnight with Christ-I'm-tired young East Side husbands who needed someplace to go to avoid screwing their wives. I used to wonder whether they ever admitted it to each other, or to little old Bessie when she took them outside for walks, one or two at a time, to turn on between drinks. Bessie took eight or ten pot breaks a night, each time with different customers, thereby guaranteeing that nobody ever went home as stoned as she was.

Richard was probably the only swinger in the place whose wife didn't really blame him for being there. I blamed myself—and that was dandy with him.

"It's a bitch," he'd sigh in his nicest monotone, "but I guess you've emasculated me somehow." And I'd lie there next to him, tears sliding sideways into my hair until he felt the wetness and lost his temper, because what the hell was *I* crying about. It usually happened after I'd tried touching him gently, quietly, dutifully trying to make his body respond in spite of him. He'd keep shielding his face with *The New Yorker* and say, "Please, Julie, don't. It's . . . it makes me uncomfortable. I *know* you're not being aggressive, but that's the way you come on. I can't . . . I don't want . . . oh Christ, you act soft and tender, and I *feel* you acting. It turns me off, you know?"

Finally I'd be able to move my hand away, hating it for being where it was, and lift my head off his chest, cringing back to my side of the bed. Then I'd wait for the inevitable aching sensation to start on the insides of my wrists. Hurt and need and helplessness. Ugly. Oh God, I must be so ugly. And then he'd slam the magazine on his night table and say, "I wish—aw, Christ, maybe I need a psychiatrist—maybe it's my fault, maybe *I'm* the one who's sick." Then he'd sigh heavily, turn off his light, turn his back to me and pretend to sleep. Or pretend not to—I never really knew.

Though I never saw it that way, it was the most beautiful solution a man could devise for keeping a fuckless marriage intact, and an unfucked wife in line. *I* was the failure. Hopelessly unfuckable. After what I'd *already* done to Richard, I couldn't even console myself by getting a lover or a divorce, now could I? So the bastard had it made.

I took up overeating, masturbation, Dexamyl, charging things at Bloomingdale's and reading textbooks on abnormal psychology. I trained myself to climb into bed with Krafft-Ebing and a whole Sara Lee fudge ripple pound cake, and I'd rip through both until I'd worked up a nice sado-masochistic fantasy, then go to work with my fingers. After a few months I'd learned to do it even with Richard lying there next to me. I was positive he never knew. Even if he did, somehow it would be less humiliating than the alternative —thrusting myself at him again, buying see-through night-gowns, stroking his body instead of mine, and trying, *trying* to understand why nothing I did produced any more reaction than that catheter they'd put on him this morning.

The nurse pulled the sheet back up and smoothed it tenderly across Richard's naked shoulders. Dignity restored. Freshly shaved, too. They'd even combed his hair the way he liked it, carefully covering the painfully thin spot on the crown and slanting slightly down across his noble but increasingly high brow. He looked like Gulliver lying there—imprisoned and asleep, strong and in-nocent; surely he could beat the pants off the rotten little creatures who'd trussed him up like that. If only he'd get up.

Ten minutes later I had settled myself uncomfortably in the little waiting room. What a shame a nice kid like you has to wind up in a place like this. It was pretty cramped, and the couch was only a two-seater, but at least in here the furniture didn't look embalmed. No pamphlets, no suffering gladioli, and from the narrow window I could just see the western rim of Stuyvesant Park. The muggers were probably all up and counting their receipts by now. It was, for no good reason, a beautiful June morning.

Focusing intently on the flaky yellow ceiling, I tried imagin-ing what Joseph E. Levine, for instance, would say if one of his highly paid Mannys actually ripped this scene out of his typewriter. Lessee now, we got Warren Beatty in this coma and Faye Dunaway out there in the waiting room. *Waiting room?* You *kidding?* No, there just isn't any market for your classic hospital drama any more. Well, sure, maybe on the TV, *if* you gotta good solid background of dirty teen-age hippies doing it to black chicks in the subplot. Otherwise, no. As for me, faithful Julie Messinger with those nice little up-turned tits, what a case of spectacular miscasting. I mean, I wasn't *ready* for a character part. Twisting a hanky in a plastic waiting room, waiting for Lefty, Godot, Godard in his wisdom . . . or Richard the Lying Heart. The celebrated de-cerebrate. I don't even *have* a hanky, and how do you twist Lady Scott facial tissue? See, I argued with the ceiling, the walls, the Formica, they'd hate it at the Fine Arts. You couldn't even sneak it in on a double bill at your RKO show-case theaters. Please, wake him up and get me out of here.

The radiator knocked softly behind me, and I said Gee, *thanks,* Mr. Mankiewicz. There's *nothing* to be scared of, right? Right. It's only a movie. A *story.* And if it has to be a hospital thing, then at least they'll toss in one of those Listerine-flavored young residents. Maybe even Sidney Poitier, to make it relevant. Any minute now his size-thirteen Hush Puppies will come stomping down the corridor, and there'll be a worried father figure panting behind him (Herschel Bernardi?) pleading, "Jim, don't be a fool! You can't use that stuff—it's still *experimental!*" But then my husband will wake up and mumble coherently, "No, not . . . Where am I? Uh, Julie, I . . . dream . . ." And then Herschel will crinkle his wise-ass old eyes and say, "Well, I'll be."

My *husband* will wake up . . . Christ, I thought, Richard

absolutely will not believe this. He'll swear I'm putting him on. And Danny Mack will bring in pictures of Elizabeth Taylor's tracheotomy scar, to see whose is kissier. And Timmy Spector, boy M.D., will pour himself a stiff one from the Chivas Regal bottle (because it really bugs Richard to see anybody swilling his Chivas Regal), and say, "Who the hell do you think saved your *life*, Messinger? And how about my reward, you sonofabitch?" Then Timmy leans over, watching me, and slides his hand meaningfully down my pink satin bell-bottoms. How about it? And both he and Richard laugh like hell.

It was Timmy Spector who had called me from the hospital at five-forty that morning, Wednesday, June 12, two days after Richard's operation. Timmy had sounded just about normal for him—one part sex, two parts gin, a dash of bitters. Anguished *tsooris*, Richard would have said. I wondered sleepily what Timmy was doing with his hands. "Hi, pussycat," he said. "I, uh, called to tell you Richard isn't responding too well. We've just had him moved over to Intensive Care—I mean, he won't be in his room."

"Mmm?" I offered. It was absolutely all I could manage.

"The, uh, nurse-patient ratio in Intensive Care is much better," he rattled on. "We'll be able to keep an eye on him and . . ."

I tuned out then, glanced at the clock and felt annoyed

as hell when I made out the blurry numbers. I was trying to think of something devastating to say about the AMA, or Medicare, or Timmy's wife's flat chest, when suddenly Timmy's voice changed. It was cold sober and scared. "I guess you better get up here as soon as you can, Julie," he said. Click.

"Shit," I muttered. "Who asked *you* to keep an eye on him?" Timmy wasn't even involved in Richard's operation. What was he messing in it now for? Would we have to pay him a damn consulting fee? That's crazy! Allergists don't get to consult about cutting moles off people, do they? Timmy was supposed to stick to the *in*ternal verities.

But he was on staff there, and he was a personal friend of Richard's—personal enough for each to wonder what kind of a lay the other's wife really was; friend enough not to have checked it out. Actually, Richard had said he couldn't possibly make it with Marian Spector: "No boobs, no soul," he said. Besides, I was positive she was one of those lifelong virgin brides. Once we'd gone to a French movie with them and she'd asked Richard what "bugger" meant.

Timmy and I had barely touched tongues either, but that was different. In moments of extreme marital discomfort, I'd been consoling myself for months now with interesting mental flash cards of Timmy raping me while Richard kibitzed; Timmy and Richard going sharesies: first one at a time, then together—front and back, top and bottom, any port in a storm. Neither ever bothered taking the cigarette out of his mouth or getting undressed. My favorite touch was Timmy making me go down on him while he phoned his wife to tell her we were coming for dinner.

Then there was the other fantasy: Richard playing tour

guide, with me as the scenic wonder. Timmy took the tour stretched out, with his shoes planted firmly on our offwhite bedspread (my mother would have died) and his head propped against Richard's contour backrest (last year's anniversary present from my sister). I had to stand at the foot of the bed while Richard rolled my clothes up or down to show Timmy points of special or historic interest. "Now *here* . . ." (unzipping my skirt just enough to rest it on my little round hipbones) "we have a rather nice belly, curved but controllable, considering she's had two kids and only does five minutes of isometrics a day."

Next, gathering my sweater up to my chest and telling me to hold it there, he'd run a finger (sometimes a pencil) lightly around each breast, then give the nipples a playful flick. "These, of course, are really superb, don't you think? More apple than pear, but that's a matter of taste . . ."

By now Timmy's eyes would be glittering, his breath coming faster, and he'd have a visible hard-on under his best Meledandri plaid slacks. Nevertheless, he'd go on lying there with his bony ankles crossed, mumbling "Mmm, yes" as if he were struggling to pay polite attention.

Finally Richard would make me sit on the crushed-velvet swivel chair in front of my magnifying make-up mirror, while he took off my clothes and started the chair swiveling. While I spun around, applying eyeliner and Blush-On, he'd wind up the two-dollar tour: ". . . thighs are still pretty firm, good for another couple of years at least. Wish her ass weren't so low-slung, though. Starts curving out too late, like an afterthought. And I really can't stand the freckles." Then he'd yawn, stop the chair, stroke my crotch absently, the way you pat the hood of your car, and nod to Timmy. "Ready as she'll ever be," he'd say, settling back in his Barca-Lounger and picking up *The New Yorker* so he'd have something to read in the dull parts.

"Oh come on, will you?" he'd say irritably after a minute or two. "You can't keep rubbing her goddamn tits all night. I know she likes it . . . You kidding, it's the *only* thing she likes, but whose party *is* this? I mean, it's my house. And you can get your goddamn finger out of her snatch, too, for Chrissake. Can't you just get in and fuck her? *Now* what? Oh, you're *not* gonna start moving the damn make-up mirrors. So it's funny! Who the hell cares about that? You wanna make *her* come? You're kidding—why? Five little quivers and she zonks out for the weekend, believe me. Besides, she'd rather do it herself when you're through. I've been there, Spector, I've *seen* her. She gets herself there and back in three minutes flat, nonstop. It's not the clitoris at all, you know. Most overrated sensation since Doris Day, the well-tempered clitoris. You oughta see her at it sometime, it's fantastic. She used to lock herself in the john, took in *The Times* Drama Section so I'd think she was just in for a crap, the stupid cunt. I actually watched through the keyhole one time, and there she was on the *floor*, rubbing it and *talking* to herself. Actual *dialogue*, like for three or four different movie characters. And whango, it was all over like a blackout skit on *Laugh-In*. I tell you, they know exactly when to quit rubbing, but they'll never tell you. She wouldn't anyway—she'd rather have you go on until you hurt her, so then she can hate your clumsy ignorant selfish guts . . ."

It was heaps of fun, really. I liked the talking parts almost as much as the action. In fact, it was my only real hobby, the only thing I really *made* time to do nearly every day in my busy life. Still, at the age of thirty-one it didn't seem quite enough. But Richard wasn't suffering any, and Timmy and a couple of our other best friends were having fun waiting for me to move on to something a little more advanced. That was some comfort, anyway. I don't know what everyone else's wife did. Marian Spector, we all figured, knew that Timmy indulged in outside activities, and didn't want to make something of it. After all, he never gave her a hard time about her charge accounts, he gave her fun furs for Christmas, took her to Puerto Rico and Nassau, and so far hadn't embarrassed her by screwing people she had lunch with—at least to her knowledge.

Timmy and Richard had lunch a lot too, usually on Saturdays, and this spring they'd taken up squash together at some midtown armory. It was one of these sweaty Saturdays that Timmy noticed the small bumpy mole on Richard's right arm. "Oughta get that thing taken off," Timmy had said. "Simple thing—send you over to Mahler at my hospital. Gideon's a good man. Probably do it for you right in his office, take half an hour." Richard, terrified hypochondriac that he was, couldn't bring himself to call Mahler for a week, and couldn't sleep until he did.

Of course it turned out to be something that couldn't be done in Gideon Mahler's office. Speedy arrangements were made at Mount Carmel instead, for what Mahler called the "minor surgical procedure" to take care of it. And Richard immediately called all our friends to tell them what he was leaving them in his will. His wire brushes, the only instrument he played despite years of longing to be a jazz drummer; his dirty paperbacks, which included all of Henry Miller's *Tropic* books, lovingly smuggled in when it really meant something to smuggle in Henry Miller's *Tropic* books; a set of nude photos of his cousin Margot, who had disgraced the family by posing for *Saga* magazine with bare breasts and a skirt so micro that she'd have to shave down there to pose the way they wanted. She was the only relative of whom Richard was truly proud, but they'd lost touch.

Everyone Richard called had something side-splitting to say about his impending ordeal. Laurie Jonas said wasn't it lucky Mount Carmel wasn't a Catholic hospital, because if it were they'd have to kill him to save the mole. Marcy Berns promised to eat only hard-boiled eggs until Richard got out of the hospital. And Timmy offered to brief the entire nursing staff so Richard wouldn't have to ring for it.

Still, Timmy had definitely not been in charge of Richard's mole; Mahler was. So there was no logic about Timmy's telling me—or not telling me—what the hell had happened to my husband since yesterday, when they'd wheeled him, whimpering and throwing up, but mole-free, out of the operating room.

As it turned out, Timmy himself didn't know what had happened. Nor did Mahler, or any other doctor in the house. One neurologist had seen him and said he undoubtedly had a brain tumor, but that was only old Harvey Wiseman, and nobody paid attention to anything *he* said. All anyone knew for sure was that at about five A.M. Richard B. Messinger, aged thirty-four if you asked him (thirty-nine if it was for an official document where they could charge you with fraud), had silently floated from his normal postoperative sleep into a perilous state of semi-death from which he could not be roused. His brain, or whatever part of it he needed in order to function as Richard B. Messinger, simply was not working. And God only knew if it would ever work again.

Mole removal qualified as minor surgery, they'd told me, because no vital organs were involved. Richard's immediate postoperative period had begun undramatically. He had emerged from the waiting room in what the nurses, as usual, called a satisfactory condition ("Only a flesh wound, sir"), except for a violently queasy stomach, excruciating pain in his poor arm and the fact that the mole had turned out to be malignant.

Funny thing about that. The cancer was the only part of the whole improbable disaster that Richard had seen coming. "Big C," he'd kept saying cheerfully all during the week between his first appointment with Mahler and the day he checked into Mount Carmel. "Always knew it would be Big C for me, kid; no heart attacks in bed for old Richie." "Oh, for Chrissake," I had finally screamed at him over my paper, refusing even to stop reading to reassure him one more time. Richard laughed his fake laugh and didn't bring it up again, but that was the night he went out for air as soon as we finished dinner and didn't get back until four-thirty A.M., very stoned. I stirred when he sank into bed still wearing his shirt, underwear and socks, and he muttered, "Drunka bum, s'all I'd ever be anyway," in his best Jason Robards voice.

We'd been going through the Big C routine for as long as I'd known him—eight years last November—and I'd always thought it was a pretty funny bit. Messinger's Message. His living faith rested firmly on the notion that something terrible was just about to happen. Squinting into the sun, he would sorrowfully predict violent rainstorms for tomorrow.

Yet when the next dawn broke, all warm and pink and beautiful, it somehow never pleased him to have been wrong.

Now it was the following Wednesday and he was right after all.

At six-thirty A.M., fifty minutes after Timmy Spector's mystifying call, my taxi coughed asthmatically down to the imposing entrance of Mount Carmel, a magnificently hideous Turkish-turreted edifice best known for its mosaic lobby murals and excellent plastic-surgery department. Even my Aunt Helena, who never descended to the lower regions of Manhattan except to consult divorce lawyers, had gone there for her chin-lift last winter. I felt clammy, goose-fleshy and much too tired, and I hadn't even had the foresight to take an extra Dexamyl spansule. "Ah, don't worry," I whispered into my collar, and hugged myself for emphasis. "You're beginning to turn into Richard." After all, Dr. Mahler—whose face looked exactly like Spencer Tracy halfway between Jekyll and Hyde—had assured me that Richard's mole was a very *young* lesion, that Richard *couldn't* have been wiser to take care of it so *promptly* and that there were absolutely *no* indications of cancer cells anywhere else so far as we can *tell*. Even the scar could be expected to heal beautifully in less than a month, so Richard could go back to the office, start work on his new children's book (*Robin's Rusty Robot*) and be hitting tennis balls in Westhampton before Labor Day.

There were, I knew, a few unpleasant beans Dr. Mahler

hadn't gotten around to spilling yet. Such as precisely how a malignant mole on the arm changed the statistical picture for Richard's living to an overripe old age. But I didn't really want him to go into that (and didn't he just know it). This way I could tell myself it was only a story, about happy people with happy problems, and Richard the Rainmaker would have *his* answer too ("Big C, always knew it would be . . .").

Timmy Spector was waiting for me at the top of the stairs. As the cab pulled up, I watched him take what should have been the last possible drag on his cigarette stub, and knew that he'd take at least three more before parting with it. He looked so illogically handsome with his illogically stiff white coat flapping starchily in the breeze. In real life I never had much of a thing for doctors—only tried one once, and hated it. What was his name, Lars? Well, something Scandinavian. A Swedish meatball, with long hay-colored hair, murderous gray eyes and one of those ripply hard bodies with thigh muscles like underground cables. But he talked medical jargon in bed. Kept saying it excited him to have me palpate his abdomen. *Pal*pate. After him I swore off doctors; I mean, I hadn't even had a *checkup* in six years.

I caught Timmy's navy-blue eyes watching me appreciatively as I climbed out of the cab and up the steps toward him. What would he do if I just slipped a hand under that coat, palpated him a little and announced, "Okay, Timmy, she's as ready as she'll ever be"?

But he was already pulling me inside the door, talking fast about Richard's condition. We rode the elevator up to Four, where Richard's private room had been, but of course he wasn't there now. A quarter of a mile of corridor segregated the private patients' wing (*pavilion*, dummy) from the Intensive Care Unit, and Timmy's monologue—I swear it was all one sentence—lasted the whole trip. Muttering the same things he'd said on the phone, about the better nurse-patient ratio, and Richard not responding, and keeping an eye on him, and like that.

I don't know why I wasn't frightened then, except that I was still too sleepy to concentrate, and besides, the whole thing sounded too nutty to be believed. "How awful," I heard myself saying sympathetically. "God, how awful."

Even when I first saw Richard, with his eyes open and fastened on some other dreadful world, his body jerking in awkward rhythmless spasms, I couldn't make any sense out of it. "But that's not how Richard moves," I protested, like an indignant theater critic. I turned to Timmy as if for confirmation. "Even when he's sleeping he's sort of fluid—you know, as if he's tuned in to some kind of slow music." I turned back to the imposter on the bed. "Richard?" Suddenly I thought he might hurt himself jerking around like that—split his sutures or something. "His arm!" I gasped to the nurse (Miss L. Farnsworth) standing coolly at the foot of the cot. She was methodically attaching and detaching a Laocoon of transparent hoses leading to and from Richard's interior. "He can't feel pain, Mrs. Messinger," she intoned matter-of-factly, not looking up from her tubes.

"But what about the, ah, incision?" I persisted.

"That is the least of his worries now," Miss Farnsworth answered crisply, heaving her snowy bosom. An ominous softness had crept into her tone. "And also the least of yours."

Timmy had left the room. Miss Farnsworth hooked up her last hose and went on to another patient, thoughtfully closing the three thin white curtains that served as walls between the beds. Richard and I were alone. "Hey," I stage-whispered at him hoarsely. "They're *gone*. It's all over. You can get up now. Oh, Richard, please stop this shit, it's not funny."

I went on like that until I heard the metal curtain rings sliding behind me. Timmy was back and this time he'd brought along kindly, tortured Dr. Jekyll, doing business as Mahler the surgeon. He nodded at me, grimacing slightly, and marched over to the bed. "*Mr. Messinger!*" he shouted. I jumped. Richard went on staring at life on other planets. Timmy put his arm around me. "*Mr. Messinger!*" Mahler yelled again, even louder. Still no reply. I noticed something sharp and glittery in Mahler's hand. Jeezus, I thought, he's going to operate on him again right now, in front of me, without even washing his hands. No, it's all right, see, he hasn't got a mask on; they can't operate without a mask on, can they? I looked around helplessly. Nobody else seemed interested. Two nurses were writing busily at a desk in the corner, and on the other side of the curtain a woman was moaning softly about what they'd done to her.

Mahler grabbed Richard's left foot and began attacking it with the diabolical shiny instrument. Scrape, scrape. I tried to shut my eyes tight enough to hurt so that when I opened them it would be tomorrow and not raining. When I was five I had tried to hold my breath and count to a hundred without peeking or letting go so Shirley Temple would appear in my room. If she wasn't there when I exhaled, then I wouldn't believe in God or wishing any more, and I'd scream and scare everybody. She hadn't come either.

But now I couldn't even shut my eyes tight enough to stop seeing Mahler's weapon scraping the sole of Richard's foot. "Oh no," I said. "Richard hates to have people touch his feet. Really, he actually *gags*." But Mahler, the bastard, was scraping so hard now that I was sure he wanted to draw blood. He didn't but Richard's foot finally jerked away. "Well, that's something," Mahler said with his most chilling Hyde-like grimace, and shoved the foot-scraper into his breast pocket. He nodded again in my direction and sauntered out.

"Be right back," Timmy whispered, squeezing my arm and racing after him.

Okay, my turn again, I thought. I bent down, carefully avoiding the cat's cradle of plastic tubes, and put my lips against Richard's ear. "YOU SONOFABITCH!" I rasped, as loud as I dared. "DIRTY FUCKING BASTARD I WANT A DIVORCE!"

Nothing.

Suddenly I felt Miss Farnsworth rustling behind me. "We'll be doing some tests on Mr. Messinger now," she said with what I thought was unnecessary enthusiasm. "Miss Detweiler will show you the visitors' waiting rooms. Doctor will be back shortly."

I nodded and trotted obediently after Miss Detweiler, wondering just what "tests" meant, and whether they did them all the time with patients in comas. Then I thought: If Richard doesn't wake up, what'll I tell the children?

Children. It was the first time I'd even thought of Matthew and Nicky since six this morning, when I scrawled emergency instructions for the day to Darlene, the housekeeper. (Her black Muslim boy friend said it was degrading to be called a domestic, so Richard called her a wild.) Dear Dr. Bettelheim: What would you recommend in the way of explaining this to two small boys, six and five? Daddy's just out decerebrating, he'll be back soon. Oh God, I promised Nicky he could call Daddy in the hospital tonight and tell him about the model plane he wants. A Fokker. My God, what do I know about a Fokker? I smiled at that. Which reminds me, where the hell is Timmy? I forgot to ask him whether Richard could . . . I mean, if there's any chance he might wake up and be . . . a vegetable.

My throat was burning and I'd worked up an Excedrin headache. Lean back against the nice cool plastic. Nauga-hyde. Nauga-hyde and go-seek.

"Cuppa coffee?" It was Timmy. I nodded, and he propelled me through another set of endless tunnels to the cafeteria. Shoving our steamy wet trays along the counter, I blurted my question.

"Richard a vegetable? Wouldn't worry about that," Timmy said. "No permanent brain damage at all."

"How do you know?" I demanded, watching him carefully.

"Corneals. Hasn't lost his corneals."

"Oh. What does that mean?"

We were in front of the cashier; twelve cents for the two coffees, nine cents for Timmy's baked apple. Never could by-pass a baked apple, he said. Though once he'd taken a baked apple in here and it turned out to be some kind of lousy Danish pastry that looked like a baked apple.

We unloaded our trays at the only empty table and sat down, Timmy expertly mopping up shreds of lettuce and blobs of tomato with the last occupants' soggy napkins. "Corneals?" I prompted.

"Eye reflexes," Timmy murmured, anxiously probing with his fork into his baked apple. It squished back and he sighed happily. "Uh . . . ability to respond to light." Squish, squish.

I pictured Timmy dissecting his first frog in anatomy class.
Same smile. "See, Richard's corneals are weak," he was saying, "but they're definitely still there. Means his brain's not
permanently damaged, like I said. Christ, that's a great baked
apple . . ."

"Oh, screw your apple, Timmy," I snapped, suddenly hating him. "How come he's in a coma, then? Doesn't decerebrate mean something to do with the brain? Timmy?"

He was looking past me, toward the door, waving vigor-
ously. I wheeled around, furious now, expecting a forty-two-
inch bust somewhere in a white uniform. But it was Mahler,
exchanging knowledgeable scowls with a thin-haired, fat-
lipped man in a fuzzy tweed coat. If he was a doctor, the
tweed coat meant he was from some other hospital.

They finally spotted Timmy and began picking their way to
us through the crowded tables. It was only eight-fifteen A.M.,
but it looked like midnight at Sardi's, except for the costumes
and the food. Dozens of white-on-white girls, dainty gold
crosses swinging gaily across their cleavages, hunched over
slabs of gray roast beef and muddy gravy. Surgeons in jolly
green scrub uniforms worked silently over mounds of oily
franks and beans. Food that looked intestinal was very popular here, I noticed; they'd probably all left a similar mess on
what Timmy cutely called the cutting-room floor. Gallons of
poisonous-looking orange soda pop hissed and swirled in a
huge automatic vat—Mount Carmel's special at only three
cents a glass. And a mysterious sprinkling of solitary old
ladies in orthopedic shoes and lumpy black cardigans nursed
eleven cents' worth of tea and dry toast, moistened scrawny
forefingers and flipped pages of newspapers undoubtedly
fished out of subway garbage cans: I learned later that these

ladies were the cafeteria's most regulars. Long ago word had seeped out through the Lower East Side that for lonely women of advanced years and pinched food budgets, hospital tea, sipped very slowly, was better than anything the doctor ordered. At least it got you out of the house.

Mahler and friend had arrived safely, and Timmy was saying: "This is Dr. Bleiweiss, Julie; Ralph—Mrs. Messinger." We nodded. He had steel-rimmed glasses, but I was sure he'd been wearing them for years before the hippies declared them groovy. Timmy added: "We've, uh, asked Ralph to look in on Richard." I nodded again. Bleiweiss' fat pink mouth looked hermetically sealed; I imagined a hissing sound escaping, like a fart, every time he let go a word.

We all began scraping chairs around to make room; fumbling elaborately for ashtrays, matches, cigarettes; sniffing for clues to each other's species.

"Mrs. Messinger," Mahler began briskly, his voice about ten decibels too loud.

"Yes, Doctor?" I half-whispered back, having decided I'd better play the scene soft and vulnerable. Huge, melting Hershey's-kiss eyes, elbows teetering daintily on the damp table rim, hands clasped tremblingly under chin.

Mahler was thrown off guard at once. He had to clear his throat, back up and start all over, carefully stringing out every word to keep from forgetting it. "Mrs. Mess-in-ger, we be-lieve . . . that is, some of the tests have just come back . . . back from the lab, you understand . . . these . . . we have . . . it appears . . . the evidence seems . . ."

"Richard's tests?" I broke in encouragingly. The others stared at me; *nobody* rushes Dr. Mahler.

"The evidence," Mahler repeated, contorting his face fu-

riously to regain control, "seems to point to a massive insult
to your husband's liver." With the words "insult" and "liver,"
he seemed to have passed his own little crisis. His words
hurtled out now, and most of his face muscles relaxed into
their normal twitch, but his eyes kept moving to avoid mine.
They finally focused on the swirling orange-soda vat over my
left shoulder and stayed there till he finished. "We believe,"
he wound up forcefully—two black orderlies at the next table
abruptly stopped slurping to hear the verdict—"the coma is a
direct result of the liver having been almost totally destroyed."

It came at me too fast. Advantage Mahler. Game, set,
match, in fact. Liver? It made no sense at all. Bleiweiss,
Mahler, even Timmy, were nodding excitedly at each other,
like a bunch of Boy Scouts celebrating their first spark after
rubbing their silly twigs together. I swallowed hard—twice, in
case I was about to throw up my six cents' worth of coffee all
over Bleiweiss' fuzzy sleeve.

Nobody gave a damn about my reaction. Mahler was tipped
back in his chair now, as if delivering a brilliant biology lec-
ture to slow sophomores. His hands had locked expansively
over his perfectly fitted pin-stripe vest (probably to control
the mad-scientist impulse to rub them gleefully), and he was
pausing to inhale and exhale deeply between phrases (to keep
from cackling?). "The damage was caused (inhale) apparently
(exhale) by some powerful foreign substance (inhale) introduced in the bloodstream (exhale) within (inhale) we
estimate (exhale, inhale) the last seventy-two hours." He finished, exhaling sheer triumph. At that moment Gideon
Mahler was a blissfully happy man.

There was a minute of silence at our table while we all
absorbed the great man's teaching. I broke it clumsily, the

instant it dawned on me what he'd said. "That means something *you* gave him *here?* He's been *poisoned* in here?" A few
spoons clattered somewhere in the room, and two of the
Puerto Rican countermen glanced nervously at the soda machine. I stared at Mahler, Bleiweiss, and finally at Timmy,
expecting at least one of them to leap up and deny it. Nobody even blinked.

Finally, Mahler: "Not poisoned, madam." His tone was a
telephone recording, distant mechanized icicles dripping
thinly from each syllable. "Mr. Messinger apparently suffered
an unpredictable *allergic reaction* to some particular medication. We are checking now to determine what he received
that might produce such a reaction."

"You don't even *know* what you gave him?" I could hear
my voice out of control now. I might even have been screaming. All the forks and spoons around us had stopped dead;
only the orange pop went on gurgling. For the first time you
could hear all the action in the kitchen behind the Mosler-
safe metal doors. Mahler and Timmy glanced quickly at each
other—consulting silently about how to handle this new case:
hysterical female; pre-menopausal; predictably acute anxiety.
Then Mahler tilted his chair back farther; he seemed to be
turning the situation over to Timmy. It occurred to me that
they respected each other professionally; for some reason, it
was an astonishing notion. Nobody I knew respected Timmy
Spector; he was *fun.* Mahler had at least twenty years on him,
and for all his crazy face-twisting, he had the authoritative air
of a man who could double-park his MD-licensed car smack
in front of the Plaza; no cop would ever doubt that he was in
there saving somebody's life. Even in bed I was sure he'd

smell like a surgical supply room. Mrs. Mahler probably had
to boil her pubes before he'd touch them.

Timmy, on the other hand, seemed strictly and perennially
pre-med, in imminent danger of flunking his finals in any
course not taught by a woman. Nobody but Timmy Spector
would come to work at Mount Carmel dressed in a plum-
colored silk shirt and a four-inch-wide brocade tie. All the
other ambitious young men wore little-boy blue or charcoal
suits, skinny rep ties and nice white Perma-Press button-
downs, preferably with frayed cuffs. Yet it was clear that
Gideon Mahler thought enough of Dr. Spector to let him
take over, at least for now.

"We think, Julie," Timmy began, flushing slightly at saying
my first name, while we all shifted in our seats, ". . . that it
might have been the anesthetic."

I felt better instantly. The nausea was gone; all I had now
was a gloriously filling sensation of healthy rage. "Might
have been the anesthetic," I echoed. "Well, that's just
great. Here's this big hospital with turrets and elevators and
. . . soda machines, but somebody forgot to put in fresh
anesthetic? No, the drug company did it. They had a nifty
half-price sale on slightly irregulars. Why not—everybody loves
a bargain. Hell, we'll try the stuff once; anything happens, we
go back to the usual brand." Something hot splashed on my
arm, and I half-jumped out of my chair, thinking it was somebody's coffee. Then I realized I was crying. "Lousy bastards,"
I sobbed, somehow angrier at myself now than at them. I had
no idea why.

"Mrs. Messinger." It was the first time Bleiweiss had forced
open his mouth. Startled, I stopped crying at once and stared
at it. At first no sound came out, but his watery gray eyes

started blinking behind the steel-rims. Warming up his engine, the dirty little four-eyed coward. "I am a hepatologist," he answered stiffly, as if correcting me.

"Your mother must be *very* proud," I said.

He flinched as if I'd slapped him, then ventured again: ". . . specialize in diseases of the liver. Dr. Spector and I . . ." He glanced at him for moral support, but Timmy's attention had wandered again. This time, when I spotted the distraction, I couldn't blame him. An unimpeachable redhead, with sensational legs mounted on black suede stiletto-heeled pumps that hadn't been fashionable for five years; when you saw them on her, you couldn't imagine why not. I'd never thought anyone could move like a Gauguin Tahitian on heels like that. Her white coat flapped open in the approved casual style and her yellow sweater-dress flashed from under it like a blinking signal light at a dangerous intersection. It might have clung to her more insistently if she'd had it knitted right on her, but I doubt it.

I reached discreetly under the table for Timmy's inner thigh, and pinched it as hard as I dared. His knee hit the table, upsetting a few spoons and the salt shaker, but at least we had recaptured his attention.

Dr. Bleiweiss, his feelings hurt again by the disturbance, shifted uneasily, but his fat little mouth kept pushing little puffs of words out. "Dr. Spector and I work together on difficult liver cases. Quite often. This particular case. Your husband is the fourth of these. That is, I've seen four of these. In hospitals this year. New York hospitals. They were all, I may add, surgical patients." The lips popped shut, then sprang open again dramatically. "Patients," he resumed, "who had been given this same anesthetic. Unfortunately. Unfortunately"—he was now fully warmed up; his eyes behind the glasses were so bright they looked feverish, and I kept expecting the lenses to fog up with steam—"this substance is now the most widely used agent of its kind." There was a note of unmistakable contempt now in his soft Boston-accented voice. "Anesthesiologists," he went on, one lip trying vainly to form a pudgy curl, "seem hopelessly in love with the stuff."

It was a highly un-Bleiweissian phrase, and on the strength of it, I decided I liked him. How lonely it must be, I reflected, to be a liver man. All the world doesn't love a liver. I didn't suppose he'd appreciate that. Still, I wanted to help. "Can't you persuade them," I offered, "to give people some sort of allergy test—a liver-rating system? I mean, so they'd know when not to use this anesthetic?"

The feverish light in Bleiweiss' eyes went out at once; I'd said the wrong thing. "There are no allergy tests for the liver," he said dejectedly, "just as there is no cure for liver damage."

"Then what the hell does a liver man *do?*" I demanded. I didn't really mean to hurt him again, but I couldn't help it.

"He does—" the soft voice was barely audible now—"what he can." Bleiweiss paused, gathering his dignity. "The liver—the human liver—is one of the most complex and unappreciated organs of the body," he began, reciting it like the pledge of allegiance. "It is the *only* organ capable of regenerating. Of healing itself."

"In other words," I cut in, "what a liver man does—what you do—is *appreciate* a sick liver. And to think—" I turned to Mahler and Timmy—"I never believed specialization had gone so far."

Timmy was grinding his heel on my instep. "Cut it out," he muttered behind his raised coffee mug, then explained me to his buddies. "Mrs. Messinger doesn't realize, of course, that liver damage such as this occurs *very* rarely. That this anesthetic is used routinely, in hundreds of thousands of operations. Not just in New York but everywhere in the U.S., England, Europe. This sort of thing happens only once in, literally, ten thousand cases."

"Aw, just this once," I repeated, feeling the anger bubbling up again. I'd had enough of all of them. "I really don't give a damn about the odds, you see. The odds against something happening aren't terribly relevant when it *has* happened. Why the hell can't any of you shut up and do something about that? The point is, you gave Richard this poison crap that did something to his liver. What the hell are you doing to *fix* it? Have you even tried pumping it *out*? What does it say on the bottle? What did the salesman tell you to do when the odds don't pay off?"

"My dear lady," Dr. Mahler replied, trying to control his mounting irritation, "the liver is *destroyed*. There is nothing to do but wait for it to heal itself—to regenerate, as Dr. Bleiweiss here has just tried to explain to you. The liver cannot be hastened in this task. It is a natural, spontaneous process. All *we* can do is our best to sustain your husband's other life functions for as long as it takes."

"You're *all* going to stand around and appreciate his liver, is that it? Indefinitely? Nobody's going to do a single—"

"*Julie*," Timmy cut in forcefully. "We'll be doing our damnedest just to keep him *stable*. We'll be shooting him full of antibiotics; we have to protect him against infections. Comatose, he's a target for all sorts of things . . . We'll be giving him total care, total support. I don't think you realize what a dangerously helpless state he is in at this moment. His liver *will* come back; we *know* that. But it will take, uh, time. We can only guard him while he's, uh, down for the count. And you've simply got to understand that this involves our doing a *helluva lot*."

I didn't understand at all, but now at least I knew there was no point in flailing at them. Besides, I was too tired. "How long does . . . will a liver take to heal?" I begged them weakly.

Bleiweiss was polishing his lenses with a dirty Kleenex. "That," he puffed, "will depend on Mr. Messinger's resources. Condition . . . other factors . . . several days . . . a week . . . perhaps longer . . ."

"Please," I whispered. "Couldn't we get out of here now?"

"Of course, Mrs. Messinger," Mahler said, relieved. "There's just one thing we'd like *you* to do at this point . . ." I nodded, expecting a warning not to bother the nurses, or to be a good girl in the waiting room. "We'll be needing blood donors," Mahler said. "Quite a few. Can you start calling now?"

"For Richard? A transfusion?"

"Not exactly," Bleiweiss chimed in, intercepting Mahler's reply, which had started to be yes. "We're going to *exchange* his blood. All of it," Bleiweiss went on, bright-eyed again. "To help rid his system of toxic substances. Normally, this is one of the liver's many functions, you see, but now . . ."

"But now, I see," I agreed coldly. "I'll get some dimes and start calling."

What does Amy Vanderbilt say about asking all your friends over for a pint of blood? Or is it better to keep this kind of thing small and intimate, strictly family, and friends can drop by later. I stood in the narrow glass-walled phone booth fingering my roll of dimes wheedled from the cafeteria cashier, and began checking off relatives. How about Richard's square twin cousins? Lester and Luke Baden, was it—or Bader? Lester was a dentist in Roslyn, and Luke was in the blouse business. Never mind, there's no phone book and I can't start calling information. Uncle Eddie and Aunt Harriet? They always sent the kids turtleneck polo shirts for Christmas. They were usually two sizes off, but at least they came from Lord & Taylor, which meant $4.50 apiece, credited to my account, thank you. But what the hell was *their* number; they'd moved.

It was getting hot in the booth and I had to call somebody. They needed twelve pints of O-Positive blood by one o'clock. What about *my* family then? Not that Richard would want their lousy blood, but somehow it wouldn't look right. Cousin Bob and his wife, Edith, weren't so bad, except we'd owed them for dinner since November. Aunt Catherine? No blood there, nothing thicker than water anyway. My sister Nina—well, I'd better call her. Although she's probably got tired blood and I wouldn't count on her waking it up for my sake. Maybe Nina knows where Mother's staying in Nassau.

Oh God, what if Mother decides to fly back early and spend the weekend sitting around here with me? "Don't you think we'd better have a really good doctor look at Richard, Julie? I'm not sure this hospital is even the place for him now that this has happened. No, *not* just because it's inconvenient, although that *is* important, but it's not a first-class hospital, I don't think. Jessica Widener had her nose fixed here and they did some botch job. Julie darling, I don't really understand how you can come to the hospital looking like that. People are going to be coming to see you—by the way, I'm having a basket of fruit and nuts sent up to you from Schrafft's, you'll want to have something for people to nibble on, won't you, but couldn't you just go home and change out of that suit? Looks like it needs a good pressing—you really have no business wearing such a hot suit to sit around all day. And I wish you'd wear darker lipstick with your hair that way. Your mouth looks sick. Like a beatnik."

Yes, Mother. So I dropped my first dime in the slot and called Calvin Jaffe, Richard's best-hated friend. Richard believed passionately that it was not enough to succeed in life—all one's best friends had to fail. And Cal, the rat-fink, never failed at anything. (Well, marriage, but he'd even escaped that with only slight contusions about the head and shoulders. Two hundred dollars a month alimony and no issue of the union requiring child support or visitation.) At forty-three, his stomach lining and his sex life seemed decidedly more intact than Richard's. There was always a spectacular girl in residence at his Playboyesque penthouse. She was never older than twenty-three, and it never lasted less than one year or more than two. Cal patiently taught each one how to serve his needs gracefully and unobtrusively. If she did well in basic training, he'd give her a heart-shaped gold key to the place, monogramed, and introduced her to the night and day doormen and the super. She could always cook his favorite zucchini-and-sour-cream dish and change the water in the pool on the terrace, where he kept his boa constrictor.

The current lady of the house was Miranda Graham, a perspiring young actress whose biggest role so far was in a Strawbridge, Mass., summer playhouse revival of *Junior Miss*. She'd played Fuffy as a latent homosexual. Miranda was the first of Cal's girls to balk at moving the snake in from the terrace to the master bathtub, where he usually wintered. Maybe Cal dug her spunk for complaining, because the snake had stayed outside this year, and Miranda was still inside, with her star on the bathroom door. Actually she was a very quiet type, not actressy like a lot of her predecessors, and she was of good, if highly neurotic, stock. A family of brilliant nuts, all creative in one art or other. Grahams were always being mentioned in the *Times* and *Variety* and the admitting list at Payne Whitney, where they usually rested up between triumphs and relieved the kind of intense depression you get from success. Miranda couldn't afford Payne Whitney except to visit her relatives, and anyhow she was still mediocre in her field, which probably helped a lot.

So Miranda and Cal were one of our more interesting couples; Richard was comfortable hating (envying) him and I was uncomfortable liking (envying) her. Also, I thought Cal was sort of pathetic, *au fond.* I mean, I think he would gladly have chucked his footloose-photographer image for a nice middle-class-but-with-it home life—like he thought we had.

The phone rang twelve times in Cal's all-beige squashy-pillowed living room. I was about to hang up when he answered. "Hanh, whosizz?"

"Cal, it's Julie—Messinger," I said. "Sorry to wake you, but . . ." (Shit, shit, there's a trickle of perspiration running down my chest. God, how I hate that feeling. I pushed my blouse against it to blot it up, knowing I'd have to keep my jacket on all day now. Probably stain the armholes on the blouse *and* the jacket. Shit!) "Richard needs blood donors, he's in a coma, nobody knows really, but can you . . . ?" I trailed off lamely, choking over what seemed to be a cotton ball in my throat, and waited for him to frame his reply while I tucked the phone into my neck. This way I could hold my arms up inside the booth and let whatever air there was circulate.

"I'll be right there, babe," Cal said gently. "Miranda too. And whoever else I can round up."

"Thanks. Bring some dimes with you," I said sideways into the mouthpiece, and barely managed to hang up without dropping my change. The cotton ball in my throat was really hurting now. *There will be absolutely no crying during the first fifteen minutes,* I announced sternly. And positively no smoking in the outer labia. (My gynecologist always loved that—I used to say it when he ordered me up on the table for a pelvic. "Spread 'em," he'd say, the cutie.)

There, better? I picked up another dime. Ping. Now who? I started dialing the first number I could think of: Pamela Howell's. Of all people, I chided myself as it started ringing. "Hello?" said Pam's soft husky voice. "Hi, Pam, it's Julie— Messinger." (Faster, dummy.) "I haven't got time to—I'm calling to ask . . . I need . . . could you or Neil come up to, uh, donate blood? It's Richard, yes. Well, if you have O-Positive it's better, but they'll take it anyway and trade it in . . . Yeah, they're not fussy, heh heh . . . Soon as you can." I forced a wry smile, hoping it would do something for my voice, which was beginning to sound like the Tin Woodsman after a night in the rain.

"But my God, Julie, what actually happened?" Pam was exclaiming. I might have known. Shut my eyes and lean against the box, nice and cool on the forehead . . . "Can't really explain it now, he's in a coma and they have to take his blood all out and give him new ones, I mean a new supply.

Yes, all of it, twelve pints they said. Pam, listen, I'll talk to you later, I've got to make some more calls, okay?"

"Of course, poor love, I'll phone Neil right now. He's at work and we'll be up soonest. Sweetie, shall I call anybody? Laurie and Bob? Marcy? What about the Macks . . . Julie, are you all *right?*"

"Sure, Pam. I'm really fine. Really, yes, call them all, I'd appreciate that, and I'll see you up here later, bless you." Click.

Pamela Howell, née Grosbart, my only childhood friend, best known for tormenting me in the second grade by telling everybody I made a stink when Miss Shutkind was out of the room. "If you don't believe me," she whispered first to Todd Blumenthal and Nathan Colwin, "just go over to her desk and *smell.* Go *on.*" They did, too, followed by Didi Tarcher and Barbara Pincus and even Beth Mandel, who wore ugly orange socks, and if only I could have died right then when I really wanted to, with Pamela's musical gargle of a laugh cascading in my inner ear and hot tears of shame and hurt streaming down my nose. They actually lined up in front of my desk, sniffing and giggling and staggering around yelling "Pew-*yew*" until Miss Shutkind came back and broke it up. "What'd you do that for," I'd asked Pamela when we were walking home. "How should I know?" she snapped. I apologized.

What if I just don't call anybody else? What if nobody comes to give any blood? All our friends could be busy, couldn't they? And my family is away. They'd still have to treat him; you don't just let a guy die because his friends are busy.

Jesus, who would he call for me? Do me a favor and just

call total strangers if it's me. I don't want anybody I know watching me like that. God, imagine being on exhibit for days, a still life with all your superfluous hairs growing out.

So call strangers. Richard's boss, that's who. Barnaby Halstead, dynamic young editor of *Household Magazine*. That bastard can send out a memo and get the entire art and editorial staff up here to bleed a little for their brilliant art director and beloved co-worker. Great idea, Chief. I called Barnaby. "Of *course*, Julie, and *please* let me know if there's anything else, anything at *all*." Well, there is just this one little thing else, sir: you could come through with the raise you promised him last year, and get around to hiring at least one assistant art director to replace the two who quit, you cheap . . . "No, I can't think of anything now, thanks. Yes, I'll keep in constant touch, sure."

Now then, what about those nice Jewish fraternity brothers from Brown University he was so ashamed of? The one with the wife in red harlequin glasses, who planted a whole flower bed of tiny plastic orchids around her sunken bathtub on Long Island someplace. With white floors which she scrubbed every day ("I get right down there with the cleaning lady, on my knees, I work right along *with* her, otherwise you *never* get it the way you like.") Oh God, no, I don't need that now. Well, the other one then, the Sanitation man. Inspector Arnie Buchalter has a goldplated garbage can that says *Waste Not Want Not*. But he must be out picketing somewhere. And let's face it, Richard has not been a good frat bro these last eight years. The Arnies and Lennys and Marvs had belonged to a whole other Richard, the one from Brooklyn Heights, with a gold collar pin and tie-tack set, and I didn't even know him then, thank God.

I scooped up the dimes. Anyway, Cal is coming, and Miranda, and Pam is calling people, and the *Household* creeps, and that's enough, maybe. Jesus, I've got to get out of this isolation booth, I'm really sopping wet now, and damn it I'll *have* to keep this jacket on all day, I'm *stuck* to it. *Keeps underarms dry up to twenty-four hours,* bullshit.

I emerged dripping, like Florence Chadwick from the English Channel, damp-haired, goose-pimpled and miserably out of my element. Calvin Jaffe, dear blessed beautiful sweet friend in need, was steaming down the hall in his filthy trench coat. "God, am I glad to see you," I said, hurling myself into his arms and embarrassing both of us with the depth charge of genuine feeling. We were, after all, only distant close friends—you know, good for dinner parties and laughs. But for tears? I don't think we'd ever even been alone before, except that one evening when he got stuck with me at a restaurant because Richard was away on some magazine junket and Miranda, then fairly new in his life, had begged off to go seize a golden oppt'y, as they say in the *Times* Classified. Richard's trip was ten days in Antigua chaperoning a hippie photographer, his model girlfriend who turned on with Estée Lauder nailpolish fumes, and *Household Magazine's* strange female fashion editor, who had designs on either the photographer or the model. Cal and Miranda had cheerfully offered me a steak and some company, but then Miranda got a better offer—a big press reception for Joe Fox, the producer, who was about to make a musical out of a Mobil Travel Guide. Miranda felt she really ought to go and try out her new eyelashes, because you never know, you know. (They were no ordinary false lashes, see, they'd been implanted, hair by tiny hair, in the lids, and then laminated with a layer of some miracle glop called Fantlashtic. The whole thing took four hours and was supposed to last three years. I can still remember the ad that launched the process at an amazing introductory offer of $375. "Up *Your* Batting Average!" it said. Within two weeks five thousand New York women had been Fantlashtuck, and the FTC had issued a warning about granulated eyelids.) Anyway, Miranda and her lashes went to bat that night, and Calvin took me to one of those swinging gaslit places called February's or October's, and we talked about Miranda and Richard and Fantlashtic. And now here we were again, folks.

"I brought some dimes, like you said," Cal began lightly, pulling fistfuls of them out of his pocket. They were all rolled in neat little packages, wrapped in thick purple bank teller's paper and stamped *10 Dimes 10.* "Used to carry one of these as a concealed weapon," he said. "Wrap your fist around it; it works like brass knuckles. Makes you feel less vulnerable in the subway." I laughed; God, it was good to have him around. "Miranda's at an audition," he went on. We were still standing in the hall, reluctant to settle any place or stop talking. "She'll be up in about an hour. Want some coffee—you look like we could use it." The last thing I thought I wanted was more coffee, or another session in that cafeteria, but there I was, nodding gratefully again. I guess I wanted even less to stay where we were, and it was dawning on me that I didn't have any other choices any more.

We pushed a chair into the middle of the smaller waiting room, and propped a note on it: *I am in the cafeteria. Julie Messinger,* thereby staking my claim to the room of my choice, and also showing how grown-up and responsible I was in not leaving the area. There was something else too, a new feeling of prickly discomfort (fright? guilt?) that had something to do with being out of reach (out of control?). The telephone in the booth might ring—I'd given the number to everyone I'd called—Timmy or Mahler or Bleiweiss might want to tell me something . . . But the note would more or less cover me for everything except phone calls, and if I missed one of those, couldn't I just be in the john or inside checking on Richard?

Even so, this unscratchable itchiness went with me to the cafeteria, as it was to go home with me that night and every other night until . . . After a while I knew when it would hit me the worst: in the cab on the way home after fourteen or fifteen hours in the waiting room; at six in the morning, when I'd wake up after three hours of sleep covered with freezing sweat (Oh God, I've been out of reach, out of control for three *hours*), and I'd have to call Miss Farnsworth or Miss Detweiler or Miss Wachtel to make sure his condition was *satisfactory*; and then at eight or nine A.M. (two more hours out of reach; what if something happened while I was riding in the cab, oh, please . . .), when I finally scaled the great stone face of Mount Carmel to report for the next day's vigil.

It took about two days to develop my complete set of co-ordinated symptoms: the itch, the clinging clamminess, the rheumatoid ache from lying in bed fighting sleep. (When I was eight I'd tried to stay awake all night on New Year's Eve; my friend Betty Lou said you had to, or else something awful would happen to you when the old year died. That was why grownups stayed out and blew horns and played music —they were scared to fall asleep.)

And the nausea, the waves of sickness in the presence of hot or cooking food. Morning sickness: I never got it when I was pregnant, but maybe it had something to do with the life cycle, after all. I couldn't stand the smell of anything broiled or fried or baked or steamed or poached or roasted or stewed or boiled. Cold stuff was okay—cottage cheese or Apple Jacks or even raw hamburger. But I couldn't feed that to the kids at night, and I couldn't not go home to fix them supper, just as if nothing was wrong, because then they'd be abandoned by *both parents*, and it was bad enough this way. So I'd race home at six or six-thirty, steeling myself for the assault of bubbling lamb-chop grease and sodden broccoli mercifully sealed in a plastic pouch. I learned to take deep breaths, and it helped some not to sit down with them where I actually had to look at their plates, so after the first couple of days I served them at the far end of the kitchen, perched on stools, while I fled to a neutral corner and force-fed myself anything that seemed tasteless enough to go down without an argument. Queasy does it.

For some reason, the only place where food didn't sicken me was the hospital cafeteria, where it sickened everyone else. Not that I could eat it, but at least I could coexist with it there. Metabolically I suppose I felt more at home than at home.

At first it was even something like fun to entertain people there; in a way, it was my turf. Cal was really my first guest; I guided him expertly around the shimmering jello, cut in cubes like faceted rubies, and steered him away from the rockpile of almond Danish and the terrible oozing pies, like an old China hand leading a stranger through Hong Kong tourist traps.

"I hear great things about their baked apple," I said helpfully. "And Craig Claiborne gave the orange pop two stars. That Puerto Rican is a spy—Royal Crown Cola sent him to get the formula." Every time I said something that made Cal chuckle, I felt all warm and triumphant. (See, Mom, he likes being with me! I can *so* talk to boys.)

"Ah, here comes our little star herself," he interrupted as Miranda appeared, all flushed and tangle-haired, at the door. "You have no idea what's going *on* out there!" she announced over the din, not making a move to join us but waving an excited mixture of hello and come-quick. We both panicked, toppling over each other to get to the door, which panicked *her*. "Oh, hey," she gasped. "No, I didn't—it's just a huge mob of *people*. God, I didn't realize you'd think . . ."

"Jesus," Cal snapped at her, "you and your dramatic entrances."

Out in the hall there was, just as she said, a mob. Everyone I'd called, everyone *they'd* called; an instant chain-letter jackpot by the modern miracle of mass communication. Dozens, maybe hundreds, of excited or worried, love- or duty- or conscience-driven curious or morbid people, all of whom, incredibly, incredibly, wanted to give of their life's blood to Richard Messinger. They were jammed into the waiting rooms, lining the corridors, teetering on the radiators, and still coming; it was like Friday night outside the Cinema Rendezvous. What could possibly be playing? *Coma!* Starring Somebody You Really Know!

All day they kept arriving, a peaceful demonstration for human self-sacrifice. Cal and Miranda and I held hands a lot and sat in the little waiting room like a receiving line or a welcoming committee. Thanks so much for coming, the blood-letting takes place down the hall, that way, yes, we'll be here awhile, sure, come on back after, thanks, thanks.

And they *would* come back after, filled with the good feeling of having done something, *really* something, for a friend or a cousin or a frat bro or a co-worker. Blood is so much more than loyalty or kindness—and so much easier. God, what other gift takes so little time, thought and effort and yields such an immediate, huge reward? You can be God, the one-shot giver of life—who's to say it wasn't *your* pint that saved him? (Beautiful—that's probably how they handle the husbands whose wives get artificial insemination. Let him know they've mixed his useless sperm in with the donor's, and tell him how the other guy's stuff is just to *stimulate* his own—you know, all we do is give it the initial thrust, sir, and then *pow*, your stuff gets shot right up there, right where you want it, and the missus too, of course.)

Not that there weren't good friends in the crowd too—yes, lots of those came. Somehow, though, Cal and Miranda were the indispensables, the ones whose comings and goings had to match mine, or almost. They seemed to think so too. At first this puzzled me; then I thought I knew. It was because, unlike Laurie and Bob, Danny and Paula, Doug and Marcy, Neil and Pamela, all of whom were either mostly my friends or at least *ours*, Calvin and Miranda were mostly Richard's, and he would have *valued* their being there. At first I missed the people *I* valued most, because it was in my honor too, sort of. But for one reason or another, everyone who really mattered to *me* stayed away. Not out of touch; they called two or three times a day, and came at least once, usually just before dinner or just after. Laurie—at least I could have cried with Laurie once in a while, between the nervous laughs. I wouldn't have had to be so damn entertaining or felt this oppressive need to make it worth the trip downtown. It was a real strain the first couple of days, just introducing myself to Cal and Miranda as this terrific witty lovable girl; no wonder Richard married her; funny, we always thought she was so quiet and cold, but she's really great, and isn't it ironic how it takes something like this to really understand someone like that?

But of course Laurie couldn't possibly sign up for full-time duty. Ever since her baby was born, she'd been having her own crisis, one of those interesting psychic things with symptoms describable only as "very Laurie." Mostly she stayed in bed consuming incredible quantities of Coke, and got up only to decorate things with Con-Tact. First she covered the TV set (including the ventilation holes); then the typewriter (*very* significant—Laurie's own brand of writer's block); then the teeny round knobs on her dresser drawers, each with a teeny round paisley-patterned dot; then the backs of her hairbrushes, the refrigerator, the telephone dial . . . One morning word went around that she'd awakened in the night and spotted her husband's toenails sticking up out of the covers, gleaming nakedly in the dark and . . . Oh come on, she did *not*. Well, only because he woke up.

As for Marcy and Doug, they were just starting their trial separation that week. He'd spent three months secretly decorating his new bachelor apartment on East 64th (Marcy and the kids were on West 64th), and only two days before, he'd made the rounds of his own psychiatrist, hers, and each of their children's, to announce that he was moving so that everyone would be ready to handle it. Doug Berns was always thoughtful that way.

So for one reason or another we all took up our positions that first day and froze there, the three of us in the center, flanked by everyone else, as if for the fourth-grade class picture. (Thirty-six perfectly still, perfectly wet-combed children

smiling at the dead birdie in the black-robed box. Only I
didn't hear the man say, "Three!" "Julie Wallman *moved,*
Miss Green!" "Julie Wallman, step forward." Miss Green's
pronunciation of my name clinched my hatred for it from that
moment. "Dear Mrs. Wallman, I am sorry to report that Julie
was inattentive during the class photographing session, and
that her movement, for which she had no satisfactory explanation, made it necessary for the photographer to take *two*
portraits of the fourth grade instead of the usual *one.* Sincerely." Pamela said why didn't I just forge my mother's
signature, that's what she did about the torn library book *and*
about the Alice Faye joke—on their honeymoon Phil Harris
says, "Why, Alice, you're not a real blonde!" So I forged my
mother's signature and had nightmares until junior high, always waking up when they were pointing and shrieking,
"Julie Wallman *moved!*")

But I wasn't moving this time. Or ever, if only . . . Down
the hall they were bleeding for me, for my love. Murray Ar-
beit, a frat bro covered with chagrin for the years of silence
between him and Bro Richard, and now this for a reunion.
Could he possibly have been in Richard's class, this weary
gray man in dusty shoes who could only be that pale if he was
a Hasidic Jew or an accountant? "Oh, yes, Richard and I
were . . . you know, like *this.* Does Richard still keep up with
his jazz? God, we used to jam together. Christ, we even recorded a few—'Honeysuckle Rose,' never forget that. Well,
gotta get home to the family—Westbury, *Old* Westbury . . .
Well, Julie, I sincerely hope everything—" "Thank you—Murray, is it?—for coming, I know Richard will appreciate . . ."

And Cousin Sid, the ear-nose-throat man, whose mother
must have Long Island Railroaded him in all the way from

Cedarhurst. That was Aunt Addie for you. She believed in a real close-knit family, never mind the dropped stitches between weddings and Cousins Club meetings. Her Sidney was the only bona-fide M.D. Richard's clan had produced (on *either* side), but Aunt Addie wore her crown with as much modesty as possible, considering. I dimly recalled her at our wedding, telling everyone what a comfort she had always been to Richard's mother after his father passed on (he should rest in peace), and to Richard, after his mother passed on (she should rest in peace) while Richard was in the Army. Aunt Addie couldn't help being a comfort, she said; it was her nature.

Now God had called on her again. Fingering his blood-donor's cotton wad like a medal of family honor, Cousin Sid did as Aunt Addie told him: as a doctor and a relative, he had to "go take a look at Richard, at least *I'll* feel better." He cleared his ears, nose and throat with otolaryngological precision and plunged in, emerging a respectable two minutes later and nodding solemnly with what passed for professional approval. Aunt Addie emitted a deep sigh of relief on behalf of the entire family, and they left.

Timmy stuck his head in the door once and suggested that maybe I should put in a brief appearance at the actual blood bank, since now the throngs were trooping there directly, and not everyone knew I was granting audiences at the other end of the hall. I went, wondering whether to just stand at the door blowing kisses like the new toast of Broadway taking curtain calls, or to flutter my hand solemnly in the dignified circular salute that Queen Elizabeth gives her troops. Moving among them would look more sincere and personal, but what if I'm supposed to know their names?

In the end I just walked in and stood in a corner, blinking, for a long time, until a few, then a few more, spotted me and came over shyly. They looked at me with a creepy kind of awe that I didn't want to fathom. A few I recognized, and they waved and nodded, or said hello in normal voices. A young guy who worked with Richard at *Household Magazine* came over to tell me about this wild thing that happened in the cab coming up. "Like this whole bunch of us from the office crowded into this cab, and the driver didn't want to take us, and then we told him where we were going and like what for, and what a great guy Richard is and everything. And you know, he not only took us, he got out of the cab with us and came in to give blood too. But that's not all—when they stuck in the needle, he passed out on the table, and now they won't take his blood. The poor old guy's heartbroken."

The human-interest material in there was unbelievable— starting with just the size of the crowd. They were actually turning people away now—they couldn't handle any more— and some of those inside had been standing waiting for two hours. I started to shake some familiar hands, to hug or kiss a few old, just-about-lost friends. But that got too sad too quickly; we were better off not touching. A young man I'd never seen before pushed toward me. "Julie?" he said very softly. "I'm Will Humphries. I worked with Richard once. I wanted to say hello." I don't know whether it was his gentleness, or what he said, or just the fact that I didn't know him and never would, but Will Humphries being there was a true thing, and because it made so little and so much sense, I knew if I stood there another minute, I'd have not just brave-girl tears but retching, gut-hurting sobs. So I fled, covering my haste by waving—all desperate energy instead of dignity. Elizabeth II, I simply wasn't.

Timmy was waiting outside. He looked tired suddenly. "We've started the exchange," he said. I waited for more, but there wasn't any, and we walked back to the waiting room in silence. "It'll take some hours," he added finally. "You be here?" I nodded.

People were going home now. I wanted to be one of the visitors at the bus stop down there, or one of the blood donors for whom dinner and peace were waiting uptown. How wonderful it must be to have finished giving, to have proved that you cared, and now to have plans for tonight and lunch appointments tomorrow. Jesus, imagine not being terrified to leave this building!

"Hey, why don't you go home and see the kids?" Cal said. "We'll stand guard till you get back. By that time all kinds of people will be here, and then Miranda and I can take a break for dinner. How's that?" Bless them, I thought, again and again.

Home, kids, Mommy noises. "So if your tooth is loose don't chew on that side."

"But why can't I call Daddy after supper? You *promised!*"

"I know, Nicky, but Daddy can't . . . because he's still sleeping, that's why . . . No, I can't promise definitely tomorrow—we'll see . . . I said we'll see."

"Do we get a story? . . . But why do you have to go back to the hospital? You said Daddy's *sleeping*."

"I know, but I have to, that's all . . . I guess . . . Okay, *one* story, okay a medium-long one, but right now in *bed*. Hey, how about *Curious George Goes to the Hospital?*" (See, how clever and reassuring, how aware and sensitive. Look at me allaying their little anxieties, I mean *subtle*, I don't even call attention to what we're doing. How come *my* mother didn't know to do that? If I drew a beautiful lady, she corrected the nose with a black crayon. "*That's* how you do a nose." But I didn't *want* that kind of nose; I just wanted two dots like I had, and she didn't even ask me. And what about my first blind date? Did she have to follow me right to the door, and then say, "What have you got on your chin right there, is that a pimple, why do you get pimples?" (Pamela said *her* mother would have opened the door, told the boy to come in, and then squeezed the pimple right in front of him.)

". . . See, they gave Curious George something to make him sleep, just like Daddy got, so it wouldn't hurt when they, uh, did the operation."

Matthew: "Yes, but then he woke up right after, how come Daddy didn't? When *will* Daddy?"

"Just as soon as the stuff, uh, just as soon as he's feeling a little better, and then he'll talk to you both on the phone and you can tell him all about the model plane. See, I haven't forgotten."

"Can I talk to him as soon as he gets up, even if it's night-time?" Even if.

I tucked them into their little Scandinavian bunks and tip-toed out. The TV was blasting in the living room, Darlene having plopped her kitchen-spattered size-twenty rear into my husband's best chair to watch the wrestling. She hadn't bothered to remove Matthew's sticky yellow lollipop. "You're sitting on Matthew's sticky yellow lollipop," I announced coolly from a safety position at the front door. "I'll be at that hospital phone-booth number in case—"

"Okay," she cut in, resenting the interruption. "Oh—sure hope Mr. Messinger's feeling better." Her gesture of conciliation. "Thank you, Darlene, and I hope *your* boy wins too," I replied, turning my freeze-dried smile toward the sweaty pretzel of bodies on Channel 9. "Hah?" she said. "Oh, yeah. Night now." "Lollipop," I reminded. "Oh, yeah," she giggled, hoisting herself reluctantly out of the chair. I let go of the door, hoping it would slam behind me hard enough to convey slight annoyance. Richard said you had to assert yourself—or rather that *I* did, because *he* needed to be totally lovable.

I had to wait for the elevator. (If I don't breathe, the telephone won't ring. That's stupid; why would they call, they *know* I'm on my way back, Cal and Miranda are there, it's all *right*, goddammit, knock it off.) But the taxi meant twenty minutes of limbo, adrift in the streets of No-phone-land, facing a card that says SIT BACK AND RELAX! But the cars ahead never move and every single light is red—they must be all broken, only they're not, and $1.95, $2.05, $2.15 . . . Christ, it'll be twelve dollars a day just for *cabs*, and what the hell does Blue Cross care?

Of course nothing had changed; Miranda was napping peacefully on the sofa. It accommodated about half her sinuous length, and two chairs took care of the legs. Cal was chortling over a dog-eared copy of the *National Enquirer*: ITALIAN DOCTORS MAKE VIRGIN PREGNANT WITH ELECTRIC

SHOCK. "That headline never would've made the *News*," he said as I walked in. "SHOCKED VIRGIN MAMA BLAMES DOCS maybe."

I smiled weakly. "Guess I didn't miss much?"

"Three phone calls. Your sister is coming after dinner; An Emily Something from Wilkes-Barre, Pa., left no message; and an anonymous masher knew enough to hang up if a man answers. Oh, and Spector said the exchange is going swimmingly, but it'll be two more hours at least. He went home to eat, back in an hour." Miranda stirred and began to uncoil. "Don't have to whisper," she said sleepily, "nap time's up anyway; I'm taking up all the seats."

"Why don't you take each other out?" I said.

"Sure?"

"Sure. Have a good din-din." I nudged them out, kicked off my shoes, curled up on the couch in Miranda's still-warm indentation, and closed my eyes.

So Emily Something from Wilkes-Barre, Pa., called, no message. Nine years, almost to the week, from the day we'd said our bitter last words in a cruddy room at the Barbizon Hotel for Women. "Have a nice life, Julie," she'd said. The flat finality of it. She hadn't expected it at all. Not that she'd thought we could go on more than another year—two at the most. But why *now*? Why did I have to kill it now? That's what I was doing, wasn't I, if we both still loved each other? Because I don't want this now, I said. It's not the same as being college roommates, sleeping together in the dorm and going out for pizza when everybody else has a stupid date. I can't live with you here and go out with boys—men—who think I'm normal. And I can't *not* go out. I'm twenty-two years old! What do I say? Sorry, my roommate won't let me?

Oh, come off it, Julie! You're the one who wants to get laid, or you wouldn't care what they thought. That's it, isn't it? You want them, you bitch; that's what it's all about. Well, go ahead—go screw them all.

Oh, Emily, for God's sake—listen! I just hate *lying* to everybody. Running away from the telephone because it's somebody I work with, or a friend of a friend who gave out my number. I feel like a criminal! At least your family doesn't live in New York. You don't have to explain all the time why you're not going on dates or trying to meet guys or saying you're busy through next January.

Come here, she said, beckoning from the iron cot. No, Emily, I don't want to. You're never going to like it with a guy—you do know that, don't you? No, I don't know that, and neither do you. (But please don't let her be right, I don't want to be that way, queer or frigid or just something missing. I never really possessed that woman, my father declared in ringing tones. How could anybody's father say that to an eight-year-old?)

But what if Emily's right? What if she is the only person in the world who will ever make me come? She never touches any part of me; just down there. Doesn't want me touching her breasts; never says why and never touches mine. Just *don't*, that's all. But she can make me come, and I can make her, and maybe that's all anybody really needs. Except I liked it when boys wanted to play with my breasts and look at them. I bet I could come just from that if somebody really wanted me to and touched me there the way I wanted him to and didn't start biting and getting rough. They never give a damn about what you really want; just for them to look and touch and kiss and *play* with you, and once in a while to say how beautiful you are there . . . and there . . .

Emily said I was beautiful, and she had strong square hands that slid softly up inside my shorts, and she'd say these are delightful little things that you wear, and then she'd pull me down on her lap and take them off. Remember how we did it to each other on an Eastern Airlines shuttle flight to Washington? Nobody could see, nobody could ever guess. Two nice girls on spring vacation, side by side, sharing a blanket. Ask the stewardess for a blanket, Emily said. I'll show you a trick. Mmmm, she whispered. Mmmm, you're so sweet.

But we're twenty-two now, Emily. We're grownups; we're supposed to get married and be normal. I've been on this lousy diet, steak and lettuce, for ten months and I've lost forty pounds, and maybe I'm even pretty now. Not just my face—all of me. You're beautiful, she said, you've always been beautiful. Why isn't it enough any more that I think so? It used to be enough, didn't it? Yes, but that was different; we were different. This is the *world* here. I don't want to be a freak in a Greenwich Village dyke bar. I'm a girl, you're a girl, you can't *marry* me. And then she stared at me for a long time. It was the only time I ever saw tears in her round tigercat's eyes, and then she kissed me goodbye with that strong tender soft mouth. Wait, I said, do you . . . do you still think I'll be famous someday? Yes, she said. Her voice was husky, but God, she had dignity, that girl. Yes, I still think you'll be, famous. Have . . . a nice life, Julie.

I never saw her again, but I heard that she'd married too and had a couple of children; once her parents sent me a snapshot of them. They still sent me a Christmas card every year;

they never could understand why Emily and I hadn't kept in touch when we'd been so close.

"The phone, Julie—want me to get it?" It was Timmy's voice. I leaped as if he'd read my thoughts, blurted, "No, I'll—" and raced toward the booth as if it were the other side of the Berlin wall. "Hello . . . Yes, this is me—she. Oh, hi, Mother, how are you? . . . Fine, thanks . . . I mean, no, he's still . . . No, please, *don't* do that . . ." (cool, *cool*, damn you), "I mean, really I'd hate for you to—you just got there, and you really need the rest . . . I'm *fine*, really, and there's no point . . . No, I really *don't* need—I mean, I've got lots of good friends and people . . . Yes, I'm sure they're doing everything, I have *complete* faith . . . No, I haven't, I don't see what good it could possibly do to have Dr. Steiner look at him . . . Yes, I *know* he's a surgeon, but it isn't a surgical . . . No, it isn't from the mole, it's from . . . Mother, *listen, will you*, it's a *hepatic coma*, from the *anesthetic*. They *know* what it is, and they're doing . . . No, not a private room, he's in the Intensive Care Unit, it's a special . . . Yes, round-the-clock nurses . . . yes. No, I don't think another hospital, absolutely no . . . Listen, Mother, the doctors are here now, I've got to . . . No, don't hold on, I'll call you if anything, really . . . Whose yacht? Oh, yes, well, say hello . . . what? The kids? Oh, they're fine, yes, this number, it's a phone booth . . . It's fine, Mother, I've *got* to hang up, okay? . . . Okay, 'bye."

Open the phone-booth door. *Open* it! That's it. Now breathe, in, two, three, out, two, three, and again, two, three, out, two, three. There you go, you big brave girl you. Now just march yourself back to that waiting room and fix your face for the nice people. It's three minutes to curtain, they're dimming the house lights—okay, you're *on*.

Hi, Marcy, hi, Doug, hi, Laurie, Bob—*Terry* love, good to see you, it's been a long time. Susie, hi. God, you look marvelous! Who brought all this food, gee and that huge plant! No, no, thanks, but it looks fabulous. Please have some. God, it's great to have you all here, I wonder if we could get some more chairs—there's another room, but it's really depressing in there . . . No, go ahead, that's what it's there for . . . What? Oh, yes, he's in there, they'll let you go in at —oh, I forgot, they're still doing his blood-exchange process, probably another hour . . . Sure, I think after that . . .

Some of them wanted to know exactly, but *exactly*, what was going on; they needed to hear all the symptoms and medical terms, and all about the catheters and the corneals. So I sat there regaling them with a perfect rendition of Bleiweiss' ode to the human liver; I gave them *lymph glands* and *melanoma*; *decerebrate* and *spontaneous regeneration, massive insult* and *stabilize* and *pumping* and *flushing*. Oh, it was one of your all-time tours de force; you should have seen their lips moving to make those words so they'd stick in their minds. Marcy, especially, and Arnie Buchalter, the Sanitation man, and a girl named Audrey Lebow whom I barely knew and hardly could stand, but who somehow decided that I *needed* her, so every single day thereafter she came and sat for six or seven hours, explaining to everyone else how difficult it was for her to spend all this time away from home, how her children were probably wandering around loose in the street, and she hadn't even done her marketing or made the beds, and her husband was bringing home somebody from the office and she'd never be ready on time. "Gee, Audrey,"

I'd say gently, "why don't you go on home? It's terribly sweet of you to stay with me but I don't really need—I mean, your *family* is more . . . Anyway, nothing much is happening, and I'll probably be going home myself pretty soon."

It's the hospital syndrome, Timmy said, when I told him about her and one or two others who seemed to have put down roots in that room, unasked and unwanted. Calvin and Miranda I needed, though I never exactly said so, and it helped to keep calling Laurie to make sure she was still there. But Audrey *Lebow?* We'd gone to three dinner parties at her house and hated every one. It was always chicken and rice, two other bland couples and four unrelieved hours of doggedly intelligent, witty small talk which she poured with the coffee in the living room, and which she seemed to have polished all week so she could sparkle like her silverware.

Audrey, said Timmy, was your classic case of hospital syndrome. Characterized by an abrupt coming-to-life in the presence of near-death. Being a sickbed voyeur is not only respectable, it's noble. For a few days the hospital friend gets a *raison* not only *d'être*, but *d'être ici.* Some place to report to, a production, rehearsals daily, and the producer never says don't call us, we'll call you. What's more, for a few of these types—the really lost and pathetic ones (Arnie Buchalter, the only forty-one-year-old bachelor in New York who couldn't make out at "Parents Without Partners")—it's a chance, maybe the only one ever, to feel luckier than the other guy. Okay, he tells himself, I'm a dumb bastard and a failure in my career and a sexual disaster area, but at least I'm out *here* standing up, and my brilliant friend with the pretty wife and the good job and the great future is in *there* flat on his back for a change, so maybe now it's my turn.

Of course there was no way to guess, that first crazy night when absolutely everyone came, which of them would develop the syndrome. Most of them showed up either because they thought they had to (it was the place to be, if they'd ever met us) or because they thought they felt something like love. Some of them did, some of them, I'm almost sure.

About eleven-thirty the crowd finally thinned out a little and all of Richard's blood had been exchanged with only one minor mishap: the discovery that one donor, Molly Hastings, assistant beauty editor of *Household*, had syphilis. She had left the hospital hours before, nobody knew where she lived, and anyway she'd mentioned having a big date (poor bastard, there was no way to warn him). Imagine if they'd dumped her rotten blood right into the pot and infected Richard. But of course that couldn't have happened; they had to screen every one of those pints for purity, body and flavor. But there was this delicate little problem of who should tell Molly. Maybe Barney Halstead could shoot off another memo? "Confidential to M.H. from B.H. Re: V.D. Dear Molly: As head of *Household*, I need a syphilitic beauty editor like I need cockroaches in my test kitchen. Let's clean this up soonest, and meantime keep your cute little rash off editorial toilet seats."

Suddenly I caught a flash of Timmy's white coat streaking across the far end of the corridor. "Something's wrong," I whispered into Miranda's ear. She didn't move, except to reach for my hand; we sat there crushing each other's fingers until Timmy reappeared, wearing his unreadable doctor's face, and motioned me outside. I got up as casually as I could. My hand felt broken in four places. That's good, I thought; maybe it will appease the wrath of whoever's unjust god was really in charge here. Timmy stared at me as I stumbled toward him. "Jesus," he said, "you love him."

"What?" I stammered. "Wh-what?"

"Baby, calm down, will you? It's all right, everything's fine. We had a little trouble—he reacted to something in some donor's blood, but we fixed it, changed his antibiotic, he's fine. We're just about finished now; may do another one tomorrow using just plasma. Depends how he does tonight, but so far it looks very encouraging. Julie, for Chrissake, go back and sit down."

He must have signaled, because Cal's arm suddenly materialized around me; I hadn't even seen him come out of the room. I sank against that arm the way a window washer leans on the harness after his first look down.

Timmy said he was going back to wind things up, and that we ought to start getting rid of the "others" now and think about packing it in for the night. Cal gently strong-armed me back to my seat next to Miranda, who apparently hadn't spoken or moved since I'd left. She'd managed to hide her clenched fists under Cal's raincoat, but there wasn't much she could do about the fright in her face. I never saw anything so vulnerable; for an instant it was like a weird mirror-image of me. We didn't have to say anything; her fists unclenched as soon as we walked in. No one else in the room had the slightest idea that anything had happened, which gave the three of us a kind of official status for what had until then been only a vague sense of *cosa nostra*.

"Spector says we ought to adjourn the meeting," Cal announced, yawning, "so Julie can go home and get some rest." There were noises of agreement, chair scrapings, solicitous goodnights, see-you-tomorrows, call-if-you-need-anythings.

"I thought they'd never," Miranda sighed, "didn't you?"

"Yeah, but what about us?" Cal replied, pulling her up. It always astonished me that, fully extended, she had three inches on him—and he was a full six feet. "Take you home, lady?" he asked me.

I shook my head firmly and hugged him. "I'll wait for Timmy," I said. "He lives five blocks from me, he's got a racy sports car, and besides . . ."

"Sure?"

"Sure."

"Don't know how it's gonna feel, just the *two* of us," he called back, halfway down the hall.

"I'll remind him," Miranda said sexily.

We all laughed, and they disappeared into the elevator. All alone, by the telephone.

I went back to say goodnight to Richard. "His color's better, isn't it—less yellow?" I observed tentatively to the new night nurse fluttering around Richard's control center—Miss P. Lopez it was, an olive-skinned lovely.

She really couldn't say.

"Cardiograph?" I asked, pointing to some cardiographic-looking machinery, and she nodded crisply. "How did he do?" I whispered—very casual, not pushy.

She, uh, couldn't say.

One more try: "Guess he's in your capable hands till tomorrow, then?" A little Latin warmth, Miss Lopez? *Poquito corazón?*

"Goodnight, Mrs. Messinger."

*Gracias* a lot.

"Hey, ready?" Timmy called, poking his head through the door.

"Coming," I said. *Adiós*, Miss Lopez. (And may the hairs on your upper lip grow and multiply.)

In the elevator I asked Timmy about the change in Richard's skin color. It wasn't my imagination; it was jaundice. "Always happens," Timmy explained, "when the liver isn't working." I thought only in British jungle movies with Trevor Howard. "That's yellow fever," he said peevishly. "Anyway, if you really want to know, it's because all kinds of crap gets washed through the blood that the liver wouldn't let in if it were functioning. So he looks better now because of all that fresh blood we gave him—his whole system's been cleaned out, in effect . . ."

Look at him, I thought; Dr. Spector is actually *high* on this case, I bet it's the biggest thing he's ever handled.

It was true. By the time we got to the doctors' parking lot, he was out of the bloodstream and into long-distance phone conferences with the only two doctors in North America who'd ever pulled anybody out of hepatic comas. Richard, he added proudly, as if he'd invented him, was actually the first case of exactly this kind *anywhere*; those others had been caused by viruses, whereas this was *chemically* induced. Anyway, there was an airline stewardess in Ontario, age twenty-six, it just happened last month, infectious hepatitis, and she was comatose just like Richard for two weeks and then came out of it on the fifteenth day like it never happened. Not a trace of damage; she's back up at twenty thousand feet dispensing tea and vomit bags, and her parents still think it's some kind of a miracle.

"Two *weeks?*" I said. "You mean it could take *two weeks?*"

We had stopped for a red light on 19th Street and Third Avenue, alone except for whoever might be lurking in the tenement doorways, and it took Timmy the full duration of the light to answer. "Every day," he said finally, with the caution of a Tiffany clerk lifting something out of the case, "is time we have to *buy* for him like we bought today. Separate *pieces* of time . . . There's no way to know how much we'll need, and it doesn't matter—it only matters whether we can keep buying it until his liver is ready to come back."

I was shivering. We turned east at 26th; I'll ask when we get to First Avenue. "What do you mean, *whether?*"

Timmy picked up my hand and stroked it with his thumb. "Lots of unknowns, Julie. General physical condition, heart, lungs, kidneys . . . being young and healthy helps."

"Oh, yes," I said bitterly, realizing how much better it felt to be angry again. "Sure, I can certainly see *that.*"

There was an awkward silence as we pulled up in front of my building. "Well, at least you didn't throw in anything about the will to live—that's a break," I said, fumbling for the door handle.

"Julie," he said, and kissed me, "*I* think he'll make it."

But his *I* offended me. "And we'll all be together again in the Medicine section of *Time,*" I said nastily. "How nice for *you.*" But then I was sorry, so I kissed him back and mumbled that it was just that I was so exhausted, and I'd see him tomorrow and thanks for the lift, and I really was glad he was handling it, all of it—*really.*

"Right to sleep," he called after me into the lobby. "Doctor's orders."

I turned and waved and nodded and stood there until his white Corvette turned the corner.

Pat, the late-night doorman, was sloshing gray suds on the travertine floor with a dirty wet mop. On this shift, he didn't get to wear his gold-buttoned uniform jacket, or the visored hat that said 421 East 83rd Street; the tenants' committee had voted to sacrifice doormanly elegance after midnight to save on janitor salaries. As a result, we were the only co-op in the East 80's that didn't have a raise in maintenance again this spring. I bet my mother would have opted for the increase, just to have someone else mop so that no matter when she came home at night a Pat in shiny buttons would salute her smartly at the door.

Well, here we are, I announced to the suddenly enormous-looking expanse of my bed. King-size really *was* obscene, I decided, and twin mattresses *passing* as king-size under the bedspread is even worse—dishonest and obscene, both.

I got undressed and pulled off the spread, but the thought of actually lying down next to that empty space . . . Darlene had changed the sheets, each side had a fresh pink-and-white striped pillowcase and matching top sheet. What do I do next week if mine has to be changed and his doesn't? Change both anyway, so they'll match? Move over and use *his* bed, so they'll be even the following week? Strip that side and put his sheets over here? Jesus, it's cracking-up time, folks. I wonder if it's too late to call Laurie and ask her how to handle it. Nobody minds *her* being crazy—she laughs about it, so it's

funny, even cute. But tragic nuttiness? No sir, you do not
see your tragic nuts at the better parties.

Then how about passing the time with a little fresh nail
polish? I see you've got a chip here and there. Look at that
thumb, for instance, and if you apply three coats, letting each
dry thoroughly before adding the next, that could take us just
about to the two A.M. mark. And then what? Well, as one
says to one's children, then we'll see.

I managed to keep the nail polish going till two-twenty,
in the interests of a thoroughly dry top coat. Then I did
isometrics, naked, every toneless muscle glaringly exposed in
the full-length mirror. Look at those buttocks, curdling like
milk, no wonder he can't stand me . . . Then I tried plucking my eyebrows. (That's what they gave me: *Best Eyebrows.*
Betsy Ritter got *Figure*; Judy Yellen got *Smile*; even Ann
("Flaky Dandruff") Hochstadter got *Best Ankles*.) Now,
about a shower? Nice hot shower? Good girl. I shaved my
legs, and then fished in the hamper for three pairs of panty-
hose to wash. Look, I'm even sparing Darlene the indignity
of white lady's dirty undies.

Wanna try reading? No, it has to be physical distraction.
Can't handle printed words with meanings. My God, it's only
three o'clock.

Well, whaddya say we try the old bed? Just *try* it, how can
it hurt, a little innocent lie-down? Nobody says you have to
sleep . . .

On the other hand, what can they do to you for sleeping?
Nobody gets points for self-induced insomnia. Fasting, yes,
but I don't think insomnia counts. Even criminals don't
have to lie there staring at the dark. They put in their rockpile time and that's it—no more expiating till tomorrow. Think

about it—what's so bad about letting yourself sleep? A purely animal function with no morality whatsoever. Unlike screwing, for instance. Hey, maybe if I . . . Why not? Masturbation is healthier than Seconal; it's not even contraindicated for persons in shock, let alone those of us who are merely upset. And like they say, you don't have to look your best.

Yes, but Richard . . . Okay, then don't then. Richard, wake up and I promise I won't lay a finger on myself until you wake up. I'll get so sexed up you'll like me again. I'll lose ten pounds and get a nightgown that pushes up my little round pale pink bosoms like the maid in a dirty Victorian autobiography. Oooh, sir. Oh, don't stop, sir.

Remember the first time we tried to fuck? It was dry and it hurt and I kept saying I can't, I can't, it's no use, it's impossible, I told you I couldn't, there's really something wrong with me, I'll never be able to, it's probably *inherited*.

But you wouldn't stop, you just kept ramming it against me and pushing and heaving and cursing, yelling, you were actually yelling, "I AM GOING TO LAY YOU, JULIE, GODDAMMIT, I AM, I HAVE TO!" Oh, please, let's quit, I can't, it just won't go in. But of course it did, finally. Look, it's in! Yay, team—only I was bleeding all over your bed, and what the hell were you going to tell the cleaning lady?

Next time you said it wouldn't hurt, but it was just as bad, just as dry, and I was still sore. Please, I don't want to start bleeding again. So you said, okay, suck me off instead. But what happens when you come? Swallow it, you said. What does it taste like? How the hell should I know, you said. Well, what if I hate it? Nobody hates it—people swallow it all the time, it's nothing, it's not even fattening.

But I couldn't force it down; I kept it in my mouth—you didn't know that, did you—and spit it out in the john, exactly the way I used to get rid of the creamed spinach and eggplant and calves' liver when they made me clean my plate. Chew, Julie, chew; swallow, Julie, swallow—so I'd pretend to get it down, and it would stay there in my cheek until after my nap when I was allowed to go to the bathroom by myself.

I didn't want to hurt your feelings, can you imagine that? If I didn't like the taste, it would be an insult to your cock. Once I held it in my mouth for a whole hour because you were holding me and I didn't want to ruin the mood by getting up. Would you have done that for me? You would not—that, or anything else. Would you kiss me there? Never once. I don't like to do that, you said, and that was that.

So I'm going to do it after all; I just changed my mind. And so what? I *know* what I said, but it was stupid—how could it possibly have anything to do with—with anything? Anyway, now I feel like it . . . Wait, a story, I want a story too. How about the evil fat monks; that's always good. ("Oh, please don't whip my titties any more, I'll do it, I'll swallow it all, I promise.")

I wonder if I could ever teach Richard just by letting him watch me. Masters and Johnson say that's the whole thing about their treatment. Ask the wife what she likes . . . This I like, and this, and this . . . and then ask her if she's ever told her husband. Of course not, she says; I wouldn't dream of it. Could you show him with your hand? Could you take his hand in yours and guide it? No. No, I don't think so. Forget about orgasms; we want you to forget about them completely. Return to sensate focus, just what feels nice. She likes her back tickled; she'd like you to play with her breasts like this, not attack them; she'd like you to stroke the clitoris, not try to erase it; she'd like you to take her clothes off occasionally, tell her what's pretty, talk about her beautiful this and her soft little that. We call it the "give to get" principle. Give her what she wants and you'll get yours.

Richard, if you wake up I'll take you to Masters and Johnson and they'll fix us. I'll ask my mother to lend us the money; I'll say, Mother, we need to have our fucking fixed. I know you gave me that nice book about animals and sex that Dr. Altman said was suitable for young girls. But you only let me read one chapter a year, on my birthday, and I was sixteen before I got to The Human Male, and believe me, it was too late. I mean, I saw the erect male penis of a total stranger when I was ten (he was waving it at me from the bottom of a hill in Central Park, where Pamela and I went sledding). Look, Pam, there's a man down there— look what he's doing. I think he's looking up our skirts. Maybe we better go down headfirst on the sled instead of sitting like this. Look at his thing—are they always red like that, or is his just cold? My brother's isn't red, but he's only twelve, said Pamela. Maybe we should move over to *that* hill, Pam; I'm getting scared. What're *you* scared for, I'm the one who started men-strew-ating, I'm the one who could get pregnant, you know. Anyway, he isn't going to do anything; he just wants to see our underpants. *I* think it's funny.

I never told you that, did I, Mother? Hey, wanna hear about the purity test we used to take every time Pam and Peggy and Amy slept over? Two points for soul kissing, three for petting above the waist outside the clothes, five for petting above inside the clothes, five for below outside, eight for below inside, and ten for blow or all the way. I didn't even know what blow was, but nobody else had ever done it either. Everybody always scored exactly the same (fifteen points), except that I lied; I gave myself five extra so they wouldn't know how untouchable I was, with my freckled arms and my awful pot and my dumb breasts that weren't big enough to be sexy like Pamela's, or flat enough to be tomboyish and graceful like Peggy's. The first time a boy ever asked me to a prom I wanted a high-necked, long-sleeved formal. We must have looked in fifteen stores, but nobody had ever heard of a high-necked, long-sleeved formal for a thirteen-year-old. Even the salesladies had to rub it in—"But *all* the young girls seem to want *strapless* now"—and they'd peer at me, trying to guess whether I had psoriasis. (It's just freckles, but they're all over; nobody else has them on their back. I can't believe I'm the only person in the world who wants a high neck; what about people who really *do* have psoriasis?) How about just short sleeves, then; it wouldn't be too bad if at least the shoulders were covered; they'd only see my arms then. "I'm sorry, all we have is just what's out here. Excuse me, I have another customer." And she'd waltz off to some creamy-smooth willowy bitch who was dying for a low-cut strapless.

We finally found it though, and it was a dream, my dream; I knew nobody else would have anything like it. It was ice-blue heavy silk with a Chinese collar and a million tiny buttons down the front, long tight sleeves and even a train like those real ball gowns in the "Modess . . . *because*" ads. God, I thought it was so elegant, and I would be totally covered, every disgusting inch of me.

And my date brought a white camellia (not a floppy-eared orchid, that looked like wilted purple lettuce, and not a

gardenia that would turn brown before we even got there).
A creamy perfect camellia, and he even knew enough not to
gook it up with silver ribbons. Oh, I love him, I just know
I do. I rescued his cigarette butt from the ashtray and put it
in my room; tomorrow I'd Scotchtape it into my memory
book, with my outstanding collection of other trophies:
Johnny Winograd's nail parings; gum scraped off Ken
Stern's shoe, and the answer to a tortured fan letter I'd written to Neil Colville, captain of the New York Rangers. ("Dear
Julie, Your request for my autograph is perfectly okay. Lots
of girls do much worse things.")

But when we got to the prom, all I wanted was midnight
and a pumpkin. There I was, the only girl in a high-necked,
long-sleeved gown. "Hey, Julie, what are you hiding it for?"
Even Pamela was in her first strapless, a white satin top and
a huge whirling skirt made of layers of snowy gauze over
three hoop petticoats circling her like a nimbus when she
danced. Beautiful; oh, why can't I be? She actually had
*cleavage* showing, and boys kept going over to her table to
drop ice cubes down her back and then she'd squeal and
squirm which made her front jiggle so then they'd try to drop
ice cubes down there.

I spent a lot of time in the powder room combing my impossible hair (it wasn't fuzzy when I left home, so now it
was fuzzy), and grimly studying a small pink hicky that
somebody had wished on my nose during the first dance; it
was blossoming like a well-tended geranium. Behind me
drifted fluffy pastel clouds of sweetheart-necklined girls.
Breathless and giggling, they sailed in and out of that mirror-
lined safety zone, powdering the cute shine on their unhickied
noses; showing each other where to dab perfume on their

unhesitatingly bared freckle-free bosoms; ruefully inspecting their dyed-to-match satin pumps to compare the scuffmarks left by all those stupid clumsy boys who kept cutting in on them—not one of them had seen her date in hours. I hadn't seen mine *or* theirs, and as for the stag line, well, who wants to have her brand-new shoes ruined by a bunch of stupid clumsy . . .

"Where the hell have you *been?*" my date demanded when I finally ventured out, praying I'd kneaded enough Pan-Stick (Natural) into my nose to cover the latest of a long series of defects. (If my mother were standing there she'd say, "What have you got on your nose? It looks all caked with something." Pamela's mother would just wipe it off.) "Oh, dancing mostly, talking to people . . . I just went in there for a sec to avoid getting cut in on again. My aching feet!" I lifted my hem to display a few cleverly self-inflicted smudges on my pristine ice-blue toes. "My mother'll kill me!" I added. "Who would believe they were all that clumsy?"

"Funny, I didn't even see you dancing," he was muttering. "I was out there the whole time."

"Well, I saw you," I countered. "That *was* you throwing ice cubes with the other *children?*" I hate him, I just hate him.

And that about wrapped it up for me and Dwight Perlmutter. He took me home, and we necked on the bench in the foyer for over an hour. (Not in the living room, Pamela said. Squishy sofas make it hard to sit up and push them away when you want to.) I let Dwight open fourteen of those little round buttons and get *bare hand,* but then he sort of dug his elbow in my crotch and tried to pin me against the wall.

Quit that, I said, that really *hurts*. He didn't quit; he just dug harder. Ow, I said, I *mean* it. If he doesn't stop, I'll bite him. He's not calling me again anyway, I know he isn't; this is just for the rotten *camellia*. So finally I bit—not really hard, but hard enough. *Jesus*, he said, rubbing his earlobe. You're a lousy C.T.! What's a C.T.? I don't even know what a C.T. is. It's what you are. Ask your friend Pamela; she's one too, but at least she's worth necking with.

And I'm not? Then why did you? Why'd you even ask me to the prom?

Boy, are you stupid! I asked you because two other girls I asked said no. And I necked with you because why not—maybe you put out.

Oh, I said. Well, thanks for telling me. It seemed to me I sounded sarcastic, which was pretty dignified. At least I didn't cry or anything. I guess Pamela would have slapped his face—I'd never slapped anybody—or said some terrific line like "How dare you!" Not me, though; hurt was how I expected to feel. It was right—I deserved it, that was it.

I waited politely till the elevator came, anyway. The next day I taped both the cigarette butt *and* the camellia into my book, and wondered if his elbow digging in my crotch counted five points.

I slept! God, I slept three hours—it's seven-thirty. In a groggy panic, I pounced on the telephone, shakily dialed the Intensive Care Unit, got a wrong number and dialed again. "Intensive Care, Miss Wachtel." "Hi, Miss Wachtel, it's Mrs. Messinger." Silence. "I, uh, guess, anything, uh, any is he . . . ?" More silence. Did she have to go look? "He's about the same, Mrs. Messinger." I exhaled, limp, drenched and exhausted. The start of another beautiful day. "Oh . . . Well, I guess I'll be there in about an hour. Is Dr. Spector in yet?" "Not yet, Mrs. Messinger." "Well, tell him I'll be there in about an hour." "I'll do that, Mrs. Messinger." All heart, that girl.

Out in the kitchen, Darlene, Nicky and Matthew were crunching Sugar Jets. "Could we send away for this rocket, it's only seventy-five cents plus two boxtops," they said, waving the container at me in lieu of Hello Mommy, how'd you sleep, poor Mommy.

"We'll see," I mumbled. Coward. Richard would say, Absolutely not, it's crummy Styrofoam, it sheds, it's worth about a nickel and you've already got three broken ones exactly like it in your room. And then he'd send away for it.

"Aw, you always say we'll see, and we never do."

"Matthew, you're bugging me again. You never learn not to bug me in the morning, and you're dripping on your clean shirt, oh God."

"Mommy, you're not supposed to say oh God either."

"No more talking. Drink your juice. You've only got ten minutes or you'll miss the bus," I retorted crisply.

"Will you be here when we get home?"

Poor babies; they really couldn't remember. It's not the loss of innocence that makes it so lousy to be a grownup; it's having all this goddam power of *retention*. "No, lovey, I have to stay at the hospital, but I'll come home for supper, okay?"

"Okay," Nicky said, but it wasn't. He'd started sucking his finger again; the grooves from those two tiny front teeth were already so deep that they looked like open cuts. Matthew didn't seem any whinier than usual, but that was whiny enough. He was the kind of second baby that made you wonder what you'd done right the first time, because it didn't work any more. Nicky never cried; Matthew never stopped. Nicky never spit up; Matthew had to be followed with a damp sponge until he was three. When he screamed in his crib at two A.M., I used to go in and pummel him in the dark. Then I'd come back a second time to pick him up, cuddle and rock him with the light on, so he'd only see the good Mommy and never be able to pick me out of the line-up as the other one.

The kids left just as the phone began to ring. I hadn't been terrified of the phone in eight years; now that was back too. I considered running out after the children, but there was Darlene's fat placid face watching me over her Sugar Jets, so I didn't wait for the second ring before throttling it like a half-dead snake. "Hello," I squeaked at it, holding it a foot away from my head.

"*Julie?* I can hardly *hear* you. Can you hear *me?*"

As soon as I recognized Timmy's voice, mine quit altogether.

"Hey!" he shouted.

"I'm . . . here," I rasped finally. Maybe my larynx was paralyzed.

"Oh, there you are. Glad I caught you. Listen, we need you to hunt for some papers and bring them up with you . . . Julie?"

I nodded, but of course that didn't help.

"Julie, you all *right?*"

"Who me?" I said; I was crying. "Wh-what papers?" At least I could talk now.

"Anything you can find about hospitalization insurance. Hey, don't *worry*" (he'd just caught on). "We need some information we didn't ask him for when he checked in, is all. Right? Julie, *say* something."

"Right," I said. "*Right.* I'll find it. Is he—have you—?"

"Oh, he's doing okay, I think. We took some tests just now. I'll tell you more when we get the reports in a couple of hours. Okay, sweets?"

"Yeah, sure, super."

Papers they want. The day he entered the hospital, Richard had thoughtfully slipped me one paper: a scrawled note from his memo pad listing the four banks in which he had savings accounts. This one for salary; this one, royalties from the kiddie books; this one, stock dividends; and the last, assorted windfalls such as Christmas bonuses and birthday checks from parents. All very tidy and anal, right down to the little rubber-banded pile of bankbooks. Once he made the fatal mistake of proudly exhibiting the bankbook collection to some of our wittier friends, who promptly christened it

Richard's Nutshell Library; he'd never heard the end of it.
Thereafter the bankbooks were filed under N for Nutshell
in the top drawer of the steel filing cabinet that made our
bedroom one-fourth tax-deductible in exchange for screwing
up the Spanish Provincial décor. Also in the cabinet were, presumably, all documents relevant to the fortunes or misfor-
tunes of Richard Messinger & Sons, Inc.—not counting what
filled the five suitcases he has stashed in the basement for
posterity. These held every work of art dating back to his
formative period (second grade), including finger paintings,
a pot holder and a clay bunny rabbit sealed in a plastic baggy.

Anyway, the suitcases were archives, while the file cabinet
was reserved for stuff in active circulation. Both were
strictly and exclusively Richard's—I had the desk drawers—
so it was something of a trespass, my barging in there. I
even had the shivery sensation that he was watching from
the doorway, and the minute I touched his papers he'd leap
out yelling "Ha! *Gotcha!*" Well, at least I'd have Timmy
as a character witness (he *told* me to!)—unless maybe they
planned it together? Oh God, am I getting paranoid now?

What did I find? There was a complete dossier on all the
78 rpm recordings ever made by B. Goodman, G. Miller, A.
Shaw, D. Ellington, H. James, L. Brown, C. Hawkins, and
the Metronome Allstar Band. Did you know what was on the
flip side of *Dr. Livingstone, I Presume?* I thought not; it was
*When the Quail Come Back to San Quentin.* Or that H.
James made a prophetic little disc called *The Mole?*

There was also a bulging manila folder of old *Life* clippings about famous artists whose genius had flowered late in
life; a carbon copy of a letter Richard had written in 1952
canceling a subscription to some left-wing magazine (who

knew when Cohn and Schine would be checking his mail-box?); all his report cards from elementary school and two letters from the High School of Music and Art (one acknowl-edging receipt of his application; the other regretting to in-form him he didn't get in). And last, an enormous collection of photographs and drawings depicting, in various stages of deshabille, a series of Outstanding Ex-Girl Friends. The big-gest batch of these was devoted to one Donna Sue Birnbaum, upon whom he had squandered nearly four years of himself and his pastel chalks, but who, though they both knew she loved him, felt obliged to marry someone a little better-heeled, even if less adorable.

One night about a month before Richard and I were mar-ried, his phone rang at two A.M. We'd just gone to bed, naked but not doing anything. It was Donna Sue; was she disturb-ing him? Well, no, what's up? Well, she just wanted to talk about *Barchester Towers*; Richard was still the only man who understood how she felt about Trollope. But what about Leonard, Richard said (she was marrying Leonard Hines, Jr. in five weeks, one week after Richard was marrying me. Leonard was both better-heeled and less adorable than Richard, as ordered). "*Leonard?*" she said, giggling, "that's pretty funny!" Richard cradled the phone in his neck so he could shrug helplessly at me, and then spent twenty min-utes discussing *Barchester Towers*. I went down on him during the last five, which made us all very happy; he got to play Sultan of the Harem, I got to play Cruelly Treated Slave Girl, and Donna Sue got some fantastic insights about Trol-lope.

So much for Drawer 1. Drawer 2 contained a sealed regis-tered letter from Richard Messinger to himself. I knew what that was: his idea for a new comic book depicting the daring adventures of a couple of high-spirited young sex organs (just the organs, no people.) This was followed by a completed but apparently chickened-out-on order form for *The Amorous Drawings of the Marquis Franz Von Bayros* ($24.95, including postage and—heh, heh—handling charges). The cover plate on the folder offering this erotic masterwork showed a ruffled-skirted lady with bare boobs being licked by her faithful dog, who obviously knew his place. "No inference," it said primly on the order blank, "should be drawn that this item is obscene (i.e.) hard-core pornography. There is no holding out that the work described herein is obscene. On the contrary, it is not obscene." That's probably what scared Richard; he thought they protested too much.

Next there was a manila folder containing fifteen typewritten pages of what appeared to be some sort of diary or expense-account record written in some sort of secret code, which I'd never seen before and which made no immediate sense. The first page was headed 1960, and had entries such as: FRIDAY, Oct. 4, 24J, lunch, 12-3, 3x: post, or; below. And WEDNESDAY Nov. 6 26J dinner 7:30-10.30, 2x (reg; or). I riffled through the whole thing. There were entries up to and including last Monday, to the day he'd checked into the hospital, with "MGM" appearing in every entry of the last six pages, but it remained meaningless. It was getting later, so I put the pages back and went on looking for hospital insurance. There was a floor plan of his old bachelor apartment . . . a bunch of aged rejection slips from the art editor of *The New Yorker* . . . royalty statements on *Melancholy Melinda* and some of her predecessors (*The Teeny Tinies, More Teeny Tinies, Teeny Tinies Come Back*). At last, *there* it was—a folder he'd jocularly marked "Live and Be Well." There were all kinds of policies in there; I took the whole thing and ran like a thief.

When I arrived at my post, Mount Carmel was already up to its majestic sun-dappled peak in midmorning traffic. It was almost reassuring to see a flicker of recognition cross so many intensively careworn faces as I made my way up. I was nodded at sympathetically in the lobby, the elevator, the private patients' wing, the corridor, and finally at the door of my own little cell, which had been dusted and re-decorated: new floral offerings, fresh water in the old ones, nuts, candies and sparkling ashtrays all in place, even some extra chairs, now that they knew how popular I was. Or he was.

Yessir, it's good to be back. With only the merest pang of hesitation, I stopped in first to see Richard. He looked just the way Miss Wachtel said, "about the same," still more healthily rosy than the sickly yellow-gold cast of yesterday. The sheet was turned down, neatly bisecting his midriff and baring most of his smooth chest and arms. I resisted an impulse to kiss some part of him, settled for touching, with one fingertip, the small hollow in the center of his chest which I had named, ever so long ago, "My place." The familiar warmth of it surprised me—I don't know why really, except that he seemed so artfully arranged—as if he should be cold to the touch and have a legend, engraved in steel, discreetly mounted on the base of his bed: *Sleeping Messinger, marble, acrylic and hair, USA, 1969, artist unknown.*

Well, Richard, I don't suppose you'd like to say a word to the folks out there? No? Can't say I blame you. Oh, *hi*, Miss Wachtel—didn't mean to startle you, I just like to sort of talk *around* him, you know; it helps me feel like he's *there*. She nodded, but I knew she wasn't convinced; nobody's fool, old B. Wachtel.

Miranda was back in her spot on the sofa; she was folded into it so precisely the way I'd last seen her that for a second I forgot she'd ever gone home. "Hi," we said, both of us suffused with shyness all over again. In spite of everything, the fact was we were strangers, and each morning we seemed to notice it again, with a sense of astonishment. I sat down stiffly in a straight chair opposite her. "Where's Calvin?" I said; that was safe.

"He had to go to the office, he's coming from there, around lunch."

Silence, and then we collided, trying to break it: "Calvin—" she said; "Would you—?" I said. And then we laughed, but it didn't solve the problem. "You first," I said. Be polite to the nice girl; maybe she'll want to play with you.

"Calvin," she repeated, clinging to the comfort of having him between us, "thought maybe we ought to go someplace for lunch—the three of us, I mean." And she blushed. (In case I thought she meant the two of them—or the two of us?)

"Like a real lunch?" I said. "Not eat *here?* Go downtown? But—"

"Hey, why not?" she said excitedly, as if it were my idea and she had to talk herself into it. "Look, there's a whole sunny Thursday out there. We could tell Spector where we are; we could be back in ten minutes if we had to be; anybody who comes can wait, and if they don't—well, so what?"

"But it's—"

"No, it's not—that's silly," she said emphatically, and blushed again. Had she really finished my ridiculous thought?

I wasn't even sure myself whether I would have said "It's wrong" or "It's not safe" or "It's tempting fate." All of those seemed to fit, and I believed them all, a little.

"Miranda," I observed impulsively, "you remind me of someone."

"You?"

"Yes and no," I replied, more or less accurately.

"Then let's have a nice lunch," she said, smiling at the way it sounded, like two ladies meeting in front of Bonwit Teller. (A small handwritten card in the window would say: *The fragrance in the air is Joie de Vivre.* And we'd breathe and say Mmmm, heaven—meaning either the fragrance, or the day, or the sun lighting sparks in the sidewalk, or a corner table in the Edwardian Room of the Plaza, with a bright yellow cloth and a window facing the park and fresh mimosa in a vase and a pretty salad with green leaves.)

"A nice lunch would be nice," I admitted. Wistful, dreamy, counting the days till he comes up for parole. Or I do. Serving a wife sentence? At least in jail you know how many days there are to go; you mark the walls 𝍩𝍫 and you know exactly when you can stop, and they can't spring anything more on you.

"I don't know, though; do you really think it's okay? To leave?" I wasn't asking what she thought; I was pleading for permission. If *she* decides, then it's not my fault.

Miranda smiled, reached over and touched me lightly on the shoulder. "I know Richard would be for it," she said.

The telephone rang: saved by somebody. I wasn't scared of it here; everything I couldn't face was on *my* end, so answering it was better than most of what it interrupted. The booth was quite far from the little waiting room, so that I had to run; you couldn't make it before the fifth or sixth ring, and most people hang up after six. I made a private thing out of trying to get there in five, and once I broke all records by catching it on the fourth, but I'd started from a standing position at the doorway so it wasn't a legitimate Roger Bannister breakthrough. After a while most of the regular callers got used to my being perpetually breathless and stopped sounding terrified when I gasped at them. In some ways it probably sounded more normal than my usual low monotone, as if I were being caught at some really climactic moment of life—which also meant that the person calling would be the first to share whatever new heights of hope or depths of despair I'd just reached. As for me, sprinting down that polished hall with my hair streaming behind me felt faintly like free-play period during school recess (after this, you have to go right back inside and sit still and pay attention for hours and hours, so run hard, get it all out of your system, good girl, just don't get overheated and *sweaty*. Sweaty: there's a word I don't think my mother's ever used in her whole life).

It was always the Symptom Collectors who called earliest in the day; they had to get a full morning report on the lab tests, the heart and lung readings, the blood count, the urine output. I got pretty good at rattling off all that stuff; I even worked up a style, like a TV weather girl, so I could make it sound zingier than it was. There was a lot of comic relief, for instance; just in the urine reading. His pee-pee is really fabulous today, I'd tell them. I mean, it's absolutely pouring out; yes, that's *good*, they say it's *extremely* good. And there was something very important called the bilirubin, which had to be measured all the time and analyzed. Old Billy Rubin's

in rare form this morning; yes, it's way down (or up, whichever it was supposed to be). Billy Rubin was great for Audrey
or Marcy, people who needed something solid and medical-
sounding to pass along to those who hadn't yet been briefed
on the really inside stuff. Being first with the Billy Rubin reading showed how close they were to the situation, and how
much I was relying on them to bring the news to the public.
In most cases, the public they brought it to was not exactly
grateful.

One time Laurie complained—only half kidding—that Audrey had just called her to tell her they were doing a plasma
exchange on Richard, and how come Audrey knew that, Audrey always seemed to be calling her to tell her stuff like that,
and she (Laurie) thought I didn't even like her (Audrey)
whereas she (Laurie) was more or less my best friend? I assured her (Laurie) that Audrey was a pest; that I had not
now nor had I ever leaked any hot scoops to her, but what
could I do when she called up ten minutes after I got here
every day and gave me a flash quiz? (The day Timmy called
Washington, D.C., to ask for a vial of growth hormone, which
was so rare that the FDA was rationing it and wouldn't let
go of an ounce unless the case was life-or-death and the doctor in charge called personally, I swear I heard Audrey actually
panting into the phone. *Growth* hormone? Ooh, Julie! They
*ration* it? The *FDA?* They're *flying* it up?)

Sure enough, the first call this morning was Audrey, although it took me two more days before I knew enough to
bet on it. I filled her in, hoping maybe it would keep her
off the premises for a while. I still wasn't tuned in on the syndrome. "I'll be up the minute I finish the beds, I *promise*,"
she promised. "I would have been there now, except Ronald

didn't get out of here until ten minutes ago. I'm not touching another thing, not even the breakfast dishes. I'll just have to do them tonight, and his dinner will be late, that's all. Julie darling, can't I bring you something? You must need something—wouldn't you like the new *Harper's Bazaar* at least?"

I didn't try to discourage her. First of all I sensed that it wouldn't work; besides, if a person has a calling, you don't tell them they're being irrational—it's not relevant. What good did it do Joan of Arc?

Arnie Buchalter was another one who checked in bright and early, propelled by a sincere belief that at a time like this I must need an excruciatingly good listener even if I had nothing whatever to say to him.

Then my sister came in all the way from New Rochelle. She had no maid now, and I could imagine, couldn't I, what it was like getting a sitter up there for the same day, just like that? Actually, I didn't mind Nina; after all, we were recovering from the same parents, although she seemed to bear fewer and less interesting scars. She'd given one of her children Robert as a middle name, after my father, and when Dad forgot the kid's birthday twice in a row, she had the middle name legally changed to John, after Lennon. On the other hand, she called Mother dutifully two or three times a week to ask, first, how she was, and second, how she'd like to repave their driveway for an anniversary present, or buy all the lounge chairs for the patio around their new pool, because she had such marvelous taste in things like that—even Jerry (Nina's husband) thought so; he still couldn't stop talking about the colors in that Oriental rug she'd bought for their den last year. Oh, and before she forgot, could she possibly borrow Mother's new white mink jacket to take to Aspen? It would look so great *après* ski.

I never could see naked greed being a good reason for calling one's parents, especially mine—though I concede that if the parents do not see what a piggy you are, and furthermore are delighted (a) that you called and (b) to shell out whatever you want, then you are not actually hurting anyone in a meaningful way. You end up not only getting the driveway paved and the pool furnished, but you also give them the terrific satisfaction that parents get when they've raised a daughter who calls up twice a week just to ask how they've been.

There was another way to look at Nina's attitude: seeing it as a demand for reparation, like European Jews were entitled to get from Germany, or like U.S. blacks from whoever might feel guilty enough to pay for two centuries of white oppression. According to this theory, by reason of having been very unloved, children should feel free to bill their parents later. Which would probably relieve the hell out of them anyway. (You mean that's *all* we have to suffer? Then I'd say we did some job raising those kids—we should thank God. Look at the terrible things some of our friends' kids did to them. Dottie's boy is a fairy; Myra's daughter had a baby and a divorce before she even wrote us a thank-you note for the sterling silver soup ladle.)

So Nina and I really did have a remarkably clean slate; neither one of us had inflicted so much as an abortion on the family, let alone a divorce. We'd both graduated from decent colleges, landed decent-looking husbands, had decent-looking children, and if we had to meet Mother for lunch at the Colony, we each had a decent mink that our husbands had managed to provide before they were forty.

Our parents had never even had to spring for a single hour of psychotherapy to insure our safe arrival at this enviable state. (I'd spared them the knowledge that I needed a shrink back when Emily and I were still tangled in our fraying post-adolescent cocoon. Out of the $37.50 I made as an executive trainee at Macy's, I had to fork over ten dollars a week (clinic rates) just to get so I could pick up the damn telephone. Good old Dr. Rosenfeld; I had him to thank for all that progress. From Emily to Richard, with blood. Just think, if it hadn't been for Rosenfeld, I wouldn't be here today. I wonder if he's sorry he told me all that crap about two kinds of female orgasms. "The clitoral, which of course you've experienced, is very nice," he said, "but it's nothing compared to the deep fulfillment of the *vaginal*. Only the male can give you that." You were a little nutsy yourself about that, Doctor, but it only hung me up another seven or eight years, until they proved there was only one kind of female orgasm after all and we could all stop torturing ourselves about not getting Brand X. That's right, ladies, no cock can do any more for you than you can do with a finger or tongue or this handy cordless plastic vibrator ($4.95, batteries extra; available in ivory, pink or heaven blue).

Nina was in therapy now, she'd confided a few weeks ago, but don't tell the folks. Four times a week, thirty-five dollars per. Luckily, Jerry's ad agency had some new company health plan that covered head as well as body repair work, so for once she hadn't felt the need to call Mother. Even if she had, she probably would have lied and said one of the kids needed orthodontia. Mother was "against" psychiatry; it did more harm than good, from what she'd seen, and besides, people should learn to solve their own problems; that's how you develop character. Now astrology was something else; she didn't pretend to understand it, but you could really get valid insights about yourself; it was amazing—and without going into all kinds of private subjects, like what you did with your husband in your bedroom, which was nobody else's business, and if you didn't see anything wrong in paying someone to pry into *that*, then you probably *needed* a psychiatrist.

When she was pregnant with Nina, Mother had consulted a really valid seer (the top man in the field at the time, I mean a *proven* authority) and he'd told her the child was destined to be a girl tennis champion, another Alice Marble. Mother spent about five thousand dollars on tennis lessons, tennis camps and little pleated white sharkskin dresses, before a kind-hearted pro at Rip's West Side Tennis Courts, where Nina had to practice for two hours every Monday, Wednesday and Friday afternoon, advised her to give up. "The kid just isn't coordinated," he said. Nina never did learn to play tennis.

She'd never played big sister either; it simply wasn't her kind of thing. There was a six-year gap between us and we were too different even to clash. Except for teaching me how to scrape my vegetables into the toilet ("I told you they'd go right down, just like 'bigs'; I've been doing it all my life, practically"), I can't remember a single sisterly secret we ever shared. She started dating when she was twelve and a half, never had the slightest trouble with boys, and couldn't understand why I was such a flop at the only thing in the world she found easy. She met Jerry Braun at a Harvard-Wellesley mixer; they went more or less steady until he graduated, the year before she did, and then they got engaged. The wedding took place two weeks after she graduated, and the only thing I remember about it was having to wear an absolutely hideous eggplant-colored taffeta dress—*sleeveless*—which was so tight that it puckered dangerously all across my midriff, and I couldn't sit down or eat anything because the seams would split. I was fifteen; I weighed one hundred and forty pounds (mostly jelly doughnuts and misery), and it was painfully clear that nobody would ever make a Bradford Bachrach bride out of me.

They had, though, or rather I had, and now that I was taller, slimmer and more confident than Nina, we seemed to have less in common than ever. We traded Jean Kerr-type anecdotes about our children, took turns honoring our parents on the major holidays, and occasionally forced our husbands on each other for an evening of unbearable dullness. "Why don't you just see your sister for lunch?" Richard would say. Because I don't eat lunch any more, and she only eats it in New Rochelle. Anyway, we don't have to face them again for six months. But I'd misjudged again; here she was less than one month later, paying her sisterly respects in my time of trouble. She fitted right in there with Audrey, Marcy and the rest of the gang, most of whom were astonished to learn that I had a sister.

As soon as the others began descending on us, Miranda withdrew into her shy, silent dignity, hands curled like fallen petals in her lap, endless legs slanting to one side—an impossibly graceful pose for such a tall girl on such a low couch. God, how she must be hating this, I thought; why does she endure it—why for me? I watched her watching them all, lowering her eyelids to half-mast, fixing her smile at some appropriate place between sad and polite. She never spoke except to say hello, or, to the new ones, "Hello, I'm Miranda Graham," and she always called them by name when they left, like a practiced politician's wife.

Timmy popped in twice, first to say that things were about the same, and then to tell us that the tests were back from the lab and everything looked unbelievably good—heart, lungs, Billy Rubin, urine output, the works. He was as close as he could get to being exultant, without showing really poor taste. I had a fleeting image of Miranda and me kneeling to kiss his NYU class ring and then lifting him to our shoulders for a triumphant ride through the corridor, with cheering, sobbing Intensive Care nurses tearing at his buttons.

Cal arrived in time to catch the last of Timmy's victory message: "So I think we're really on top of it now—it'll still be a *haul*, my guess is a week at least, but both Bleiweiss and I" (how modest, how scrupulously fair he was) "are breathing a lot easier right now."

"Gee, that's great!" Cal exploded, enveloping me and Miranda in a suffocating bearhug. "Would you say we've earned our lunch now—would you?" He squeezed, and we both laughed, and said yes! God, yes! And laughed again, all of us, half hysterical. "The Plaza!" I gasped recklessly. "Oh, yes! Perfect!" And Cal pounded Timmy on the back, and I kissed him recklessly on the mouth, and Miranda just looked at him with her great tender eyes, and we said we'd be back at three and then we were running for the elevator, still laughing and clutching each other, not wanting to let go.

In the cab we couldn't stop giggling; the driver kept staring nervously at us in his rear-view mirror. The Plaza sobered us up a little, though; there was something about that lobby which challenged you to look classy and lower your voice, or it would sneer. Richard and I had spent our wedding night there. We hung around the lobby newsstand waiting for the city edition of *The New York Times,* then bought two copies and took them to the Oak Room to read our wedding announcement over steak sandwiches and champagne. " 'The bride carried roses and stephanotis,' " Richard read aloud. "No kidding!" " 'Linda Bauman Weds Physician,' " I read aloud back. "*She* carried phlox." "I thought they had a vaccine against that now," Richard said. There we were—how cool can you get on your wedding night—each of us behind the *Times,* like a *New Yorker* cartoon, when an old friend of Richard's spotted us and came over to say hello. What's new? Well, nothing much, we said, casually lowering our papers, except we just got married three hours ago. His double-take was a classic—our proudest achievement of the day.

"I wonder if they still float rose petals in the finger bowls," I said to Miranda. The *maître d'* had obviously recognized our special need, if not our deservingness, for he bestowed

on us the northeast corner table, with the best possible view
of those decaying horse-drawn carriages lined up to await
spoiled prep school kids and their dates and families from
Ohio carefully holding onto their white hats. "If it's not on
the menu, we'll order it special," Cal promised. "After the
eggs Benedict and champagne, right?"

God, no, I couldn't go that far. That was what Richard
used to have with Donna Sue; it was their Sunday lunch
thing for years. I'd never been here with him for lunch, not
even the morning after our wedding. We'd flown to St. Croix
at nine-thirty A.M., and that was the last time we'd ever set
foot in the Plaza together. Not that I didn't want to—how
come I never rated eggs Benedict like Donna Sue? I once
came right out and asked him. "Because it's the kind of thing
you do with a girl when you're twenty-three and crazy in
love," he said. But I'm twenty-three and crazy in love, I reminded him. Yeah, but I'm thirty-three and married, he said,
which of course ended it.

"Just a chef's salad, I guess." I surrendered the velvety
crimson menu with its gold tassel. What the hell was I doing
having lunch at the Plaza? "And coffee."

Undaunted, unmarried, Calvin and Miranda ordered the
eggs and champagne. But then they stopped laughing too,
whether because I had or because suddenly it all seemed
like a bad idea, after all. Outside it didn't even look sunny
now. We had to start force-feeding gaiety to each other, as if
we were GI's who'd taken all kinds of insane risks to go
AWOL together, only to find ourselves feeling homesick for
camp. There seemed to be nothing to talk about, except
Timmy Spector and Dr. Mahler and the waiting-room visitors
and how impossible it was to sleep last night. I told them

about the stewardess from Ontario who'd taken two weeks to snap out of her coma, and about my suspicion that Timmy was convinced he and Richard were making medical history.

Finally the coffee arrived, and I had to help them finish the champagne. We were running out of time and material when I remembered about all the funny stuff in Richard's filing cabinet. So I threw that into the awkward silence—the Nutshell Library, the collected rejection slips, Benny Goodman, the drawings of Donna Sue, the pornography . . . And then there was this crazy diary which he must have been keeping for years . . . No, not a book, just a bunch of typewritten pages in some kind of code. "What kind of code?" asked Cal, interested.

"I don't know; it's got numbers and letters and abbreviated words. Hey, maybe Richard's a double agent and this whole thing with the mole and the liver is some fantastic SMERSH plot to keep him quiet while they—"

"Like what kind of numbers and letters, for instance?" Cal asked.

I dug in my handbag for something to write on. Cal handed me a pen and I jotted down some of the symbols as I talked. "First there were dates, like Friday, October 4, then initials, J or N; then sometimes numbers with x after—2x or 4x. And sometimes words like post or flag. And then in the later pages, like from 1967 on, everything had MGM, like: 'Wednesday, December 28, MGM, 2x or post.' Or something."

"That's wild," Cal said thoughtfully. "How many pages?"

"I don't know—fifteen or twenty. I didn't really study it, but it was pretty much all like that. You think it's an expense account? There are a lot of lunches and some dinners. Flag could be for parades; Richard loves a parade."

"Let's see," Miranda said, leaning over. She studied it, frowning, then pushed it back. "Expense account—sure, it must be. Can't we go, though? It's after three o'clock." She was still frowning; I couldn't tell if she was puzzling over Richard's code or worrying about getting back to the hospital. Anyway, she got up from the table before the waiter came back with Cal's change, and started for the door.

Cal watched her curiously, then shrugged when she stopped at the door, waiting for us. "Very nervous girl I got there," he said.

"Well, but why wouldn't she be? Look at what she's— what you're both going through, and it's not even your . . . I mean, for my sake—Richard's and mine. Miranda, you realize she doesn't even *know* us very well? So she's even further away. At least you're an old friend, which means she's mostly involved because you are. I don't know how to even tell you what I'd be like right now if it hadn't been for you two—"

"Oh, Julie, knock that off, that's . . . shit, I don't think I could *not* be going through this with you. Richard is— Christ, he's not really a close friend, he's just a great guy, I dig him. He . . . enjoys. I dig that. Remember when he got that big black leather Eames chair, with the footstool— you gave it to him for Christmas or something? I never saw anybody get such a goddamn *kick* out of a thing. We were up at your house for dinner, remember, and he was swiveling around in this big chair like some little kid, with tears in his eyes. You just don't know guys like that—*alive* like that— just sitting there making their own whatever it is—happiness, joyfulness—out of a chair. So he's a sweet guy we see sometimes, and I'm glad he's somebody I know, but who thinks about him—about it *mattering* that he's around? Listen, this is the honest-to-God first time I've even talked about it! Miranda and I haven't said word one—I don't know why, but we haven't. So I guess I needed to think why am I going through this . . . whatever it is. And *that's* why. I'm making myself *see* it matters that Richard exists. I'm showing him, or you, or somebody—myself—that I value him. Did I ever face that before about any friend? I guess not. I guess none of us ever had to." He stopped abruptly. "Christ, am I making *sense?*"

"Yes. Too much," I said, explaining why the two tears I'd been trying so hard to blink back into place had defied me and rolled right down. I stopped one with my tongue; the other landed in the champagne. Cal was still talking. "About Miranda, though, you're wrong—she's not involved because of me at all. She doesn't . . . it's so hard for her to show herself. It's that kind of wrapped-up coolness—dignity, whatever it is—that makes her look so turned off. Like you, in fact; you both probably got that the same way. Shy."

I nodded, glancing shyly toward Miranda, my newly appointed soul sister. She was still standing near the captain's station, leaning against a mahogany pillar, with her hands behind her, all coiled tension and helpless calm, like a sixty-dollar-an-hour model freezing to death in a bikini. Cal was saying, "I've never seen her this caught by anything. Anyone." He laughed. "Not even me."

We looked at each other, embarrassed again. I had no idea what he was telling me, and I wasn't sure I could handle it, regardless. "Guess we'd better go?" I suggested.

"Yeah, so it seems," he agreed, still studying me and not getting up.

Didn't I see this with William Holden once? "Then come on," I said, forgetting how it was supposed to end, and stood up decisively.

"Well, hi there," bubbled Miranda when we finally reached her.

"Sorry, babe," Cal said, ignoring the sarcasm. He reached up and touched her hair. "I just got wound up, like I do."

We emerged via the revolving door on 59th Street, linked arms and walked confidently to Fifth Avenue, where we split for opposite corners—who knows, maybe one of us would appeal to some hard-up cab driver. One finally took pity on us, seeing as how Mount Carmel was only two blocks from his garage.

Driving back in slow-torture traffic, we were a different crew from the trio of hopped-up kids last seen whizzing up to that fancy hotel a couple of sunlit hours ago. Could that really have been how we felt? Nothing on our idiotic minds but eggs Benedict? Only Miranda seemed to have retained the power of speech. She kept calling our attention to passing Kodacolor slides, cropped by the taxi window like so many tiny squares on a glossy contact sheet. Small boy losing turquoise balloon; weeping willow resembling long-haired hippie, grooving to breezes; little girls with "Footsees"—no, it's not a fungus, it's a plastic ankle ring toy. Chalk hopscotch marks —you never see kids play hopscotch any more—they look like Stone Age graffiti. We didn't give her much feedback though, so after a while all three of us just listened to the meter and studied Al Eisenberg's hack license for the rest of the way.

We were back in the waiting room at ten minutes to four. A whole new batch of well-wishers had gathered, many of them first-timers known only to me and/or Richard, not to each other. Somehow they'd managed to introduce themselves and advance to the nervous-chatter stage of early guests wondering where the hell the maid was with their first drink.

Marian, Timmy's wife, was there, apparently fresh from the beauty parlor, where they'd teased her hair so mercilessly that it lay on her head like a golden goose egg. Barney Halstead, pipe clamped safely in teeth like the permanently erect member it stood for, had arrived with a protective convoy of two pretty girls from the magazine's food department. (Or maybe they came to make us fudge brownies?) Laurie, sweet nutsy Laurie, had brought up a queen-size shopping bag full of Con-Tact, and was parked in a corner quietly pasting yellow-green abstract floral designs all over the clay pot that contained Aunt Addie's hydrangea.

And for some reason Pamela had felt moved to dig up our other best elementary-school friend, Peggy Pines, now a Mrs. Myles Mumford from Mount Vernon. We hadn't seen each other since we were sixteen. The two of them, Pam and Peggy, had met for lunch before coming up to surprise me—sort of a fun sympathy call. Peggy still had that leggy straight-edge build, only now you'd have to say she could use some fiberfill in the bra. And the teeth had worked out after all—perfectly white, even, slightly buck. Everyone had talked her parents out of straightening them. (So what if the bite is bad, she'll look just like Gene Tierney.) She had taught me about vaseline on your mouth (we were the last two in the class to be allowed to use lipstick at school), and she had presided at my first successful insertion of a Tampax, which I believed was the single most grown-up feat, short of going all the way, that you could accomplish at fifteen.

On that memorable day we gobbled our lunches in ten minutes so we could spend the rest of the period in the john. Pamela was posted at the outer door as a guard, and Peggy stood on the other side of my locked cubicle. Inside, we carefully taped the instruction folder from the Tampax box just above the toilet-paper dispenser. The diagrams—terrifying cross-sections of the female interior, full of squiggly Suez canals—showed a cute little cotton wad nestled in there like an eensy white mouse with its tail hanging down and out. That was supposed to be the tampon, properly inserted in the right canal zone.

"Ready?" Peggy called through the door. I'd been fidgeting for five minutes.

"I guess so," I said doubtfully. "Wait—my hands are sweating."

"Never mind that," she snapped. "Just don't get the cardboard soggy. It has to glide, like." God, she sounded experienced.

"Peggy," I called forlornly, "did *you* have trouble the first time? I mean, finding where to *put* it? I can't seem to—"

"For *Pete's* sake, Julie. You really *can't* put it in too many wrong places."

"Well, that's fine," I said, trying not to sound really upset.

"But so far I can't find *any* place. I mean, I don't think I've got one. Oh, help, now the cardboard's *bending!*"

"Honestly! You're not supposed to poke around with the cardboard, stupid—use your finger!" she commanded sharply. "Here, better take another one; that won't work now." A new Tampax appeared under the door.

"Sssh!" Pamela signaled, "somebody's coming!" Peggy deserted her post and started making hand-washing noises.

"What *time* is it?" I called anxiously.

"Quit worrying, will you," Peggy replied; I sensed everyone's patience wearing thin. "Okay, they're gone . . . Now *listen*—you really have to concentrate now or else we're quitting. Okay? Use your finger, right?"

"Okay, okay—hey, I think I found it! It's right *here!* Eureka—I'm a girl!"

Peggy was not overwhelmed. "Good. Now take the thing with your *other* hand and put it *right there*. Don't lose your *place!*"

"Okay, but *now* what?"

"Now push it in."

"Ow. It doesn't fit! Oh God, now what?"

"Try standing, like in the instructions. One foot up on the john seat."

"I can't find the *place* standing up," I wailed. "Anyway, how do you know it's not different if your hymen isn't broken? Maybe you went horseback riding more than I did last year."

"Because it's not different, that's why. It even says so right in the instructions."

"Where? It does not. It says about unmarried girls, that's all—that it's safe for unmarried girls. They don't even *men-*

*tion* the word hymen. Maybe it's designed not to go in if you're a virgin."

"Oh God, did you ever?" Pamela groaned. "Listen, I don't *care* if she gets it in. Do I have to stand here wasting a whole lunch hour?"

"And me—what am I, in the Tampax business or something?" Peggy demanded. "You wanna give up, go ahead. Just don't tell me how you hate sanitary belts and how *icky* it all is and you wish you could swim with the curse like I do— just don't give me that any more, okay?"

"All right, I'm *sorry*, I'll try again, please stay . . . Peggy?"

"All right. Now relax and do what I tell you . . ."

Half a box of bent cardboard tubes and wasted tampons later, I stumbled out of the cubicle, exhausted, every limb and muscle aching from acrobatic contortions and emotional stress, but securely, triumphantly Tampaxed.

Peggy had long since slumped to the floor. Pamela was crumped out against the door. The three of us jumped around the john, whooping and laughing and pounding each other, and then we beat it back to class, making it just as the final bell rang.

That night I took Parker pen in hand and inscribed, with an elaborate flourish and turquoise-blue ink, in my memory book: "Today I became a woman." If only I'd thought of it, I would have saved the cardboard tube.

J ulie?" I had not been paying attention to Barney Halstead, who was mouthing some sort of apology around his unlit pipe. ". . . So I hope you'll forgive me for bringing them." The pipe swiveled toward Bobbie and Jill, the two little wide-eyed food editors who were whispering outside the door, as if they were mustering courage to ring the bell and admit they were selling Girl Scout cookies.

"Aren't they coming in?" I asked Barney. "I mean, they're welcome."

"Well, that's sweet, I really have to get 'em back to the office, probably left the stove on or something, ha, ha, I just wanted to drop in myself and say hello . . ."

"Sure, well. Nice to . . . I appreciate—"

"And anything at all you need, I mean that," he said, backing out behind his pipe. "You know how we all feel about Richard."

"I sure do, Barney," I said, hoping I sounded less phony than he did. "'Bye, girls."

"Food editors sure look full of homemade goodness, don't they?" Peggy remarked, as their little behinds twitched down the hall.

"Julie." A solemn Timmy stood in the hall, beckoning. Oh, no, I thought. I was learning to read him better—much good might it do me. He was carrying some kind of printed form.

"Trouble, right?" I blurted the instant I cleared the door.

"Now take it easy," he said, noncommittally. "Let's duck in here a minute." He was steering me across the hall, through a door I'd never even noticed before. It looked like a supply closet—one of those shallow locked cupboards nobody ever quite went into, so much as stood in front of, tinkling glass beakers. But it turned out to be a whole room that had nothing much in it except an examining table, a chair and a desk. "So this is your secret hideout," I chirped quickly, to fill the silence. This silence is Occupied, Occupado, Occupé. Please wait until Libre. All I wanted was to buy a little piece of Richard's time for myself, to put off whatever Timmy was about to tell me.

"Julie, we've decided to dialyze him." He flashed me a quick look and decided to plunge right ahead; maybe I'd just let it go and not ask what that meant. "There's nothing *wrong*, so don't . . . We just think it would be a tremendous help. It'll take the strain off his kidneys. They're being overworked and, well, it's just a good idea to *rest* them if we can. So essentially it's a *safety measure*, that's all."

"Cross at the green, not in between," I said.

"Huh?"

"Nothing. How do you dial—dialyze—whatever you said . . . ?" With that, my voice went again. Every word wedged in my throat like the cherry pits I'd always been terrified of swallowing but never learned to spit out before I choked on them.

"It's *not* a big thing, I promise you . . . Here, sit down a second and just listen calmly."

I sat.

"Now," he said, leaning back against the examining table and rumpling the clean paper on it. "Dialysis is just a process, a way of automatically flushing the kidneys continuously. It will do what we did with the blood exchange—same thing, only with less of a shock to the system because it's *continuous*."

"You said that. But what are you going to do to him?"

"Well, it's really not complicated. We just have to . . . drill another hole or two, thread the tube into the kidney and out again. And that's *it*—that's all it is."

"Oh, well, if *that's* all." Heavy on the irony, I was. "Then why did we have to come in here?"

"Well, because you need to sign this." He pushed his paper at me.

"Sign? What is it?"

"It's a form, that's all, saying it's okay for us to do it, that you're permitting it."

"How come I didn't have to sign for any of the other holes?"

"Because none of the others involved voluntary surgery. It's purely a technical thing—Julie, you're getting upset again, I can *see* it."

"Not me, I'm about the same," I said, controlling the quaver beautifully. "See, my condition is satisfactory, just like all the other kids. I need your pen, unless you want me to sign in blood or something—ha, ha, just teasing."

### CONSENT FOR OPERATION

Date_____19__

I, _____, bearing the relationship of _____ to patient _____ hereby give consent for the operation known as _____, with anesthesia, if necessary, and for any modification of the operation deemed necessary by the surgeon.

Signed: _____

Address: _____

Witness: _____

"With anesthesia, if necessary!" I read. "Well, I guess we don't need to worry about that part, anyway. I mean, you already did that to him—in spades, you might say. Besides, if you hurt him bad enough to wake him up, then we can all just go home, right?"

"Julie—"

"Yes, Timmy? Forget something else you had to tell me in here?"

"No. Just take it easy. This is not something we're, uh, pulling on you. I've been leveling with you, haven't I? More than I would with anyone else. Haven't I?"

"Oh, Timmy, you're such a damn liar," I said wearily. I felt too tired even for wisecracks. "He's not okay at all or you wouldn't need to do this."

"That's not so! We are doing it as a safety—"

"—measure. I know, I heard you."

"But that's the truth! The kidneys can't perform like this indefinitely, and it's foolish to take a chance. We don't know how long it'll be before that liver starts moving—"

"Which means it *is* worse than you thought! You all said a few days—a week. Then last night you said two weeks, and now you have no idea—"

"We never gave you a time limit! Bleiweiss—"

"Bleiweiss my foot! Not one of you says anything the same way twice! This morning you said he was unbelievably good —all you had to do was wait for the Nobel Prize! I just wish I'd recorded it all because who would believe it? It's—Jesus, it's Hospital *Gaslight!*"

"Julie, if you don't calm down—" (That's it, take a firm tone with me.)

"—You'll what? Send me to the principal? Call my mother? *Dialyze* me?"

"Sign the form, Julie," he commanded sternly. "And cut it out. Christ, you've been so *great* up to now."

"Aw, hey, that's nice you said that. Here." I signed and then stalked out, wrapping my anger around me like a warm sweater.

Back in the waiting room the party was chugging into high. Pam and Peggy were still reliving the horrors of childhood; Laurie had finished working on the flower pot and had moved on to a fruit basket, and the Macks had arrived with the Bernses, who, though separated, were dating. They'd all been taking turns telling funny hospital or doctor stories. Danny Mack was into a lengthy one, so I waited at the door for the laugh to explode, then arranged my face into a with-it smile and dashed to my seat so fast that I had no time to notice who had moved in next to me. It was Marian Spector and her golden beehive. Miranda, she said, had wandered down the hall and lost a quarter in the cigarette machine, and Calvin had gallantly gone to beat it up.

Marian bestowed upon me her gummiest smile; there was lipstick on her teeth, and I was just going to sit and stare at it—that'll show Timmy. She was a giggler, that Marian. Ordinarily the acoustics in our living rooms were good enough to muffle her, or maybe it was just that we'd never sat this close before. The chirpy noises she made, like a series of damaged hiccups, caromed off the walls and the plastic upholstery like those blobs of lit-up sound at the Electric Circus.

"Timmy's so excited about this case," she squealed. "He just can't talk about anything else!"

"That's nice," I said.

"Well, I think it's wonderful that we're all friends—it makes it even *more* exciting! Don't you?"

"Don't I what?"

"Think?"

"Oh, yes, indeed," I said. "Friends are much more exciting. I mean, if he's saving Richard's life, it's really good that they're basically compatible."

"Yes!" she agreed. "That's just what I was saying before you—"

"On the other hand," I went on recklessly—look, Ma, I'm a bitch!—"if he *isn't* saving it, we may find it a little awkward at dinner parties."

That stopped her in mid-giggle, along with everyone else's private noise. Even the strangely comforting sound of Laurie peeling off adhesive backing ceased, and she looked up from her work, bewildered. "Hey, Julie," she reproached me in soft dismay. Peggy and Pamela exchanged glances, but neither seemed happier with the one she traded for. Why did I have to go and spoil everybody's fun?

"Sorry, folks," I mumbled into the tension. "It's just that I'm bushed, I guess, jumpy—and that I have to go home and face Matthew's hamburger."

Oh sure, they understood, exhaling loudly; even Marian managed a giggle of forgiveness. At which point Calvin and Miranda reappeared, scars of battle on their knuckles and shoes, a flush of hard-won victory on their faces. They'd rescued their quarter from the evil cigarette machine. "Look," they said, holding up the shiny evidence. "It's an omen!"

At ten o'clock that night Richard caught a virus—from the dialysis, or another reaction to something, or he'd built up a tolerance to some medication, or the new holes made him more vulnerable to sneak attacks by UFO's. It could have been anything. I knew better, of course; he'd got it from my lunch at the Plaza.

Once again I grabbed Miranda's hand in our secret sorority grip. (If she digs her nails into my hand hard enough, if it hurts enough, if it actually *bleeds*, then everything will be all right.) We kept the hand-mangling routine hidden in the folds of our skirts, between the seat cushions. So nobody would feel hurt that I hadn't chosen some other hand? Or because she and I didn't want to see ourselves punishing each other like that? I mean, why *were* we doing it, anyway?

The only other time in my life I'd tried to wrench salvation from another person's hand, I was seventeen and over-emotional, and that hand too had belonged to a stranger—name of Rita Hohaus. I had known her for two weeks, and after the crisis passed I never saw her again. We were classmates of sorts, having enrolled on the same day at the Irma Fontanel Charm School for a two-week desperation course. We both weighed a hundred and forty-eight pounds the day we registered, and we were the only girls in the group under forty-five years of age and two hundred pounds. Other than that, I don't remember anything special that drew us together.

On the first day of the course, supple-limbed lady Fontanel instructors weighed and measured us, holding the tape very loose so it would look like we'd lost more when they measured us again at the end of the two weeks. The worse you were *Before,* and the better you were *After,* the more Irma Fontanel could be proud to display your record in their flowered reception salon. "Fontanel graduates lose an amazing average of twenty pounds and four to six inches from waist and hips." For final measurements and weighing-ins, you were forbidden to eat *anything*—not even a swallow of rinse water after brushing—and they pulled the tape measure so tight it often snapped, but you lost your required four inches.

My hips were forty on registration day, even before they slackened the tape, and I was pushing thirty-two in the waist. When I was seventeen, never mind Frank Sinatra, it was a very bad year. As a college freshman I had slipped from an uncomfortable size fourteen to an irreparable sixteen, and now I really hated myself in any dress. On campus I got away with jeans and loose shirts with flapping tails that hung discreetly over the worst parts. I didn't really look fat because I was so tall and had long slim arms and legs. People thought of me more as *big.* But somehow that sounded worse, because fat you could change by not eating any more doughnuts or cutting down from five meals a day between snacks to just five meals a day or just snacks, while big was something you were born to be, a congenital defect. "You've got those broad shoulders; you're a big girl, you can carry it" was what the salesladies trying to be kind said when confronted with me. But nobody *else* had to carry it. I thought of myself lumbering through life like a star fullback who didn't want to turn pro but couldn't get out of his pads. "Big bones" was another curse they hung on me. Aunts and uncles liked that one; it sounded strong and healthy, the product of enriched protein bread from America's heartland.

I had great legs, though, and this was a terrific point of pride until Dwight Perlmutter (the one whose cigarette butts I'd saved) said, "What a *waste* those legs are on you, when a beautiful girl like Beryl Sideman gets stuck with a pair of tree stumps. Boy, somebody sure balled up *that* order."

During freshman year my mother kept sending me huge CARE packages of date dresses. After a month or two I'd convinced her that jeans were the only thing allowed for classes, and that *Glamour* and *Seventeen* didn't know what they were talking about with all those plaid skirts and Bermuda shorts in the August back-to-school issue. But what could I say about date dresses except the truth: I didn't *have* dates. Still the boxes came. I opened them so that I could say thank you for the black velvet or I love the pink taffeta, but I left them with their sleeves crossed in their flat tissuepaper sandwiches, and simply slid the box neatly under my bed. Occasionally some large but still possible-looking girl who actually did have dates would come in and borrow something, so most of the stuff looked lived in by the end of the term. (This model was used only twice, by special arrangement; its owner never got asked to the Dartmouth Winter Carnival or the Harvard-Yale game or even Hobart-Trinity.)

I held the all-time dorm record for dirty underwear. I never washed anything; it became my badge of distinction. Pants, socks, shirts—I just wore them until they called attention to themselves, then balled them up and threw them in the closet (after all, there wasn't anything else in there). When everything was too filthy to get away with one more time, I turned things inside out and wore them that way until they got even all around. By then it was either time for vacation, when I could go home and get all new ones—"It's not *my* fault the laundry loses everything . . . I *did* sew the name tapes on . . ." (I'd thrown them out). "It happens to everybody, honest!"—or else I'd con some friend in another dorm (where they didn't know about me) into lending me a couple of pairs of whatever until after vacation, when I could pay her back out of the new stuff.

That summer I tried to go straight. Resolved: to stop being a fat pig. Or bust. Out of my own allowance I paid the Irma Fontanel Charm School to change me into a thin princess. The reason was one Blair Johnston II, a blind date from Babson Institute who had turned out to be a dead ringer for Phil Watson of the New York Rangers, except he didn't play hockey or curse in French. Blair was all chiseled and strong-jawed and khaki pants and crew-neck lamb's-wool sweaters and little sharp pointed dog-teeth and flashy blue eyes. He was *handsome*. And he called me *again*. Oh, he was dumb; he had to be *something*, or what would he be doing calling me? And who cared, anyway? Once I tried forcing him to be bright, but it didn't pan out at all. A girl in my dorm had been going with a Phi Bete from Harvard Law School with whom, she bragged, she could park and just talk about justice. That was what I wanted too, so one time Blair and I parked and I said, "What do you think about justice?" He said, "I don't know; what do you think?" I said some deeply felt stuff about Plato's Gold Men and Silver Men and how Nietzsche scared me but also made such powerful sense. And he said, "Yeah. That's more or less what I think."

After that I decided I really didn't care if he was smart.

I went to beer parties in his fraternity house, and football games, and gave him hand jobs in the car, and progressed to petting above and below, *inside*. And at last I had something to say when Gloria Stewart and Brooke Taylor and the others in the dorm talked about whether you should go all the way if you were really in love, and how did you know when that was? (Blair didn't *want* us to go all the way; everyone in my dorm thought that was beautiful.)

So the only hitch, besides his dumbness, was that his parents, Mr. and Mrs. Blair Johnston I, were shocked and dismayed when he wrote home to tell about *us*. They lived on a mink ranch in Green Bay, Wisconsin, and they had certain feelings about certain things. Her name is *Wallman?* they said. She's not Jewish, is she? She is? Oh. Does she, uh, *mix* with the others in the dorm? You know, *we* had one in the dorm when I was in college. We said hello to her, of course, but we didn't really *mix*.

Blair wrote back to stick up for me and our love. Honestly, Mom, he said he'd said, she's wonderful! Of course she mixes; she's very popular. (*I'm very popular!*) Sure she's pretty. (*I'm pretty!*) And *very* intelligent. ("Oh, they're *all* intelligent! I *figured* she'd be *intelligent*," he said she'd said.) Anyway, I just wish you'd let me ask her down this summer. I really want you to meet her; I know you'll feel different when you meet her. (Blair had come a long way from the mink ranch, though he still got "nauseous" on the train, he said, if a colored person was eating in the dining car at the same time. He knew it was silly, and he was really trying to get over it, but he still couldn't help it; they'd *taught* his stomach to turn that way.)

Mrs. Johnston finally wrote to invite me out for inspection. "Blair tells me you would like to come out here to visit him" ("That's some invitation," my mother said)—so three weeks before the end of school I began training for the bout. *Total* starvation, for starters. I was the first freshman ever to stay up all night cramming for exams on an empty stomach. Somebody said I should eat saltines wrapped in Kleenex; it filled you up and didn't get absorbed into your system. I tried that. Also enemas and once Ipecac, to throw up a mushroom pizza I had yielded to in an agony of self-pity after a bitch of a geology exam.

And every Sunday I attended Episcopal services in town with Barbie Wilson and Gretchen Leacock, two of the cleanest-cut WASPs who mixed with me in the dorm. They were coaching me in hymns and responsive reading, so at least I'd have a feel for the amens and the congregation rises when Mr. and Mrs. Johnston watched me for false moves in church.

Barbie and Gretchen also took me to the local suburban branch of Lord & Taylor, into which I'd never before set foot, to choose something "Wisconsin-looking" in a size twelve ("For my *sister*—she's thinner," I explained sheepishly to the salesgirl with the curling lip). All the dresses in those Pandora's boxes under my bed were for a sophisticated New York type (i.e., Jewish); clearly nothing like that would do. "I see something pink and crisp," said Barbie firmly. "And a white straw hat with streamers," Gretchen added. "Oh, *no*," I wailed finally, gazing at my unzipped, unbelted, pink-and-white-streamered reflection. "I look like Honey Bunch!"

"You do not—you look like a rancher's daughter-in-law," Barbie said.

"Exactly," said Gretchen. Two against one.

When exams ended, I had dropped from 161 to 148, and

also from a C to a C-minus average—which at least showed that I wasn't so disgustingly *intelligent*. However, there were still those twenty pounds I had no intention of carrying to the mink ranch. I needed to break 130 to zip the pink dress and close the belt, and a two-pound margin to exhale.

So Fontanel Charm School it was. In two weeks they would remold me into something poised, confident, charming and beautiful. Basically their method was a snap, provided you were desperate enough not to cheat on weekends. They weighed us daily and measured us on Mondays, and we had to stay there from ten A.M. to five-thirty P.M. daily, surrounded by mirrors (lest we forget), learning how to cross our legs, thwack our thighs, walk on our buttocks, squat, throw out our pelvises, reshape our brows and smile without crinkling.

There was a half-hour lunch break (one teaspoon of mineral oil and lettuce), and every night we got a printed homework assignment telling us what to have for dinner, which exercises to do fifty of before retiring, and what to do to our faces before sleeping. Mineral oil was prescribed three times a day; we were expected to move our bowels more than any other part of the body.

On the twelfth day they told us how to prepare for graduation. Black one-piece bathing suits with built-in bras were required; also high-heeled black pumps. Hair was to be professionally shampooed and set, and there would be full make-up and manicure inspection at eleven A.M., followed by *After* photos. (*Before* photos showed us wearing any grubby thing at all, preferably something that made the worst of that we'd come there to make better. I had brought my old high school gym suit to exercise in; it had bunchy elasticized bloomers

and perspiration stains. "Oh, that's *perfect* for the *Before!*"
the instructor chortled when I unveiled it. "Get her profile
with all those folds over the rear end!" The cameraman
zeroed in for posterity. They also took front, back and head
shots, pouncing greedily on every jowl, crow's foot, oily
blackhead and unplucked hair.)

The *After* portraits took five times as long, because for
them we needed to be carefully posed, angled and lit—the
object being to show the dramatic contrast between our
glamorous new selves and the shameful spectacles we'd been
just two weeks before. Considering that your average Fontanel student weighed in at 250 to 300 pounds, and weighed
out at 225 to 275, that photographer deserved a Pulitzer for
sheer genius in the darkroom.

After the *Afters*, Miss Fontanel herself administered the
last rites. Ageless Irma (pick a number from seventy-five to
infinity) ascended the mirror-rimmed stage flanked by her
own six reflections. She always wore black, which draped her
all-in-one boned torso like a bolt of cloth basted to a dress
dummy. The hair gleamed like real patent leather, and her
eyelids were so weighted with beady mascara that she appeared to have given up trying to pry them open. First she
delivered the commencement address. The thirty-four graduates sat in the first two rows, like a herd of quivering hip-
popotami dressed up in Lastex bellybands. Faculty and other
students sat all around us (too late, we're trapped).

Miss F. glared down through her closed lids at the land-
scape of fleshy mountains and foothills—her kingdom—and
then spoke.

"Fat!" she shrieked at us. "Fat! Fat!" (We cowered and
shifted precariously on our dinky folding chairs, which hadn't

been designed for this audience.) "Does every one of you hate that word?" Miss Fontanel demanded. (Mute, terrified, nodding.) "Do you *despise* it?" (Yes, oh, fervent yes.) "No!" she screamed. "Not until you have destroyed it layer by layer —the fat that you have heaped on your own—bodies! This—" she paused, flinging out her arms (which were carefully covered to the wrists) as if she were Billy Graham welcoming us to Glory—"this is only the beginning!"

Then came the certificate awards, starting with the honor roll ("girls" who had dropped upwards of fifty pounds). The biggest loser was a Mrs. Cirker, whose varicosities covered her great thighs like alternate routes on a map of New England. "310 Pounds Before—255 After!" There was deafening applause as we all rose for the musical salute (*A Pretty Girl Is Like a Melody*). Mrs. Cirker, wobbling on her tiny heels, heaved herself gamely to the stage for her prizes; a chrome car-ornament Venus and a scholarship (twenty percent off) if she re-enrolled for another two weeks. This was valid up to one month after graduation, provided the winner did not regain more than ten of the pounds she'd just taken off.

Those who didn't make the honor roll were called up in descending order, according to their measure of success. Rita Hohaus and I were borderline cases; neither of us had reached the passing twenty-pounds-lost mark the day before, and this was our last chance to make good. The final weigh-in was conducted right on the stage, with the whole school watching and Miss Fontanel herself sliding the indicator with one of her merciless scarlet-tipped claws. If, God forbid, you were still not down to par, she handed you your discharge paper in

withering silence, and there was no pudgy hand-clapping from
your peers. You were a disgrace to your bathing suit.

Which was why Rita and I sat together cringing through
the exquisite suspense. Perhaps mutual knuckle-mashing
would burn up a few more calories; in any case, we ruined
each other's required manicures by chipping the fresh polish.
I had been three pounds above target yesterday—131. In a
frenzy of guilt and panic I had skipped my entire dinner
(three ounces white meat of chicken, no skin) and taken an
extra dose of mineral oil instead. Two BM's this morning
ought to be worth something, if there was any justice in the
world. (What do I think of justice? It's a lady with a scale
that says I lost twenty pounds.) Oh, please, *please* make me
be 128. Otherwise, that's the end of Blair. That's what it
*really* means—it's destiny's way of saying no. I'm not even
going to Wisconsin if I don't make it; I'll just take that stupid
dress back in September and say my poor thin sister died
from malnutrition.

"*Julie Wallman*—148 Pounds *Before!* Miss Wallman, please
step forward for final weigh-in!"

Oh God, I can't. I'm *sick.*

"Go *on,*" Rita Hohaus whispered hoarsely, pulling her hand
away with one last dig at my pink thumbnail. "You *have*
to!" she added. People were starting to swivel around. I forced
myself up off the chair, advanced shakily into the aisle—and
passed out.

They mailed me my certificate two days later, with the final
weight left blank. According to my bathroom scale, it was
128.

A few days later I made it to Wisconsin in my thin dis-
guise. I could even look down and see my whole belt when

I was sitting down, a heady experience I hadn't had since eighth grade. I was a model guest, too—made my bed before breakfast, helped clear the table, called her ma'am and him sir, and daintily hung my conspicuously rinsed nylons in the guest bathroom. On Sunday night, as Blair and I were leaving for the train, he hugged his mother and whispered happily in her ear, "Well?" Mrs. Johnston did not favor us with a smile. "Well, I hope your friend enjoyed her visit," she said. "I don't think I won her heart," I murmured to Blair as we got into the car. "Aw, sure you did," he protested. "You'll see."

The next day he called me in New York to announce that he'd been forbidden to see or "maintain contact" with me unless he wanted to drop out of college right now and support himself—or me. "I still love you," he said, crying into the receiver, "but I'm only a junior!"

In September I went back to college weighing 145, and I was up to 160 again by Christmas. The week before my sophomore year ended, Blair called me. I told Emily, my friend, my love, to say I was out.

They conquered Richard's virus by pumping a series of different antibiotics into his bloodstream. Victory came in less than an hour. Timmy charged in to tell us, wearing his Eisenhower VE-Day smile again. "He's got *fantastic* resources," he reported. "You should have seen the slide—we took some cultures to see what was happening—and it was absolutely incredible. The antibodies just swarming over that virus within *seconds!* Honestly, none of us ever saw anything like it!"

I turned to Miranda; her eyes looked moist but not runny. It struck me that I couldn't picture her crying, rumpling the smooth planes of her face, disturbing its peace with random puffings and swellings. We both smiled as the pain went away. "Fantastic resources," I echoed, liking it. "How about that?"

"It's from loving music," she replied almost inaudibly.

The night visitors had advanced and receded even before the virus; now that things were quiet and "under control," Timmy thought I should be taken home.

Miranda got up like a good girl. "No," I said. "I'm not going." I stretched out, unknotting my cramps on the couch, and kicked off my shoes. "I have a feeling," I explained, "that he's going to wake up tonight. And I think I should be here."

"Julie, that's silly," Timmy said, like a slightly annoyed daddy. "He isn't going to wake up like that all of a sudden —tonight or tomorrow or any time. It's a *gradual* process; I thought you understood that finally. The reflexes will start to come back little by little, stronger and stronger. A coma sort of lifts off, like fog."

"I don't care," I said. "I'm not going. I can sleep here." I closed my eyes to demonstrate.

"Good evening," somebody said dourly at the door. It was Dr. Mahler.

I fought an impulse to stand up respectfully, or at least put my shoes back on, and deliberately did nothing except turn my head. "Hello, Dr. Mahler. This is Miss Graham,

Mr. Jaffe . . . uh, friends of ours." Did I have to explain what they were doing in his hospital?

They all shook hands, mumbling appropriately, but Mahler kept frowning toward the elevated bottoms of my feet. Were they clean? I tried to remember without looking. Or was it that I shouldn't have them up on the furniture? I argued it out with myself. (Look, I have a right to relax. Yeah, but not sprawl. Well, is it my fault I have to hang around here till midnight in a state of exhaustion? Who said you *had* to? Well, they act as if I'm supposed to. I feel they expect it. That's tough—but it's your problem.)

One of us lost, and I swung my feet down into my shoes. Mahler cleared his throat until everything was decently covered, then focused on a lamp at the other end of the room. "I, uh, just dropped by to, uh, tell you we received some good news from the lab a while ago. Sorry I couldn't get up here earlier. It's about the lymph nodes . . ."

"What limp nodes?"

"*Lymph*. Your husband's—we had them removed, you remember? The chain of nodes from the area adjacent to the, uh, melanoma? The mole? To examine for evidence of metastasis?"

"Pardon?"

I'd earned my first grimace of the evening. "Spread of the infection," he said, remembering to simplify for us slower students.

"Oh, sure. I remember . . . I guess." I shrugged, which caused several of his key facial muscles to twitch.

"I believe we told you in some *detail*, following the excision of the melanoma. Mole."

"I said I guessed I *remembered*. Anyway, could we hear the good news?"

"The lab study . . . of the excised lymph nodes . . . reveals no invasion . . . of the malignancy. Not . . . one . . . cell. In other words, it was all localized in the mole; it had not spread. He was . . . he is *clean*."

"Hey, that's wonderful!" Calvin began cheerleading.

"Yeah," I said numbly. "But then how come—I mean, why didn't they just leave the lymphs alone? If he was clean, couldn't they leave him alone after they took the mole off?"

Timmy answered without raising his hand. "You can't do that with a melanoma. You have to take out the lymph nodes in order to tell if they're clean."

"Why?" I persisted. "They *were* clean. Who cared if you could tell or *not*? It's like the tree that falls in the forest, where nobody hears it make a noise. Who says it *needs* to be heard?"

"That's cute, Julie, but you just don't sit around philosophizing about melanoma. You look to see, or else you risk the guy's *life*."

Mahler didn't seem to want any more of Timmy's help. He had an announcement. "Mrs. Messinger," he began, forcing one of his Jekyll grins. "I can tell you now, with a certainty I did not have before, that your husband exercised great prudence in reporting to us when he did."

"Prudence," I mused, groping for the logic in it. I couldn't seem to find any right off, so I confessed I didn't see it that way. "Let's say he hadn't been so prudent," I began slowly, feeling my devilish way. "Say he *didn't* report to you and you *didn't* dig out his lymph nodes, which were all so nice and clean? Then, as I see it, nobody would have given him such a prudent dose of that anesthetic, and none of this—"

"Forgive me, Mrs. Messinger?" Mahler interrupted, not even pausing to see if I would. "You're not being precisely rational just now. I quite understand, believe me, and I urge you to go home and rest. This is all extremely trying for you, and it seems likely to grow more so before it is over."

There was something menacing about his oily tone now. "Why do you say that?" I demanded.

"Because it is true," he said evenly. "Now I must say good-night. I trust Dr. Spector can persuade you to get to bed." He nodded stiffly to "Mr. and Mrs., uh . . ."—meaning Cal and Miranda—and left us.

"Well?" Cal challenged sternly, all imbued with Mahler's delegated authority. "You gonna disobey him?"

"No," I said meekly. "I'll go quietly."

"It really is good news about the lab report, isn't it?" Miranda asked Timmy. It was a plea.

"Of course," he said. "Now who gets to take Julie home?"

"You," I said. "I mean, if you can."

"Sure, why not? Give me ten minutes." He did not seem delighted, but I really didn't want to go with Cal and Miranda. Something about its being late at night and going home; I felt oddly three's-a-crowdish and burdensome. Besides, maybe Timmy would tell me something. Anything.

But when he did, all the way home and for fifteen minutes parked in front of my house, I wasn't ready for what came out: a tongue-lashing about my behavior and general attitude—toward the nurses, the hospital, the doctors, him and "God knows who else." I was childish and destructive, stubborn and stupid, hostile and uncooperative. Didn't I know the entire hospital was practically *mobilized* for this case?

That people were pitching in, *volunteering* time and effort that wasn't even called for—people who had no reason to be concerned? Somehow Richard had become a war effort for Mount Carmel; Timmy had never seen such total involvement there over the fate of any patient. Nurses—the Intensive Care Unit girls—had I even noticed the way they handled him? Mahler and Bleiweiss, and now the kidney man, Tompkins, and maybe a dozen others I didn't even know about, the lab people—did I have the slightest idea of the *hours* these people were spending? The *research* they were doing on their own time? Did it even occur to me once to be, if not *grateful*, at least not *bitchy!* What the hell made me start acting like this, anyway? Some kind of hysterical self-pity? Who the hell was I trying to get even with? Him? Mahler? Richard, maybe?

After a while he switched to what I was doing to myself, which was even worse. "I think Richard's going to make it," he declared again with his usual breezy omniscience. "But I don't know if *you* will, at the rate you're going."

"What exactly did *that* mean," I yelped defensively.

Simply that I was turning myself into some kind of bitter, pathetic weirdo who hung around the hospital day and night —not that I didn't have a right to, but what was I proving by making it my life work? It was like I'd taken holy orders or something—I was never going to go anywhere, I was just going to sit there forever berating everybody for making me sit there forever, was that it? Because if it was, I needed either a spanking or a head-shrinking—maybe both.

"What do *you* think I should be doing, going dancing?" I asked.

"Maybe," he retorted. "Out to dinner, seeing people—anywhere but that plastic tomb you've sealed yourself into. Jesus, you sit there like a spider waiting for your little friends. It's the creepiest act I ever saw, and I've seen a few creeps up there."

"Is that about it?"

"Yeah, that's it. Julie? I'm sorry I had to be rough; I didn't mean to hit so hard; it just came out that way."

"It always does," I murmured; I hurt all over. "Oh, it's only a slight concussion, sir. I can set the broken leg myself."

I got out without looking at him, and dragged my bruises upstairs. He's right, of course, I decided in the elevator. If Richard makes it, what will I have contributed? And if he doesn't, ditto.

I went through all my bed-postponing rituals, and gave up at ten past three. When I was four or five and afraid of sleep, all I had to do was think about things I hated, like which meal I'd hated the most that day. I would run through the breakfast, lunch and dinner menus in my mind, trying to decide whether the soft-boiled eggs had made me gag more than, say, the calves' liver. Or how about the bowl of lumpy Farina with the wisp of smoke trickling up out of its middle? I used to be served that on a tray in bed when I was recuperating from something. My sister would leave for school at eight o'clock, and at noon when she got home for lunch, there I'd be crying into the same mealy mess, now cold and lumpier. The single spoonful I'd taken was always wedged solid in a corner of my mouth. I was not allowed to get up, see, till I'd finished breakfast. Farina tastes much worse cold than hot, in case anyone wants to know.

Richard *liked* Farina. Also Ralston. I still gag when I smell it, so he used to cook it for himself; it made him feel warm and loved. Food equals love, Dr. Rosenfeld said; love equals food. Richard's whole food orientation was childlike: milk and crackers at bedtime; Hostess Twinkies for dessert. Before I met him when he went to Chinese restaurants he'd order lamb chops because all that other stuff looked funny. It took me two years to convince him that Moo Goo Gai Pan couldn't possibly disagree with him any more than chicken fricassee. (Even plain broiled chicken was a problem; I had to cut it up so it didn't look so "human"—with actual wings that once flapped or legs that the damn thing used to walk around on.)

Food equals love. Maybe that really was why I went on what Rosenfeld called my sexual binge the summer before we got married. Stuffing myself with men instead of jelly doughnuts. But that wasn't how I thought of it; I just didn't want to be the kind of girl who sleeps with one guy and then marries him—the acceptable updated edition of a virgin bride. Richard had all those grainy blowups of Donna Sue Birnbaum's classic tits and other mastered pieces, whereas I . . .

Besides, Richard and I had gone to Provincetown together, and he'd left after a week to think about whether or not he really wanted to marry me, or whether he was still caroming off Donna Sue's last farewell. So okay, go think, I said bravely; I'm staying. I had another whole week before Macy's could put me back in the basement. (I was now assistant budget hosiery buyer in charge of "Irregulars." It was not exactly a meteoric career, but as Richard said, it was better than heavy lifting.)

The night he checked out of our rooming house, gallantly paying the landlady for "my wife staying another week," I checked into the singles scene at the Ropewalk Bar, assuring myself that I was thin, pretty and socially secure. After all, we were somewhat engaged, so I wasn't really *looking*, like all those other girls in there furtively checking their mirrors. Also, I knew people, because Richard had insisted on spending at least an hour a night listening to their jazz piano player. His name was Milt, and we'd talked to him enough to know that he was married, but only nine months a year. Summers they split; she went around singing Nellie Forbush, and he came up here to make tranquilizing background noise for all the editorial secretaries who hadn't lined up a dinner date yet.

Milt said his wife had a liberal attitude about fidelity during their off-season, which made marriage much less of a drag. Richard liked that a lot; I emphatically didn't, but secretly I found it sort of interesting. Besides, Milt had a sexy sad mouth and the backs of his hands weren't hairy. So him first, I decided coolly, entering the Ropewalk alone that night. It was the first time I'd ever felt so sure I could "get" a boy— and equally sure that I didn't *need* him.

It was easy, but I can't really say it was fun. Milt finished work at eleven, we drove around in his car, parked and necked, and then he asked politely whether I was "protected." Of course not, I said. (I hadn't even thought of wearing my diaphragm to cheat on Richard.) So we had to drive to his rooming house to get his Trojans, by which time I really didn't even want to. I went through with it, though (no C.T., I), right in the front seat with the steering wheel and gearshift, and cold and messy, and no place for my elbows or knees. And I really didn't even like him; all I thought was, So there, Richard, so there.

The following night I went to a house party with a boy named Steve I'd met on the beach. Nobody even bothered to

ask anybody else's last name, but there was a lot of vodka
and grapefruit juice, and the lights went out about ten o'clock
and people started pairing off into bedrooms. I don't remember much except that Steve's breath smelled like hot corn on
the cob and that when we started thrashing around I pulled
my face away and yelled, "I'm not protected! Not *protected!*"
"Don't worry," he panted, stifling me with corn fumes, "I'll
never come, I'll never come!" Richard always said that was
bad for a guy's health, so I pulled away again and panted back,
"I thought that was bad for your health!" He started laughing, forced open my mouth, and said, "Don't worry, honey, I
got Blue Shield!" I swore off corn for the rest of that summer.
So there, Richard.

There were two others before the week ended. "Higamous,
Hogamous," Richard used to recite. "Hogamous, Higamous,
men are polygamous, Higamous, Hogamous, women monoga-
mous." He also said that women were flowers; they were supposed to stay in place and look open and beautiful for the bee.
My Provincetown protest was against that too. Look at me
prove how wrong he is! Screw male arrogance! Nobody gets
to plant me in any mudpile, cooling my rooted heels while he
buzzes around on his fuzzy little wings. Knock knock, it's
your winged Messinger; you know you got the best nectar in
this whole tulip bed, baby.

Well, I can fly too, see. But had I really? Would I ever?

I didn't tell Richard about that week, but somehow he
sensed a difference the minute I got home. For the first time
in our fourteen-month romance, I realized suddenly that I
could "get" him too. And what's more, I thought to myself
with a tremendous burst of brand-new pride—like when I

first crossed a street alone—I don't *need* to! It was a surge of feminine power, the thing I knew other girls had, which explained how they could get boys to do things—or to stop doing things—whenever they wanted.

If I hadn't learned to fly, at least I'd sprouted something that passed for wings. The next day Richard said he'd made up his mind, and we got married four weeks later. As for the wings—well, I never really got to try them after all. Had I.

W hat day is it now, Mommy?"

"The third—I mean it's Friday. June, uh, fourteenth. Why?"

"*See*, Matthew? I *told* you it's not Saturday yet. Mommy, what are we doing Saturday?"

"We're, uh, I have to . . . I'll be visiting Daddy most of the day, but you could . . ." (Oh God, there goes the finger in the mouth.) "Nicky, sweetie, don't suck, *please*, look at your poor knuckle." (The more you call attention to it, the worse you make it. Besides, you've got *your* finger for a consolation prize; why can't he have his? Oh, shut up, I just don't want him pushing all his little teeth out of whack. Bulldicky, you just don't want people to see your kid sucking. Tsk, tsk, there goes that anxiety-ridden little Messinger boy; his mother must be— Oh, that's not *fair*! Matthew doesn't suck! That's because you gave Matthew a pacifier. You should have given Nicky one, but you hated the way it would have looked—that big plastic thing stuck in the middle of his beautiful tiny face. You didn't care so much about Matthew's face, right? Anything, even a pacifier, to shut it.)

It was Richard's fault; Matthew bugged him crying all the time—*that's* when he started cutting out every night. He couldn't stand being boxed in with that screaming kid on the other side of a thin wall. Nicky was so smily and quiet; it was no sweat being a nice daddy with that one. He even tried changing Nicky's diapers a few times. Not if there was poopee, though; he gagged if it had poopee. But he never went near Matthew, even when he was clean. "The minute I touch him he spits up! It's a goddamn reflex, I tell you. I don't *care* if you just changed him; he still smells. He'll go to his college interviews smelling like that!"

So then Richard would slam out into the night, and I'd sit there blaming it all on this smelly, squalling baby, who'd just spit up again on his nice yellow terry-cloth pajamas. (Yeah, but whose fault was it that you had him? Who was it that spouted all that crap about its being unfair to Nicky to wait for two or three years, that he'd be spoiled rotten. And if we had another one right away, adorable Nicky would never have to go through all that lousy adjusting to the little sibling; he'd never even remember its not being there. Oh, it'll be a cinch having them really close together. Remember all those stupid reasons? (a) We'll get it all over with quicker; (b) we won't have to put all the equipment away—the potty seat and bottles, the plastic pants and stroller—and then get it all out again three or four years later. And (c)—oh, c was a beaut— they'll always have each other even if they're not popular. And if this one's another boy we don't ever have to move; they can share a room till they go to college! And if it's a girl we can still leave them together five or six years. Who cares if they touch peepees, anyway; at least we'll know where they've both been!) It was me, all *me*. Richard only said okay. That was all: "Okay."

"*What* could we?" Matthew was demanding. "You didn't tell about Saturday."

"We'll see," I said lamely, infuriating them both.

"Aw, but—"

"*Not now.*" My rising tone indicating absolute authority, dangerous if crossed. "Schooltime—we'll discuss it *tonight!*" Benevolent despot. I kissed them goodbye. (There, all better? Hardly, Mommy, you big bully.)

I took the bedroom phone off the hook to start the day by loading something in my favor. Ha, ha, can't catch me. What if—hey, what if I played hooky all day? Just like that. Timmy had practically ordered me to stop suffocating in that plastic tomb. Womb tomb waiting room. Impulsively I grabbed the phone again, jabbed its little buttons until the dial tone replaced the whiny out-of-order noise, and called my hairdresser for an appointment. Then I congratulated myself nastily in the mirror. Yessir, you're some fine upstanding wife, you are. Oh nuts, I replied defensively. Now I'm not entitled to have clean hair? I have to sit there while it gets limp and stringy? That shows I'm a good wifey? Bug off, will you? Even the Army gives R & R to keep the troops fit to be shot at.

I picked up the receiver again. "Cal? Hi, it's me. No, everything's okay. I just wanted . . . Timmy Spector says I should get out more with actual live people, so could I play with you and Miranda tonight? I don't care what, anything. A party? Oh, not a party. No. God no, I couldn't do that. But dinner, just us, not even *out*—just not home or the hospital . . . Your

place—great . . . No, I'm still home . . . I don't know. I
mean yes, *sure* I'm going up there . . . Now, I guess . . .
What? She can't . . . All day? She say why? Okay, tell me
later."

Miranda wouldn't be around today. At all. So? She's allowed to go do things too. I hadn't signed her to any run-of-
play contract, had I? I shrugged and finished dressing. But
Cal had sounded funny. I probably woke him up.

So it seemed I wasn't playing hooky after all. Chicken, I
sneered into my magnifying mirror. Look, I'll just check in
and out; I mean, how, how could I not go at all? Just go
straight up and . . . look at him, stay awhile . . . and then
leave. Take a cab to 57th and Fifth and just walk around—
look at windows, maybe even buy something. Why not? And
then clean hair, just like a real-life lady getting ready for a
real weekend. How could they do anything to me for that?
(Yeah? Look at what they did to you yesterday, just for a
lousy chef's salad. And if you're so damn sure it's okay, why
don't you just *call* the hospital, give them the hairdresser's
number and tell them you'll check back later. Why do you
have to spend five dollars on cabs?) Because I'm chicken,
right? Right.

Because I have to see him at least. (You mean because you
have to show your face at least to the nurses so they won't
think you're a cool heartless bitch? No, that isn't it.) It's just
that I have to pay something to make it be okay. Suffer in advance: five dollars in cab fare, plus an hour of lousy travel-
ing up there and back, plus another half-hour—all right, a
*whole* hour—on active duty. Then I've really earned the R &
R, they can't hurt me for it, they'll see how badly I *need* it,
just like Timmy said.

(Oh, who are you kidding? The truth is you *are* a heartless bitch. Refrigerator cookie—if you were breastfeeding, the baby would be sucking ice. Suppose you run into somebody you know downtown? "What are you doing in *here?* I thought Richard—?" "Well, yes, but I *needed* a transparent jumpsuit for this party I'm going to. I *needed* a shampoo; I *needed* to look at all these white summer sandals in the windows, you understand, don't you?" Try one of those on Aunt Helena. I dare you. Darers go first.)

I took three Dexamyl spansules: one for Smith, one for Kline and one for French, who made this brand of sustained release possible—"Ten to twelve uninterrupted hours of smooth mood elevation, starting within thirty to sixty minutes."

Cal Jaffe called the corridor phone booth at ten-thirty; he couldn't get down there this morning either, but would I consider meeting him somewhere for lunch? Not the Plaza again, though; you never know what they put in the food there, ha, ha. I hesitated; I was going to do some, uh, things downtown, and I've got an appointment at, uh, this afternoon . . .

He broke in, sounding funny again. "We could make it a quickie then. Wherever you say. Please?"

"All right, but *really* a quickie."

"I swear, on my ex-mother-in-law's life—"

"Okay," I capitulated, "twelve-fifteen and out by one-thirty?"

"One forty-five. How's the Regency Bar?"

"Super." I hung up, sighing. I'd really wanted an all-by-myself indulgence this time—no reminders, not even of Cal and Miranda, a pretend-it's-a-real Friday just to waste. Testing the thirty-nine-cent frosted lipsticks on the back of my hand in the Five and Ten. Agonizing over marked-down sweaters in Bloomie's because I bought one full-price only last month—or feeling virtuous and glad all over because there's the one I tried on and *didn't* buy.

Well, so I'd have an hour and a half less of that stuff, and just this once maybe the rotten hair routine wouldn't take a whole two hours. All those lavender-rinse Friday regulars can keep their little pink rollers on while he works me in. "I'm sorry, Mrs. Baumgold, I promised this lady I'd take her next . . . I know you have to be out at three, but she has . . ."

"She *has?* Then how can she be in here having her hair done?"

Oh Christ, leave me alone. It's a morale emergency, okay? It's a terrible ordeal she's going through; you have no idea.

Cal was halfway through a Bloody Mary when I got to the Regency, and I wasn't even late. "First?" I asked.

"Second," he confessed.

"I thought you couldn't drink before lunch?"

"I can't but this is before breakfast. And besides . . ." He gulped the rest of it. "Here, before I forget—Miranda sent you a crumpled note." He fished it out.

It said: "Dear Julie. I love you and will do any rotten thing you want. Sorry about today. M."

"I guess I'll have a Bloody Mary too in that case," I said, recrumpling it. He ordered two; he was watching me like an actor who knows his part cold but isn't sure of the cues.

"Perhaps you're wondering why I've asked you all here tonight," I said.

He wouldn't play, though; he just sat there smiling irrelevantly into the pretzel bowl. "Cal?" I prodded gently.

The drinks came and he rallied a little. "Oh, there you are," he said.

I nodded encouragingly. "Me Julie," I added. "We've met."

He took a great swig of his third drink. "Yeah, you're the happily married one. With the kids. Husband's got a black leather chair, right?"

"Right," I said. "It swivels."

"You ever, uh, cheat on Richard?"

"No." For some reason the question didn't surprise me. "He ever?"

"No." What the hell . . . uh-oh, Miranda's probably got another fella.

"Sure?"

"Yes."

"How come you're sure?"

"Oh, I just am. I just know Richard. What he's like, what he needs to do. What he's capable of. Besides—"

"What?"

"Well, there'd be some indication if he did. There's always

—husbands who fool around, their wives know. Blond hairs, working late at the office, things in their pockets, phone calls —same as in the movies." I shrugged.

"Yeah, I guess so," he said, draining his glass. "Let's eat. I'm full."

There is probably no sanctuary in the world like a big French menu. The *plats du jour* alone are good for five or six minutes of inviolable silence; then you've still got *les grillades, oeufs, buffet froid, legumes*. Cal stayed hidden in there so long I thought he'd fallen asleep, but he finally reappeared, looking as if he'd literally digested it all and was already sorry.

"What if . . ." he began, and then to the waiter, "Oh, eggs for me, fried. And bacon."

"And the lady?"

"Chef's salad."

"Anything to start, sir?"

We shook our heads and he wrested our menus from us, leaving us alone and unarmed. "What if . . . ?" I prompted.

"What if I told you that Richard . . . that Richard and Miranda . . ." He trailed off, with a feeble wave indicating he couldn't go another step but that the rest of the expedition should carry on.

"Oh, come on, Cal, that's just ridiculous." I wasn't even sure he wasn't kidding.

"Yeah, I know," he said, in a mixed tone that included pain, his own incredulity, and vast relief at getting it out. "The most ridiculous part is that it's true."

He looked terrifyingly sober, which didn't necessarily mean he wasn't either crazy or the victim of some crazy other person who had a summer job as a sadist. Unless *I* was supposed to be the victim? I looked at him again, hard, to see if there was maybe a telltale gleam of cruelty in the eyes or around the mouth. Nope. Unless he's got one of those secret portraits back home, getting old and ugly for him.

"Well, I just don't believe it," I said finally, brushing the whole thing off as miserably unfunny, whoever's idea it was.

He laughed—hollowly, as they say. "Just repeat it three times, baby, and make it go away."

The food came and we sat staring at it. Was there anything wrong, sir? No, no, it's just fine. The two gelatinous eyes of Cal's eggs reminded me of something. What? The swinging doors of the Intensive Care Unit.

I stabbed at my salad; reality is shreds of tongue and chicken on a bed of spiky greens. "Okay," I said. "Go on. There *is* more? Such as how you received this CBS bulletin?"

"Miranda," he said, poking the eye out of one egg. I squirmed as the yellow bled slowly over his plate. "Told me last night."

"Why?" I said. (That must be it; *she's* crazy.) "I mean, if it was true, why would she tell you?"

"She said she just had to tell somebody. She was . . . she couldn't keep it to herself any more. Going through all this torture in the hospital, and nobody understanding what it meant to her. And being with you—suddenly finding how much she *liked* you—which made the nightmare even worse, because you didn't know she was sharing it."

"Did she . . . did she want you to tell me?" I was still chewing but I couldn't taste any more. The only sensation I had came from the noise of my teeth crunching and sliding on the slippery lettuce.

"No. She didn't say anything about that. I doubt if she

thought . . . All she seemed to want was somebody to listen."

I stopped chewing finally. The plate was empty, so apparently I had also swallowed. I had no idea what to do now.

"All night," Cal went on, "I spent hassling with myself. Should I tell you? What good would it do? Would it hurt you? Would it hurt you more *not* to tell you? Maybe you already knew? Or suspected. *Something.* Anyway, why did I want to tell you? I decided around eight o'clock this morning that I wanted to for one purely selfish reason: I wanted there to be two of us feeling the way I feel."

"How do you feel?" I asked, so I'd know what to expect when my internal Novocain wore off.

"Had," he said. "Duped. Stupid. *Used.* April Fool for all seasons. They've been . . . you know how long they've been at it? Since last summer! If this . . . if he weren't in the hospital, they would have just gone on like that for who the hell *knows* how long!"

It struck me suddenly: Richard was married, but Miranda wasn't. Why didn't she just break up with Cal Jaffe? He wasn't even supporting her! She had her own apartment and an allowance from her family; it didn't make sense.

Cal was coming to that. "At least you were married, with kids—there's some logic in his trying to have it both ways. But Miranda—can you figure that one? Why the hell didn't she just tell me and clear her goddamn nylons out of my dresser?"

He came up for air, and then answered his own question. "She's crazy, is why. You know what she told me? She used

to kick him out when I was due home! You ever hear anything—"

"Maybe she wants to marry you?"

"Then why the hell *tell* me now!"

I didn't know. I was tired. Even with three Dexies I was
tired. "Listen," I said. "I was going to the hair . . . to get my
hair washed. And go shopping. You . . . we were . . . there
was a party tonight, you said."

"Still is," Cal said. "And we could still go. Can't we?"

"The *three* of us?" At least I could still register shock.

"Christ, no! Just you and me," he said. "They *owe* us a
party, don't they?"

Richard and Miranda, I re-
cited under the dryer. Miranda loves Richard. The sound
melted inside my protective helmet of hissing hot air. I could
have yelled and still not heard it—even though I felt it in my
throat and all the shampoo girls turned to see if I was calling
for a manicure. Hey, it's got a nice irony to it; even my best
friends tell me, even *I* tell me—and I still don't get the
message.

Why couldn't I get fighting mad, like Cal? How dare you,
Richard, you rotten bastard, you balding father of two? Did
you tell her your wife doesn't understand you? Because that's
a fat lie, Richard, and you know it. So then what was it? More
screwing, that's for sure—but why not me first? I'm not any
uglier than I *was*, am I? And any time he wanted—*any*

time. How many wives can make that statement? All right, so I hated getting up to put the diaphragm in—sleepy, stumbling around, slathering the damn cream on it, hurrying with slippery fingers so he wouldn't change his mind before I got back—oh, I resented that, sure, but did I ever tell him? Did I *ever* say I was too tired? No, sir, sometimes I kept that damn thing inside for days, just in case he wanted to. So I would be ready when the master rang.

That was my Story of O period: learn masochism at home. Lesson 1: You are a thing. A thing does not expect pleasure; it is used for the pleasure of its owner. But after a while I resented that even more—wearing it for days, constantly at the ready, and nothing ever happening. The master never rang. He did not wish to avail himself. To use the facilities. Finally I took it out and put it away.

Richard didn't really care, anyway. I was getting better at swallowing, and that was what he seemed to want, so we sort of made our peace with it. "Shall I go put the thing in?" I'd volunteer. "No, never mind." I'll use this part of you instead.

I wonder if Miranda's on pills. Would *that* make a difference? That's a crazy thought; nobody commits adultery just to try an alternate method of birth control.

I wandered through Bloomingdale's in a daze. Should I go back to the hospital right now before I've even sorted out my feelings? My God, what if he wakes up today and I can't look at him? He'll think it's because he's sick. Well, how am I *supposed* to act? I don't even know what it means. Does he love her? ("Julie, I just couldn't help myself—you must know I've never done this before." Must I? What if he did it a lot? That's insane; he couldn't possibly—where, when would he have had time? You're kidding. Any night. *Any one of those nights.* Oh God, I don't believe it. Yes, you do.)

Hurt. I've got that; check. Sorry for myself; right, got that too. What did I do to deserve this, a nice wife like me who never even complained about his cutting out every night like that. On weekends I let him sleep late, let him be alone, got the kids out of his hair, didn't bug him to come to the park and be a daddy. He's bushed, he's a creative person, he needs to get away from the screaming, from being a middle-class husband who's pushing forty in a five-and-a-half-room co-op and not even happy in his chosen career. It's stifling, and if you love a person you don't stifle him more. You loosen his collar so he can breathe, so he doesn't feel the goddamn thing throttling him every second of his life. (Like the one that's throttling me, for instance. But I never said that—not once: What about me! Who cares if *I* breathe? I'm the female, right? Flower; tuberous vegetable; hot-house-wife. I get to lie in the bed of roses, and the maid will make it in the morning.)

That's good, let's get a little warm resentment going, at least. Woman scorned, hell hath no fury like. Resentment is okay as far as it goes; it's like anger in B-flat minor. Margie and Josh Firestone used to have fights and throw plates— just the open-stock Wedgwood, not the Royal Doulton. I always envied them that. Also they *pushed* each other, the way little kids do. Oooh, you! I never pushed anybody. When I was six I used to try pummeling my sister; shaking with fury, I'd flail at her, and she'd just grab my wrists and stand there holding on, laughing. When I'd worn myself out struggling and screaming, she'd let go. It only took a few of those humiliating defeats to teach me I was better off holding it in.

Resenting you can do alone, all you want—like masturbating. You get secret throbs of pain in all your joints; you can sob in the closet against the clothes or the autographed pictures of Frank Sinatra, who'd be on your side if only he knew. And when you have to cry really loud, you can take a long shower and run the water full force; if you do it face up into the downpour, it sounds like you might be singing or gargling; also there's something soothing about a torrent of hot water mixing with your tears.

I got off the escalator on Three, and headed automatically toward Sports Separates. There's a bank of phone booths next to Blouses. Should I call the hospital? It's almost four o'clock; am I going back up there? What if—oh, damn it, just call if you're calling; otherwise get the hell away from here. I'll just ask how everything is and if Timmy's there.

Everything was about the same. Dr. Spector was not around just now; there had been several calls for me: a Mrs. Sloan, a Mrs. Berns, Mr. Halstead, Mrs. Jonas, Mrs. Braun, Inspector Buchalter . . .

Did anyone, uh, were there any visitors? Miss Wachtel believed so; there were a few notes in the waiting room.

"Thank you, I'll be up in about an hour, I guess." (I guess I'll have to, or what will they think?) "Just briefly, I have, uh, an appointment this evening, so—"

"Fine, Mrs. Messinger. Thank *you*."

What's fine? Thank me for what? Was the bitch being sarcastic? Oh God, what was the Billy Rubin reading this afternoon? I hadn't even asked.

Well, are you buying something, or do you feel all guilty now and Jiminy Cricket says you have to leave this minute and go right up there, and how can you arrive carrying a shopping bag that everyone will know must be full of something for you, not for him. With your *hair* done, what's more!

It could be something for the kids, couldn't it? Or the house? What the hell do I care, anyhow? I'm not supposed to shave my head and sit there moaning. Timmy even said I was overdoing it, and that was *before*—that was yesterday!

Now you're talking; that was a nice little spurt of indignation there. Let's hear it for self-respect, and civil rights for the wronged, and you'll show him.

Normally I'm a fantastic shopper; I operate on a kind of radar which I must have developed as a reaction to all those years of suffering in clothes, or hiding under them. Now that I was a perfect size 9 and could walk around impersonating a pretty girl, dressing was a sacred privilege, something entrusted to me. Girls who have cried into their mirrors are never really sure what will happen if they smile now. Won't the mirror send you right back to your old self? You tremble in ecstatic stage fright every time you enter the try-on room with the curtain that doesn't quite close. Don't be silly, you really *are* pretty, see? Oh, but *that* isn't me!

Anyway, for me shopping is a work of prayer and sacrifice. I have to go alone or it doesn't work. All these women who make sociable outings out of picking a new spring coat are another species. "You really think I can wear pink, with my coloring?" "Oh, divine, darling, don't you love pleats?" "Well, for you, yes, but with *these* hips . . ."

And the ones who can use the salesgirl, shamelessly calling her in for a conference or a pep talk. "What do *you* think of me in this?" I'd die before I asked anyone. I can't even tell them what I'm looking for. I'm looking for "it"; when I see it, I'll know.

Today I was distracting myself; my whole system was mal-functioning. But I wasn't quitting; this time my honor was at stake. You're not leaving without "it"; you have half an hour, so you damn well better hurry. Doggedly, viciously, I tore at things, rack after rack, hardly seeing what I pushed away; I was flying on instruments and dangerously low on fuel, not knowing whether my internal pilot light was even on. Everything looked god-awful, as if some buyer had made a killing on schlocky rayon lining material. Slimy to the touch. Even the display dummies seemed more sullen than usual. The entire Fashion Third floor had been summer-decorated to look blindingly cold and shiny, like the inside of an ice cube, and the junior department had added Muzak rock that shrieked at you from between the hangers. I made up my own litany as I picked my way through unbearably hot pinks and insufferably cool greens. One-piece, two-piece, see-through, *bra*. Lace slacks, no backs, that's too *blah*.

Hey, what's that? It was a vest. Little teensy pearls all strung out like a trellis, and you just tie it on with a satin shoe-lace. Over whatever. Or *nothing* whatever: your bare trem-bling body. Twenty dollars? "It" rang. Miss? *Miss!* Charge and take, I'm in a *terrible* hurry. Over and out.

I checked into Mount Carmel at five, clutching my package like a nervous fence with a hot mink. Riding downtown I felt higher than I had all day on the Dexies—a combination of making out at Bloomie's and being terrified of seeing Richard now that I knew. I had this awful premonition that he was going to open his eyes and say "Miranda," right in front of Miss Wachtel and Dr. Mahler. Who would revolve slowly, wearing their ghastly expressions, to demand an explanation from me. And what could I say?

However, Richard chose not to disgrace me. I hovered at his side for God knows how long, all my ill-sorted reactions thudding and colliding soggily in my head like heavy blankets in the washing machine.

"Hey," I said to him sadly, reproachfully, "why'd you have to go and do that, anyway?" Forming the words hurt my throat; I knew the sound, soft as it was, could trigger a crying jag, but talking to him was still better than leaving it all jumbled and unsyllabled in my head. I wasn't asking why he had to go and *fuck* her. Because why *not*, what's so far-fetched about that, it's no different from anybody else we know. Adultery!—the first family game that would outsell Monopoly, if Parker Bros. could only find a way to box it without running afoul of the obscenity laws . . . So I'd buy that part of it, Richard, even from you. You who used to talk about the marriage contract, in your lovable jazz talk: "Once you sign up for this gig, you gotta play it," you said. You changed your mind, was all; you found out you could hum a few bars and then fake it.

I'm not even asking why'd you have to fuck *her*, because that's why not too. It's part of the kick, I see that. When you get Cal Jaffe's girl, you get Cal Jaffe. It eases the pain a little for Cal's having the good free life when you're all hung up with children who are not returnable for exchange or credit, and a wife who—well, who . . . And inviting them over all the time, I even dig that. Blowing pot in Mommy's bathroom is groovier than turning on ten miles away where she couldn't possibly catch you.

But why all that *other* stuff—what you did to *me*. The guilt, the lousy lies about my "emasculating" you with my strong personality, about my destroying your manhood! About how I made it impossible for you to function *sex*ually! You couldn't, you just couldn't; I'd loused up your whole system with my blunt little hatchet. Remember, once I even asked you. "If I'm such a ball-breaking bitch, how come you're not out screwing somebody who isn't? I don't see how you can get totally impotent from me."

And you sighed heavily—oh, it was too much, too much what I did to you—and you said, you self-righteous bastard!: "If a man has one sexual relationship and he becomes impotent in that *one* relationship, he doesn't cure it with another relationship; that would just create another *problem*. How could I prove myself by betraying you? What happens to *us*, then? Don't you see, Julie, I have to work this out with you!"

There were tears, actual *tears*, in your eyes. "Ah, Julie baby, you're so good, in so many ways. You don't know how I hate this, hurting you. I *love* you, I love us married. And the babies . . ."

The babies, poor pussycats. Well, if we get a divorce, at least there wouldn't be a custody fight. Not over Matthew, anyway. Custody: dividing up the spoiled. And the records: you take the jazz, I get the Broadway show albums. But what about the Beatles and the Stones? Oh, it's too silly; I don't want *anything* if I have to get demarried. I'll just take the babies and move out. Yeah, but what if Miranda moves in? I don't want her glorious mass of curls cascading on my pink-striped pillowcase. Let her go to her own damn White Sales.

Oh, Richard, you fink. Crying on cue without onions, like Margaret O'Brien. Give the girl a break; tell her something that will get her off your back. "Maybe it's just some male premenopausal thing, a phase, something that'll go like it came. Maybe it just happens to guys and nobody talks about it." That was pretty good, Richard. And then you tried gallantry—just in case I wasn't guilt-ridden enough. "I'm probably unfair as hell, blaming it all on you," you said. "Maybe a lot of it isn't you at all. I don't know, maybe I'm overworked, overworried, overover." Sir Walter Raleigh, you were, offering me a *choice* of cloaks for my puddle. Pick one from Group A, one from Group B, here, here, just take what you want and go play with it, go see what you can make with this, there's a good girl. Now maybe the stupid cunt will leave me alone for another three weeks.

Oh, damn you. Why couldn't you just go do your rotten thing and let me, let me . . . There's gotta be something in the Geneva Conventions against what you did. No fair torturing POWs. Jake Barnes wouldn't tell Lady Brett it was a hell of a place to be wounded if he wasn't hit there at all . . . And you did even worse: you said, Look, *you* shot it off. Now sit right there and love it and feel sorry for it and maybe it will get better. At least Brett managed to go out and get laid; not me, though. Not faithful little Julie, the stupid cunt who signed up for this gig and can't stop playing it.

"Hi," said Timmy, sneaking up behind me. I jumped. "Anything?"

"N-not so's you'd notice," I said, gathering my shredded composure.

"Hey," he said, startled, sliding his hand down to mine and leading me in my teary blindness away from what he thought was my trouble. I stumbled obediently in his wake, gulping to keep the noise of my sobs down to something that might pass for violent hiccuping or *petit mal*.

"I'm . . . sorry; I'm all right," I gasped, "I don't know what—"

"Here." He handed me a rumpled tissue; it wasn't quite clean, but what can you expect from a dirty young doctor's pocket. I wiped and blew; he nodded. "I'm leaving in half an hour; want a lift?"

"No," I said, trying to remember why not. "I have to leave right now—I, uh, I mean, I told him, them, I'd be ready by eight. And I want to see the babies. The kids." I stopped and inhaled. "Timmy, you're *sure* it's okay for me not to come back here tonight?" I looked at him as carefully as I could through the stinging haze of salt-watered eye make-up.

"I'm sure," said Timmy, healer of the sick, patron saint of wives about to leave the waiting room. He kissed me: a blessing for my night of freedom. "I'll be in touch with the hospital from home," he murmured. "Don't call; if there's anything, I'll call *you*. And there won't be, so don't worry." Another kiss for amen.

In the cab I remembered Miranda's note, which I'd stuck somewhere in my bag. Somewhere, in that cavernous mess of lost cleaner's tickets,

154

trading stamps with fuzz on their stickum, long cash-reg-
ister curls from The Cake Masters, D'Agostino's, the A&P,
Bloomie's . . .

There it was. I reread it, still incredulous. "I love you and
will do any rotten thing you want. Sorry about today. M."
Sorry about *today*? How *about* that girl? Maybe she's just
some new brand of mixed nut, like the rest of her bobo family.
Could she possibly still want to be best friends till this blew
over? And then we'd go back to being—well, whatever it was
we were to each other *before*. Harem mates? Not if one of
us lives out, I guess.

What rotten thing would I want her to do, I wonder? Wash
my undies? Give me the answers in the Social Studies final?
Give up Richard? Well, there's something.

Why don't I hate either of them? It's insane that they've
done this nasty, dirty, cheating, rat-finky thing, and all I feel
is *hurt*. My stupid feelings are hurt. The nice girl didn't really
want to be with me in the waiting room; she didn't care about
me after all; she wouldn't even have come if it hadn't been for
*him*. I would have been there all by myself with Audrey
Lebow and Arnie Buchalter.

First I tried on the lacy pearl
vest over a dress. Pretty. Then I took off the dress and put on
a white linen pants suit, with the vest over a shirt. Also pretty.
Then I took off the shirt and put the vest over me, plain. Oh,
yes. I hedged the bet by adding the jacket, unbuttoned. When

I moved, it was clear I had nothing on under the vest; on the other hand, there were no nippies visible.

I wrote Cal's number on the message pad, propped it on the kitchen wall phone and kissed everybody except Darlene goodnight.

Halfway to the elevator I turned around, went back and took another Dexamyl. That made four today, a record. Well, it was a very special day. And I won't drink. If I drink I know I'll black out. This way I'll just appear slightly more light-headed than your average everyday comatose adulterer's wife.

I arrived at Cal's apartment feeling not only light-headed but overwound, like a mistreated watch. (*Caution:* The following are unwanted reactions considered possible with dextroamphetamine: Overstimulation, restlessness . . .") "Where's, uh, Miranda?" I asked uncomfortably, eying the dents in the white sofa.

"Her place, I guess." Cal looked extremely handsome; one of those impossible, smooth blond men whose green eyes always have changing flecks of something else. Strong face, good teeth, arrogant jawline—all that stuff I had automatically never looked at before I was married because it would never look back. "She's pretty upset," he said, "I told her that I . . . about our lunch. She . . . It's funny, she really *likes* you."

"Yeah, lots," I said, lowering myself carefully onto one of the dented cushions. It was, I saw, going to be somewhat difficult to keep decently covered without closing the jacket, which would kill the whole *point.*

"No, I mean it," he persisted, sitting next to me. I tugged again at the jacket. "She, uh, admires you, is what it really is. That first day, when she went up to the hospital? Wearing, you know, her usual sloppy off-duty actress uniform, the way we both go around—dirty raincoat, jeans, whatever. Then she started studying you, what you were wearing, how you looked, even your hair. Next day she showed up a whole different girl—a new dress, *stockings*, the hair. Even a pocketbook. She never carries a pocketbook—just stuffs her hairbrush in my coat. She was *imitating* you. Hey, wanna drink?" He got up and started toward the kitchen.

"Um," I said. "Are you?"

"Yeah, I think I need. Should I do something funny in the blender? I've got some rum and a rotten banana I can throw in."

"Okay," I surrendered. "Whatever." I felt really strange now; if this was an amphetamine high I was not impressed. More of an askew, I'd say. I kept looking toward the corners of the room where Miranda or Richard might be lurking, or an elaborate alarm system that would go off if either of us made a false move. Cal didn't seem at all uneasy, though, which was a help.

He came back with two huge glasses of some thick yellowish concoction, each topped by hissing foam. "They're passing for banana daiquiris," he announced proudly. "Don't tell."

It was good, like a fresh fruit punch. Plus four Dexies, I mused. Oh, well.

Cal sat down and put some records on a machine. He kept all forms of entertainment—hi-fi, radios, TV, magazines— flat on the floor, either piled up, built in or planted on very low custom-built swiveling platforms. He liked to live things down, he explained; it kept him from losing touch with his roots.

"Where's the snake?" I asked.

"Back in the tub," he answered morosely.

We wandered out to the terrace, where I began pacing ("overstimulation, restlessness . . ."), waiting for the alarm. He noticed, finally. "Wanna eat, you hungry? I got a steak in the fridge. Or we could go out . . . Or we could take a chance they'll feed us at the party, though I have my doubts. It's a hard cheese and Dipsy Doodles crowd."

"You decide," I said. "But not a steak; the smell . . ."

"Yeah, I forgot about you," he said. Which reminded him: "Miranda, uh, said she had letters. From Richard."

"Mmm?" Hard to concentrate. Must tune in . . .

"I saw a couple . . ."

"Anything . . . he ever write anything about me?"

"Not much about either of us. Once something about his 'roommate':—'My roommate thinks I'll be on location all week.' They were planning some weekend jaunt."

"'My roommate,'" I repeated.

We were standing at the doorway, paying our cliché respects to the cliché New York terrace view: silhouetted buildings like irregular staircases ending abruptly on the twentieth zig or thirtieth zag, occasional slivers of yellow light piercing the flat blackness, indicating occasional life. We turned toward each other and said "Hi," and kissed hard, each pressing hurt and confusion and lostness against the other. I was crying again, but this time it was all liquid—no sobs, no heaving shoulders—as if my whole essential substance had simply begun to ooze.

We walked back into the living room and sank down onto the sofa, still clinging. Hansel and Gretel in the forest, their entire trail of breadcrumbs eaten by the birds.

Now what? I reached up and touched his face. Good face. Why would she want to hurt a face like that? I kissed him again. It was an apology. On behalf of my husband and myself.

He reached under my jacket, under the vest. Stroking me. "Soft," he said. "Who would have thought you had such a tender kiss for me . . . ?" He reached across me and flicked the button on the lamp base. The terrace door was still open, and the distant slivers of yellow were all the light we had. He leaned back, pulling me gently with him. "Miranda," he said, "does not have a tender kiss like yours."

"Cal," I said. "Don't talk about them."

"Then kiss me again." I did. And then. And then. I watched myself from some backstage prompter's post, as if the me in front were auditioning for the coveted lead role. Can she meet this challenge of her career? Can she play the wife who has an affair? Demure, ever-faithful Deborah Kerr, actually unbuttoning her own blouse, untying her own pearl vest, for a man other than Richard, her lawfully wedded Messinger. Look, Richard. Look—he's kissing them. My married titties. Wake up, Richard, and tell me to quit, that everything's all right and you didn't do it and I can stop. Ah, but I can't; I signed up for *this* gig now and I'm . . . going . . . to . . . play . . .

Cal, silent, laboring over the making of love; suddenly I was aware of his forehead glistening, creased with concentration, bringing to the task of caressing my body the dedication of a Peace Corps volunteer assigned to a hardship post. Perspiring. It was slow, heavy work: fingers, mouth, tongue grazing me, tracing their paths as if following directions to a stranger's house in the suburbs . . . should be a turnoff here, a crossroads, a Mobil gas station. His touch was light and warming; I felt my skin responding, but there was something

—the effort of it, the urgency—something wrong. "You like
. . . this?" he murmured. "Kissing you here . . . here? Tell
me . . . I want to make you come."

Sweet, he was. His hair damp; cool strands of it sweeping
over me. "What about you?" I said.

"Sssh, don't worry. Here . . . this, you like . . . ?" Untiring
skillful fingers, years of training in the manual operation of
sensitive female machinery . . . Oh God, stop him; I'm not
going to. I stirred and shifted, reaching for him; here, I'll
guide you home . . . But touching him—oh, no—he was, it
was, in no condition to be guided. Sweet Jesus, I thought in a
flash of horror and shame, I can't even turn *him* on—I'm a
*disaster* . . .

He reclaimed his hand then and gently pushed mine away.
By his own hand he was going to demonstrate how to breathe
life into a limp cock. Furious flying fingers. "Let me," I offered, ashamed. (I know how; I can do that.) "No," he
snapped. "No!" Was he angry because I'd failed? No sense;
it made no sense.

His fist, blurred like motion under strobe lights, was still
going. I raised myself on one elbow and bent my head to
take the poor thing in my mouth; maybe that would—

"Oh, sweet," he panted, "you . . . are . . . so . . ." and he
sank back, permission granted. How long I labored there,
God knows; it seemed I gave it the best year of my life.
Thanks to Richard's rigorous training I knew I was good at
this—even he, the master, had acknowledged it. "You're a
natural," he'd said, "it's a gift."

Cal, one hand resting lightly on my hair, breathed in the
rhythmic cadence of a lulled infant. I didn't dare raise my
head to look at his face lest all my work be for nothing. On

and on I pressed, until finally, it seemed, was it slightly, ever so slightly, harder? What do I do now? Oh Christ, I want to stop. His eyes fluttered open; he was watching me now, trying to read me. What did he *want?*

Then he sat up, turning me, forcing me back, burying his face in my stomach, moving, inexorably, down. "No!" I cried, wriggling away. "Don't! It's all right!"

Relief and exhaustion: it's not me, it's *him!* He's . . . *that's* why . . . he . . . she . . . oh Jesus, what a group. "Cal," I said tenderly, "listen, it's . . . we're both . . . It's been an awful day, it's nobody's fault, Cal . . ."

His head was still embedded in my stomach; he was crying.

We survived the next minutes ministering to each other's wounds and avoiding eyes. His refuge seemed to lie in curling up again inside his rage: Miranda, that bitch, that faithless cunt. I couldn't really contribute much, but I was glad not to have to. As long as there was a refuge to repair to, I was grateful. Neither of us wanted anything except an excuse to not talk about what had just happened, or why, or what it meant, or what we were going to do now—if anything. You just instinctively start removing traces of some things the minute they happen, like stains that can't be permitted to set or they'll never come out. (Though I'd have given a lot to have him reassure me just once that yes, indeed, he did have this, er, problem, and it wasn't me, no sir, couldn't be *me* because I was so fantastically sexy and feminine; why, any normal guy would be . . . So while he ranted against Miranda, I kept up a running interior monologue, desperately trying to convince the jury that it was so, it *had* to be so, that the whole bizarre incident should be struck at once from my record as incompetent, irrelevant and immaterial, your honor.)

At last Cal got up like a corpse at the end of the play and began to take curtain calls: possessive caresses, casual nuzzling and kisses—the whole postcoital bill of intimacy rights. It was as if he'd sent the mess out to a one-hour dry cleaner and got it back all spotless and steam-pressed. Tomorrow he'd remember nothing except that we had comforted each other with a little harmless fucking—or maybe even simply that he had comforted me.

"Still want to make that party?" he asked solicitously (I hope I haven't tired you, love). He was, *mirabile dictu*, cheerful and refreshed. Talk about your remarkable recuperative powers. Only I was stunned and still reeling, too numb to leap out of my corner, punching holes in the air with ridiculous swollen mittens because the fans wanted me for one more round.

"I guess not," I said. I couldn't possibly. All those noisy glistening faces. Too many differences now between them and me. Between everyone and me. A species gap. "But why don't *you* go?" I suggested. "Do you good—I mean, do us *both* good, but I'm . . . really, I can't. First time in days I feel a real need for sleep."

He hesitated gallantly. "Aw, sweetie, let's just peek in for a half-hour. I'm tired too, but how can it hurt us? Just a half-hour of comic relief?"

"No, please, but I wish you would go—for both of us. Like you said, they owe us a party." I smiled weakly.

He still wasn't sure how to do right by me. "Tell you what," he said, handing me pieces of clothing for a start. "We'll point a cab uptown. On the way I'll work on changing your mind. You're on 83rd; the party's on 89th. Maybe we'll even compromise—like on a hamburger at 86th." He grinned, pleased with himself. Pleased with me too, watching me tie the pearl vest over my gleaming bare self. "You know, that's some groovy outfit," he observed appreciatively, applying a proprietary kiss to the back of my neck. "Damn shame to waste it."

"Yes. Well," I murmured uncomfortably. I wasn't sure which I was more acutely aware of: the damn shame or the waste.

It was just after midnight when Cal dropped me off; by then he seemed positively aglow with contentment. Having done all his own cutting and designed the credits, he had a beautifully edited memory of tonight, and he was about to get rid of me, the co-star whose acting was still a little out of synch. Besides, I had finally managed to become a drag. He was about to run for Life of the Party; I, despite my sexy costume, would have been the lifeless. So when I got out of his cab, by mutual consent, it was all he could do to keep his sigh of relief to himself.

There were two messages upstairs—one from my mother in

Nassau, the other from my sister in Westchester. Nothing from Timmy; my reward for extreme heroism under fire. Unless . . . oh, don't start *that* now. You know he'd have called if . . . wouldn't he? Yeah, but . . . How about I just call the hospital and say hello to Miss Lopez? I'll sleep better with that lilting Spanish-American lullaby in my ear—"Heese about de sem, heese condition no change . . ."

I collapsed into bed without benefit of exercise, laundry, shower, nail polish or troubled thought—and at four-thirty woke from my dreamless depths, damp, shivering and entangled in the sheets like a carelessly prepared mummy. "Diary," I mumbled aloud, and staggered up.

That's what it was: a diary—"MGM" is for Miranda Graham. I stumbled around in the dark—where the hell did I put it?—too groggy to think of putting on the light, slamming drawers on my fingers, shaking. Maybe I didn't want light, just a comic-strip bulb over my head marked IDEA. Except that in the comics there's no such thing as a *bad* idea. The bulb always gives off those little radiant porcupine quills, as from distant stars and buried treasure. But whether there was anything good about the idea of getting up to decode Richard's diary—if it was a diary—now that I thought I had the key—if it was a key—I didn't know or care. I *had* to look, *now*, right this predawn sleep-coated minute.

I found it at last and stumbled back to the bed, still unwilling or unable to turn a light on. I sat there teetering on the edge of the mattress and of wakefulness and of scary certainties, holding that stupid sheaf of stupid papers in my stupid hand. Go ahead, why don't you? I double-dare you. Look, she's scared stiff. Know what happens to scaredy-cats?

You put Ajax on their stomach like they did to Dottie Lubin. Rubbed her skin right off, remember?

But it's different; this is grown-up scared. It's for a good *reason*; it all *counts* now. What if—?

What if what, you dumb bitch; he's already done it all. The tree already fell in the forest; all you'll be doing is reading the initials on the rotten trunk. RM loves—

No, wait—*listen*, will you! What if . . . Well, obviously it isn't just Miranda, it's *lots* of initials, there's a whole bunch —And what if I think I know who but I'm not sure, and I start staring at every person who comes to the hospital? It's like some horrible crazy game—who knows, who doesn't know, what about her? And what about all the ones who *don't* come—why aren't they, is she, could they be avoiding me? The whole thing is insane, I can't sit in that waiting room and go through that on top of everything else. And if I'm right, if it really is that kind of a diary . . . I *know* I'm right, I can't not be . . . MGM for lunch and MGM for dinner . . .

Tear it up then; don't read it. Ha, ha.

Maybe I will.

Yeah, I'll bet. You want to know why you won't? Because you've already seen it, already guessed some of it; you're already in the game. If you throw it out now, you don't change anything. You're stuck; you're still *it*.

I went on like that till after six o'clock, then fell asleep again without deciding anything—not even whether I had anything to decide. At seven-fifteen I woke up for keeps, still holding the damn papers. Whittaker Chambers playing Hamlet; whether to stuff it all back in the pumpkin, unread, or not to stuff it . . .

Better put it back, at least temporarily. It'll be in escrow;

I need a little time first; I can't look at it now, is all. I'm being sensible; I can't handle it today; I know myself; I haven't even digested last night yet. I'm going over there early, and I'm sitting there all day and calming down, and then we'll see how it goes.

But what about Cal and Miranda, what do I do about them today? There isn't any them today, dummy. We're all in separate hells now, remember? Hey, Miranda, what do you want to do today? I don't know, Cal, what do you want to do today? Let's go screw Julie Messinger, one way or another, just for old times' sake.

As a matter of fact, I hope she does show up. I want her to. Do you realize we haven't exchanged one single first-person word about this whole thing? The entire event has been brought to us through the medium of Calvin Jaffe, who is probably a security risk.

So when do I get to confront The Other Woman? To call her a shameless hussy and a homewrecker? No, love thief— that's it, love thief. Don't I get my picture taken, like Debbie Reynolds after Liz stole Eddie? With diaper pins eloquently stuck in my housedress, madonnahood intact. Sybil Burton got those condolences too, with that white hair and all, until she ruined it by getting sexy. Seventy percent of the women readers in the prime twenty-to-thirty-five age market (most responsive to magazine advertising) would prefer that she stay home crying into her stainless-steel sink; the other thirty percent would forgive her if she went right out and shot him in the heart.

The only thing you can't do is sneak around trying to correct the conjugal imbalance sheet: doing unto others what I did last night. The sheer symmetry of it scares people; how

can they tell the victims from the perpetrators? In the dark
they are all to blame.

But would Miranda even talk to me? Subject herself to my
wrath, my tender-pink nails raking across her two faces? Why,
sure she would! She *loves* me, remember? And will do any
rotten thing I want. Well, I want . . . to know things.

First I called the hospital. Oh, yes, he was in satisfactory
condition, and how was I today? Well, Miss Farnsworth, I
don't know quite how to tell you—there's been a slight
change; nothing alarming, but I've lost all my best friends.
Terrible accident, very sudden, the Lord giveth and the
Lord taketh away, that's that kind of hairpin He is.

Miranda didn't seem at all surprised when I called. Which
threw me. The soft voice was exactly the same: not a tremor.
(What did you expect—rueful tears? Protestations of innocence? I repudiate that confession. I am not now nor have I
ever been Richard's . . .)

"Miranda?" I croaked.

"Yes, hi," she said mellifluously.

"It's Julie."

"Yes, I know. Hi."

"I wondered if you were, uh, planning . . . to come over to
the hospital. I mean, any time today? I mean, if you could?"

Pause. "Would you want me to?" Still not surprised. Not
humble or apologetic or even worried. Does she care? She
does not. Bobo. She's really bobo.

"I'd like to see you."

"Then I'll come. What time?"

My God, now she's going polite on me. I had a lovely time
at your lovely party. "I don't know—ten, eleven? I'll be there,
you know, all day I guess."

"About ten, then?"

"Okay." Jesus, what did I do that for; what will I *say* to her? Miranda Graham, you are accused of adultery with intent to commit adultery; how do you plead? (She doesn't plead, she wouldn't know how to plead; she simply gets or doesn't get what's coming to her; she *accepts*.) All right, how about "Where were you on the night of April the twelfth? Tell the court what you did to him and what he did to you, to the best of your recollection."

"We made love, your honor."

"Speak up so the jury can hear."

"We made love, your honor. He didn't have any, and neither did I. So we made some. It was good."

"Objection! Oh, please, objection. He did so have some—what about what *I* gave him?"

"I don't know anything about that, your honor. Maybe she did give him something . . . maybe he used it all up. Maybe it didn't taste the same any more. Maybe . . ."

"All right, that's enough—but I still don't understand. What did *she* give him?"

"Probably just one of those fabulous flights. With unobstructed exit doors and a loosely fastened safety belt in case of turbulence. In-flight entertainment, smiling attention, non-stop service, food and beverage, wine and spirits, blanket and pillow, upright and reclining. And she always reminded him—still smiling, of course—to take his belongings when he leaves. Thank you for flying Miranda."

Of course I couldn't play that scene at all. I'd end up with a hung jury or a mistrial. DOR—Dismissed on her Own Recognizance, whatever the hell that is. I spent a whole hour in the waiting room going over my lines and trying to work my face into something righteous or wronged. Also I fidgeted, like a Houston debutante practicing her curtsy for Her Serene Highness' visit to Texas. I must have opened my handbag twenty times for consultations with my compact mirror, to verify key portions of my face. (Yeah, that's her—that's the wife.)

Luckily nobody else was around yet; I hadn't even considered how awkward it would be if Audrey or Pamela or Timmy were to pop in during the question-and-answer period. I tried staring out the window at discarded sheets of newspaper swirling in the warm dust. New York's largest daily circulation. Must be breezy out. Must be a thirty-mile-an-hour gale on Cal's terrace. Cal. The crazy irony of his caring so desperately about *my* orgasm; the double irony that his caring made it impossible. Would it have been possible otherwise? The one time in my life that a person literally knocks himself out for my entertainment pleasure, and all I feel is embarrassed. *Appalled.* I can't stand the attention. There he is, riveted to it, the Queen's Guard at the Palace gate, eyes neither right nor left but straight up under the old busby. And what do I do? Freeze. My legs feel like Good Humor Dubl-Stix. I'm dying of exposure. How could he stand wasting all that time; how could he think it was worth it? Oh, please don't *bother*, it's all right, really, it's too much trouble, there's no point, it's stupid. Don't you see, I don't look good enough to be watched like that, I don't want to be *concentrated* on, you'll start noticing all the parts that aren't . . . open to the public. And you'll be sorry—you won't like me then. Listen, I'll do anything to you, anything you want. I'm good at that; I'm terrific. Hey, let me up, I'm too flat-chested in this position; please don't go there, I have no idea how I look there; oh God, I forget whether I shaved my legs and . . .

What I'd hated most was that he was so *solicitous*. Conscientious. All that awful plodding patience, and the careful fingers. It's so easy, you stupid jerk; why does it have to be such a fifth-grade science project, anyway? It really takes about three minutes by the clock—*three lousy minutes!* Good old American know-how?—I've never met *one* who knew how. Except Richard, finally; Richard—and Miranda didn't teach him; he got there before—all by himself, with just the Kama Sutra or the Kami-kaze or I Ching or Sun Luck East. Or maybe *I* did it; maybe I finally let him get me there because I believed that he loved me. That he really cared if I did. As Dr. Rosenfeld said: "If he's secure and he loves you, he'll value your orgasm more than his own. Because giving you one proves that his penis works." (My rod and my staff, it comforted her!)

No, Doctor, it was pretty to think so, but I had no business buying it. I knew better *au fond.* I still think every male sees a cunt as a velvet-lined safe-deposit box. What's valuable is what *they* put in there, and how nice it feels. So unfair—it's all so unfuckingfair.

She was wearing amber sunglasses and her pale face was almost chalky; she looked like someone just shaking off a

twenty-four-hour intestinal virus. "Hi," she said. "How is he?"
(*Our* boy.)

"The same," I said. Timmy had just stopped in to tell me
about the growth hormone. Magic mushrooms. "I don't believe in it really," he said, very blasé. "But I figure why not; it
can't hurt to try it." It was supposed to stimulate human tissue. Help build strong bodies twelve ways—guarantees taller
dwarfs in two weeks or return the unused portion. Grow new
liver faster; amazing results when used as directed. The stuff
was still so rare that the National Institute of Health kept it
in vaults; not so much as a dropperful could be released
without orders from the top. Washington had called Bethesda
to release some for my Richard. "How much will you need,
Dr. Spector?" they'd asked in hushed long-distance life-or-
death gasps. "I could use six ounces," he replied. "Yes, *sir*,
we'll have it on the noon air shuttle," they'd said. Sealed in
dry ice, police escort waiting at the airport, motorcycles with
sirens, everything but ticker tape on the East River Drive.
Oh, Richard, if you only see one motion picture all year, make
it this one. People are talking about . . . the spectacular arrival of priceless growth hormone for New Yorker Richard
Messinger, still fighting for his life in Mount Carmel Hospital. Meanwhile, outside in the waiting room, locked in another mortal struggle, his wife, Julie, and sometime actress
Miranda Graham, with whom Messinger was reported late
yesterday to be linked romantically . . .

Should we go have some coffee on that? How about starting all over? Let's take it from last Wednesday in this same
identical cafeteria. I was over here when you came in. You
were looking for a friend, and for a minute I thought . . .
never know who your friends are, how true. But that was in

another movie, and besides the wench is dead. Ding dong, the wicked wench is dead.

Now, as I see it, between then and now nothing has actually happened between the two of us . . .

(Pamela Howell and I had been playing Snow White in the john during recess, tucking our long hair inside our turned-up Peter Pan collars and pasting little gold gumbacked paper stars across our foreheads. When the bell rang we changed back into ordinary people, but each was to keep one small gold star on the back of her hand, as a royal birthmark, until after school. Hide your hand in your pocket or under your desk; if anyone sees the star, the spell will be broken and you'll never be a princess again.

She picked Grace Martin to leak it to. I saw them whispering, but what secret could they have compared to *ours?* But then Grace came over and said, loud and clear, "How come you've got that gold star pasted on your hand?" How could she have seen it? Silently I implored my royal playmate. Explain me. Pamela shrugged. I was stunned; *there was no star on her hand.* After school I asked only where it was. "Oh," she said carelessly, "I took it off—I'm using it as a bookmark.")

. . . Nothing has actually happened between Miranda and me. Not a shot was fired; the junta merely usurped the palace in a bloodless coup, proclaiming total victory for Dragon Lady, a former friend of the family.

"Do you have a middle name, Miranda?"

"Yes, but I've always hated it."

"Me too. Mine is Hope. Julie Hope spring eternal." (Notice how she didn't tell hers.) "Uh, you went to Bennington, didn't you?"

"Yes."

"Did you know Margot Cantor? I think she was there around your time."

"I don't think so."

(Well, smarty? It's your turn again. Look, you got double sixes. Go directly to jail. Do not pass Go. Do not collect two hundred dollars. Do not even look at her. She is wearing dark glasses, and even if she were not, it would be impossible to tell what she was thinking. I'm sorry, Miss Graham cannot come out from behind those; she is *in cognito. In cognito* there is strength. No pictures, please. Miss Graham has no further comment at this time.)

"Miranda, could you tell me about you and Richard?"

"Tell you what?"

"Just anything. What it was . . . is. If it's true."

"It's true. That we love each other is true." She spoke in a soft, monotonous voice. (No matter what the eleven o'clock news is, the voice of CBS does not convey any emotional policy.)

"Did he . . . does he want—plan—to stay married to me? Or—"

"I don't know. He . . . we've been talking about it. Whether I'd marry him. If I would, he'd get a divorce. I couldn't decide. I wasn't sure—"

Why is it that nobody ever mentions me—even now? It isn't *my* divorce, just his and hers. Something they'll order at Georg Jensen as soon as she picks out the pattern.

"—until this week. This week I decided to say yes."

"This week? Because of the operation?"

"No, because I thought . . . I was pregnant. I thought if that happened, then it would mean . . . you know, that the decision had been made for me . . . that it was out of my hands. So if I was, I would say yes. I went for the test Monday, the same day he—"

"Yes, I know." (I'm the wife.) "Well, are you? Pregnant?"

"No. False alarm." She smiled; why does she smile at all the wrong things?

"I guess that's a break, anyway."

"Why? I wish I were pregnant."

"But suppose he—?"

"—I know. Even so."

"Oh Christ, I don't understand. When was he . . . when was I supposed to be told?"

"I don't know."

"Didn't you ever talk about that? About telling me? About the children?"

"Sometimes he talked about the children. Nicky—he said he would miss Nicky."

"But not me, not Matthew?"

"No, not very much. I mean, he just didn't talk about you or Matthew very much."

God, wouldn't you think she could tone down the brutality just a little at a time like this? Please, somebody tell her I'm bleeding . . . So he didn't talk about me. Not even "I love my wife, but—" Well, it *could* mean I wasn't so bad. He didn't have to run to her with a bunch of complaints about what Julie did or didn't. In a way he could have been protecting me —trying to keep the two things separate, not betraying either of us. That's a nice idea, isn't it—Sir Galahad in double harness.

Now Miranda was talking about how it started. She had been out of work, filling in with some modeling: a fashion spread for *Household*, a couple of business lunches, and . . .

I tried to picture them together; it still seemed impossible. Richard is two inches shorter than Cal; she must tower under him. A Mickey Rooney complex? "Listen, Miranda, I'm trying to see . . . trying to put myself in your . . . and I can't—I just can't. How could you . . . for instance, how could you stand the four of us having dinner, going to movies?"

"It was . . . well, it was a way to see more of each other. Better than nothing."

"What about . . . then what about this, here—sitting here with me, day after day—?"

"That was hard at first; it really was. I wished I could tell somebody . . ."

Not to confess; God, no, why should she feel the need to do that? Absolution is for people who at least send their regrets. This little girl does not say she is sorry when she is not sorry.

("Apologize to your friend. See, you hurt her."

"Where?"

"There."

"I don't see anything."

"Of course not. It's inside. Anyhow, you have to apologize."

"Why?"

"Because people are supposed to. You wouldn't like her to do it to you, would you?"

"I don't know. What would it feel like?"

"If you don't apologize, you'll find out."

"Okay." I don't think she ever did, though . . .)

Once my sister Nina threw a full pail of sand at me, scoring a direct hit to my head. "Why'd you throw that pail at your little sister?" my mother demanded. "I didn't throw it *at* her, Mommy, I threw it *to* her and she missed it," my sister said. "Oh," said my mother. "Well, next time watch how you aim." "Okay," said my sister.

No, Miranda hadn't wanted forgiveness. Only recognition. Someone to see through her ridiculous pose as a common friend, and restore her inalienable right to over-the-title billing. The wife is clearly an imposter; see that she is removed. But my husband is still in a coma! Sorry, madam, the coma now belongs to the woman he loves.

". . . I didn't really think about you being Richard's wife during all this. I never really knew you before. And then . . . well, I started to like you. I don't have any women friends— mostly I don't want to. But you were . . . I was glad I liked you, and after that it wasn't so hard."

Now what? Do I thank her? Would someone please tell me why I feel like thanking her, as if the queen has just conferred birthday honors on me? Is it possible I'm as crazy as she is? Because, God help me, I like her too. Oh, damn you, Richard! Damn you both!

She stayed with me most of the day, but after that we didn't talk much. We were like women who have been in the labor room together. Each has seen the other enduring horrible pain—writhing and screaming, cursing her obstetrician, her husband, her baby, God, and the nurse who keeps saying she's only two-fingers-dilated. When it's over, neither remembers her own pain or how she took it; the fact is, neither wants to. They can never really discuss what they've shared; yet somehow they're tied by an unspeakable bond, like fellow passengers who were the only ones to panic when the *Andrea Doria* started sinking. We drew comfort from each other's silences, and later from the noise of the Saturday matinée crowd. A big crowd it was, too: lots of people who had come the first day but not again since; others who had just heard; the suburbanites who hadn't been able to make it into town all week but now felt they had to.

The growth hormone arrived with a modest flourish of trumpets at one-thirty, and was promptly administered. Some hours later the pathology lab found no discernible effects on Richard's sluggish liver tissue. Timmy was not surprised—but had the liver sprung into immediate throbbing action and sent forth blossoms, I doubt if that would have surprised him either. Still, spirits were high. Even Mahler stopped by toward midafternoon with what for him was an encouraging word: he believed that Richard now had "a chance." "Why *now?*" I asked. "Because," he replied with chilling Mahlerian candor, "I didn't think he would survive this long." As for Bleiweiss, the liver man himself, he never wavered in his childlike faith: "The liver *always* comes back." It was months before I realized that he had never promised it would come back *in time.*

I had taken four Dexamyls again, this time within seven hours and without hesitation. (Anyway, how do you know what an overdose is with these things? Especially on three hours' sleep. *One* is probably an overdose if you've got a decent metabolism, whereas I seem to need two before I can even wake up enough to feel depressed. One drink and I crump out. Without Dexies, I might have missed this whole experience, just like Richard, instead of giving a magnificent tour de force, exhibiting boundless courage, matched only by my superb control, and calling on deep resources of spirit, humor and energy never before seen in a woman of such gentle birth.

Just to top things off, Cal Jaffe called. How was I? I was okay; how was he? He was okay; how was Richard? Richard was the same. And Miranda, in case he wanted to know, was also okay—right here, in fact.

"Jesus!" was all he said to that.

"I asked her to come," I explained. "I wanted to talk about . . . things."

"And?"

"And we talked."

"Julie, are you . . . could we have dinner tonight?"

"Gee, no, thanks, really. I'm sort of so exhausted today, too many people, and I think I should stay home with the kids. I haven't, you know, seen them very much."

"Well, if you change your mind, call me, will you? I'll be home. I'm not feeling too outgoing myself."

"Oh, how was the party? I forgot."

"It was . . . anticlimactic. Only stayed half an hour. Couldn't get into it. Julie?"

"Mmm, I'm here—"

"I missed you."

"Thank you." (Yech, how can he talk that way after . . . ? I've got to hang up; I can't stand this.) "Oh, there's Timmy —listen, I have to go talk to him, okay?"

"Julie—"

"I really have to hang up now—"

"Should I call you back? Later?"

"I . . . all right, if you want . . ." (Why can't you just tell him to bug off? Because, stupid, you don't know how. You never did and you never will.)

Actually, Timmy was in the vicinity, busy talking to Miranda. People were starting to go; it was past five. Only the late shoppers were left, having come directly from Saturday funtime at Ohrbach's or Saks, toting their new bathing suit for the July Fourth weekend, itching to go home and try it on for their husband. But they couldn't leave before paying the recommended half-hour visit. Besides, it'll be impossible to get a taxi here now; if you just wait for me a few minutes, I'll drop you. We can leave soon, everybody's going, Julie's probably sick of all this company anyway—she looks worn out, poor kid, what she's been through this week . . .

Even Miranda left before six; after all, it was Saturday night in the real world. I wondered bitchily who else she had on tap, and where, but then I remembered that she'd mentioned something about staying with her father, who had just been let out of Payne Whitney. I kept forgetting she had an apartment. Was that where she and Richard . . . or had they mostly used Cal's? And if there, the bed, or the white couch, where I . . . ? There goes your fearful symmetry again, tiger.

Timmy was ready to take me home too. Would I like to stop for a drink at his place? (Let's see, am I numb enough to withstand twenty minutes of Marian Spector's gummy solicitude? I guess so, and maybe a drink would bring me down some; I could still be home by seven and eat with the kids.) Sure, I decided, why not?

In the car Timmy rattled off his latest News of the Week roundup on "the case," sounding more than ever like a bright ten-year-old showing off for company. With *expression*, as in

Mrs. Barmash's speech class, and dramatic flourishes of his free hand (two when stopped for lights) for emphasis. Things were "completely under control" at this point. Tomorrow he'd be ordering a new series of lab tests. "And I told Tompkins to stop in . . . And we'll be calling Bleiweiss for another conference . . . We have to feel our way on some of these procedures; we're moving now into uncharted territory. Not even the Canadian team handled it quite this way . . ."

Somehow it all slid over me more easily tonight—partly because of my higher Dexie content, but more because I thought maybe he'd begun to earn that piece in *Time* after all. Richard's condition did seem to be stabilized at last; in his fashion, even Mahler had conceded that. If they'd made it this far, they must be doing something remarkable. And even if there was still no projection, based on the early returns, as to when the victory speech might be telecast, at least there was a clear consensus now that we should stay tuned.

In two days the pathology microscopes had yielded no alarming new blobs on Richard's culture slides. His custom-designed plumbing system appeared to be a plastic marvel of intravenous ingenuity, flushing the good stuff in and the nasties out with the perfect, mindless discipline of a captive ocean. Dialyzed, the human body flows with the same magnificent regularity that allows us to chalk those omniscient notices on the lifeguard stand at the beach: High Tide will be at 4:48 P.M. today. Even the nurses had been subtly filling in their blank stares for the last day or so—like kids in the chorus line kicking ever so slightly higher after a sudden spurt at the box office. The show will not be folding tomorrow.

So if Timmy needed to file another dispatch about the view from the Matterhorn when he was still two treacherous miles from the peak, I could be gracious this one time. "You've really been fantastic," I offered. "And I'm sorry—I know I've been making it tougher." He squeezed forgiveness into my hand: Oh, that's all right, honey, my sainthood isn't even official yet; it still has to go through all that Vatican red tape.

Marian Spector wasn't home. I forced a few polite syllables of disappointment through the delight that didn't belong on my face. But I'd had no idea how anti-Marian I was feeling tonight until we walked into her brocade cream puff of a living room.

Everything was what Marian called *authentic* traditional. Rich and soft, in that order. The pillows were filled with down, not shredded kapok, and they were always fluffed up, just as the gleaming wood surfaces always reeked of Lemon Pledge. As Richard used to say, the only piece on the premises that didn't have a hand-rubbed finish was Marian herself. She wouldn't admit having had a professional decorator, even though her mother bragged about it. "Mother doesn't understand; I just used a friend's AID card to get around in 'the market.'" To Marian, having your apartment "done" was an open admission that originally you were from the Bronx. Which unfortunately she was, and which unfortunately she couldn't fix by taking a lifetime subscription to *House Beautiful*. She never wore a print dress; it was "flower-sprigged." She liked a bath towel to be "velvety," and she was constantly dropping auctions and periods. "Wait, let me guess," Richard had said when they got their new sofa. "Alvin Quatorze?" Timmy howled, but Marian was furious.

"Vodka and—?" Timmy asked.

"Fine."

"And what, though?"

"Anything."

"Well, tonic, Bitter Lemon, orange juice?"

"Any of those is fine."

"Well, pick one, then, for Chrissake."

I always exasperate people about that. Why should ordering a lousy drink be so hard? I don't like to drink, I'm no good at it, but that doesn't explain why I can't even make a selection. "Pick one for me, would you? I'm just not up to it."

He handed me something colorless, which meant he had settled on tonic. I sighed, wishing he'd picked Bitter Lemon. Not enough to have told him, of course; that would have been pushy. God, I'm an idiot, even when it doesn't count. Never dare say what you want or how you want it; who the hell are you to have a preference? Or else it leaves you wide open for being turned down. Or—maybe worst of all—you get what you ask for and find you can't stand that either. Nothing really *is* too good for me; how come *he* doesn't know that? Take a simple little thing like this drink. What if I had asked for something straight out—"I'd like a vodka and Bitter Lemon" —and he says he's sorry, but he hasn't got Bitter Lemon. What right do I have to make somebody sorry he couldn't please me? All I do is make him uncomfortable—*and then he won't like me.*

The fact is he probably won't like me anyway, but the least I can do is not ask for anything; then maybe it will take longer for him to decide. I won't give him any trouble; I'm a very cheap date, I'm a fairly easy lay; if he stops calling, I won't call him; I can confine my crying to the early evening hours so as not to disturb the other tenants in the building who may be enjoying themselves, or, preferably, each other. So please don't encourage me to say what I want; all I want is not to have to say. In *or* out of bed. If you'd just tell me, I'll do it to you. Thanks very much, but I'll never tell—I'd rather die. Or rather, I'd rather do without. I'm fine this way . . . Yes, I'm sure—*really*.

But really I'm lying again. Why doesn't anybody ever realize I'm lying? Because they don't care to. Julie didn't get any. Well, but she didn't *ask* for any. Does everybody else ask? Or do other people always know what everybody else wants? Am I the only one whose communication lines are down?

I felt the drink after two sips: a what-the-hellish sensation about the head and ears. "Ask me anything," I used to beg my blind dates, when I got high on half a drink. In my teens, it never took more than that. "Ask me," I would plead with boys who had absolutely no desire to ask me. Oh, please ask me; I want to tell you beautiful secret truths about what I feel. Ask me to talk from way in here, where I'm beautiful and interesting, where I'm all liquid and light and have no freckles. I'm clean and clear-skinned, bone and sinew; I turn golden in the sun; I get blond streaks. Furthermore, my brain is full of those springy little curls marked Good Sense of Humor, Good Personality, Good Dancer, Good Sport, Fun to Be With, Does not Get Runny Nose at Football Games, Will Not Clam Up at Parties. Want to talk about something neutral, not love? How about Latin poetry then. Poor Dido, I know just how she felt watching that bastard Aeneas sail away the next morning. *Fato profugus*, my foot.

Maybe it was a good thing those boys hadn't asked me anything. I really was a royal pain. I never opened my mouth when I was sober, but with one drink, beer even, I couldn't shut it. If I wasn't crying about love, I was upchucking or out cold. At least that got me out of the lonely corners and into the john or bedroom. People who came in to pee or get their coats would ask me how I was and could they get me anything and who was my date and did he know I was in here being sick? I always assured them that I was fine, thanks, and that Stan or Jimmy was probably busy somewhere and don't bother him; I didn't want him to see me like this anyhow.

I never got ditched, though; Stan or Jimmy always mustered up enough chivalry to take me home. After all, the poor kid . . . And in that condition, maybe she'll . . .

Ask me anything, Timmy: Go ahead. Which of my dark secrets would you like to hear?" I hadn't come very far since high school, but at least now I could make it sound light and sexy. I had developed a nice bantering delivery, which was the verbal equivalent of keeping my fingers safely crossed while opening the rest of me. See, I had fins; I don't have to go on.

"How do you feel about Miranda?" he said, watching me closely.

"Ambivalent," I said quickly. "Why?"

"I thought *I* was asking. I'm not through."

I'd failed to dazzle him with my footwork. "Sorry, sir. Go on."

"Would you define her as a close friend?"

"Yes and no. Mostly no, I guess."

"How come?"

"I think I need another vodka."

"That's how come?"

"No, but it's how you can get me to answer that."

He took both glasses to their clever bar, one of those old wooden dry sinks with wormholes for character, doors for storage and hinged shelves lined with burnished copper. But Marian had labored over it so lovingly with Copper-Glo that it was no longer merely burnished—it shone with an abraded pinkness like new kitchen pots.

"As you were saying?" he prompted, surrendering my re-filled glass.

"I wasn't saying yet," I countered, stalling. "But I will in a minute. Where is Marian, anyway?"

"Visiting her family. It's Father's Day tomorrow, and she has to atone for being ashamed of them. She'll be back around seven; we're eating out. Want to come?"

"No." (Boy, did I ever not.) "I really have to go home. I promised the children."

"Well? Your minute's up."

"Why do you want—? Oh, I forgot—I'm not allowed to ask you. Though I must say, I don't think it's fair. I didn't agree to it, either."

"Okay, how about if I let you ask me anything after five questions? But we're still only on number two, right?"

"Mmmm." I was getting a little slow on the uptake now;

it was harder to keep track. "Let's see, the question was how come something about Miranda?"

"About being good friends. More no than yes?"

"Close friends, you said."

"Okay, close."

"Because of Richard."

"What? Why?"

"Because she and Richard . . . Richard and she . . . are love . . . lovers. Having a loverly time. Wish I weren't here."

"Who the hell told *you* that?" He was thunderstruck— obviously not by the news but by hearing it from me. Now why was that? I stared at him, trying to filter it through my rapidly thickening head. I told you two drinks is two many. Are. Too. Many many tekel upharsin, weighed in the balance and found wanting. That's me, all right, but found wanting what? Someplace to lie down would be good for starters. I swung my feet up and closed my eyes, the roar of illegal-drug-and-alcohol traffic in my ears.

"Julie! Hey, don't!" He shook me gently, trying to peel me off and transfer me to something chemically treated to resist stains and accidents. Finally he gave up and carefully removed my shoes.

"Not ticklish there," I said. "Richard is, I'm not."

"You all right?" he said, pushing my damp hair back off my clammy forehead, as if that would reveal the answer.

"Sure I am. Yessir, that little girl is *all right*. Everybody says so."

"Julie, don't pass out."

"Why not? Oh, I know, because you get one more question."

"Two more; you didn't answer the last one. But I don't want you to be sick—"

"—on the Alvin Quatorze sofa? Marian will spank? I'm okay, don't worry. And here's the answer I owe you. Always pay my just debts. Cal told me, is who. Miranda told him. One more question then my turn, right?

"*Cal?* Why would that sonofabitch tell *you?* At a time like this?"

"Because misery loves company. That's five questions and it's my turn! You knew before I said—you knew the whole thing?"

"Yes. But I'd never have told you. What a goddamn lousy thing to do."

I shook my pounding head. "Nope. Don't see that. Think he did me a big favor. Why wouldn't you tell me? Never mind, I can guess that—never tell wife; what she doesn't know won't hurt you. Keep 'em ignorant and well fed. We treat our slaves real good as long as they know their place. Empty head and a belly full. Which reminds me—think I'd better throw up now."

When I raised my head the room was in total eclipse. Timmy half-carried me to the john, but I managed to push him away and lock the door before collapsing over the beautiful bowl.

When it was over I flushed it and lay down in a limp curl around the cool base of the toilet. Oh God, I promised the kids ice cream! It's Saturday—everything closes at six. I wonder if I can stand up yet. Carefully I rolled away from my rotund comfort station. "From down here you look pregnant," I told it. That's either funny or symbolic—if you can still be funny without being symbolic. Slowly I let go of the tile floor and rose to my knees at the count of nine. Then I heard Timmy pounding on the door, calling me. "Julie, let me help! For Chrissake! I'm a doctor!"

"Get hot water," I said weakly. "The baby's coming."

"Julie, will you open the damn door!"

"No," I said. "Use the other john. I was here first."

"You stupid bitch, I'm trying to help you!"

"Then get me some ice cream. I need a pint of vanilla or two Dexie—I mean Dixie cups, vanilla and chocolate. And the time—I need to know the time."

It took a minute for him to react. "Dixie cups?" he said finally in a cracked voice. A man with a psychotic female locked in his wife's bathroom; who would believe that for once he was innocent? I began giggling; suddenly the whole thing was a black farce. Filmed entirely on location in the Black Farce of West Germany. I sank back on the floor and laughed myself all the way into tears, picturing poor bewildered Timmy out there wincing at every hysterical sound.

Finally I stopped, weak and sore from prolonged overexercise of unused muscles. "Timmy, I'm not crazy," I panted. "I'm all right. Timmy, what time is it?"

"Six-thirty. If you're not crazy, what *was* all that?"

I struggled up and opened the door. "See? Same old Julie, just a little the worse . . ." He led me back to the living room, eying me nervously in case I was being crafty so as to catch him off guard. As I reclaimed my old spot on the couch, he demanded, "What about the two Dixie cups?" Stifling another giggle, I explained, "For the kids, I promised —and the supermarket's closed."

"Oh, thank God," he said, closing his eyes. "You bitch." And he kissed me for making the bad dream come untrue.

He'd been trying to do the same for me. So I returned it. An even exchange.

But wasn't there something I needed to ask him? Wait— it was seeping back. Miranda. He knew about Miranda. "Hey, I had four questions left," I said, startling him.

He backed off, disconcerted, like a pigeon who can't touch the crumbs until the person who scattered them has the decency to quit moving.

"Yeah, I guess so," he said, scowling, and picked up his glass. "No more for you," he added firmly, by way of getting even.

"Now that it's my turn, you want to play something else," I retorted. "Cheater!"

"Sticks and stones," he said, smiling slyly over his shoulder. He poured the drink, tossed in more ice and tipped the glass toward me. "Here's to your four questions. Shoot." He leaned back against the bar, draping himself in a parody of every slouching cowboy star waiting for the other guy to draw.

"How long have you known . . . about them?"

"Since it started, I guess." He shrugged. "A year, maybe?"

"Did he tell you?"

"Sure."

"Did he . . . do you know if he wanted—wants—to divorce me and marry her?"

"I don't think so. Maybe *she* thinks so, but that doesn't mean anything. One of your incurable romantics, old Richard. Everything always has to be love."

"*What* everything always?"

He didn't answer right away. Was he weighing whether

he'd told me more than he meant to? Then, very quietly,
he reminded me: "That would be your last question?"

"Oh, is it?" Flustered, I tried to recount, to think up something better, or else find a loophole. "Wait—I withdraw it
then. No, I don't. What *did* you mean, everything?"

"Sure that's it now?"

"Sure."

"Well, just that every time he bangs a girl he calls it love.
It seems as if he *has* to. It's . . . he's got a nice-Jewish-boy
hang-up about that. I *think*. Like if you don't feel something
big and beautiful about the girl, if she's just a quif, you've
got no right to bang her. It makes her a whore and a nice-
Jewish-boy doesn't go to whores. He's too sensitive . . .
and clean."

"Maybe it's that whores don't come kosher," I cut in, and
promptly regretted it, because he suddenly stopped talking and just sat there frowning into his drink.

"Every time—you said every time he bangs a girl," I
prompted. "Other girls . . . That means others, besides her?"

Another sly smile . . . and another sip of the drink. He
sipped very slowly, the bastard. He shook his head. "Uh-uh.
No more questions."

My cheeks were flaming, I had a headache, and I felt dizzy
and feverish. Please, I don't want to be sick again. He couldn't
be doing this; what sonofabitch would do this? "Tell me!"
I screamed. "You bastard, you have to tell me!"

"Listen, you little bitch," he shot back, "I don't have to
tell you any fucking thing at all. Richard is my friend, my
*best* friend, and what he tells me—has told me—is nobody's
goddamn business. Not yours, not any-goddamn-body else's.
Where do you get off demanding—screaming at me like a

goddamn fishwife!—that I tell *you!* Things you have no right to know. Richard, my buddy Richard, up there in my charge, my *patient,* and you're—and I'm supposed to stab him in the back? For what? For whose benefit? Yours? Who do I owe my loyalty to, my sick friend who trusts me—or his jealous bitch of a wife who happens to feel like snooping around? Suppose *you* tell *me!*"

I couldn't. The fight was over. Battered contender fails to respond to the bell. Spector wins by a TKO in the second, calls challenger "hopelessly outclassed."

"I'm sorry," I said stiffly, rolling it over my smashed teeth and bits of broken mouthpiece. It was very hard to see (both the challenger's eyes were swollen shut; it looked as if her head had taken most of the punishment). "Could you just tell me . . . I found a—something that must be a diary, I think . . . it might be a record of . . . Could you just tell me if you know about that—please?"

"Oh, sure," Timmy said cheerfully (champ will consider rematch). "I know about that. Like I said, he's got these nutty hang-ups about his sex life. That was another one—writing it down every time he got laid. Who, what, when, where and how. Even the positions, and how many times he came. I kid the hell out of him about it, but he says he can't help it. He likes to *store* things."

"Next to the bankbooks," I mumbled, nodding with painful recognition. "Another Nutshell Library. Jesus, filing his own orgasms."

There didn't seem to be any more to ask, except "What time is it?"

"Quarter to seven."

"I have to go home." I got up uncertainly and picked my

way through the wreckage, which had been strewn for half
a mile beyond the site of the crash. Timmy unhitched himself from the bar and loped over to me. "Julie," he said,
and pulled me against him. "Come here, poor baby." I was
whimpering, and he began to stroke and nuzzle me, as one
would a wounded or badly frightened animal. I shivered in
response, and he whispered comfortingly in my ear, "Richard
loves you. Don't you see, he needs you. That's why he took
such care . . . not to let you find out." I continued to shiver,
aguelike, whether from the cold sense of irony, or from the
erotic stimulus of his warm breath on my neck, I couldn't
tell. Not being of sound mind or body, and under the undue
influence of person or persons known . . .

What I felt like was one of those Slinky toys, a large useless
coiled metal spring that seems to have been designed for
no purpose except its own destruction—to be playfully
pulled and stretched until, tangled in its own misshapen
loops, it can never bounce back again. That was where I was:
Slinky Julie, twisted beyond recoil. My spring had sprung.

Come on now, Julie, how do you show the nice doctor you
appreciate his hurting you? He only did it for your own good.
Here, like this; suddenly he was pushing my head down
gently . . . and gently, obediently, I dropped, grateful for
the prescription that would make me all better tomorrow.
I was down on my knees, struggling with a stuck zipper.
Timmy's fly zipper! On my knees trying to take my medicine like a big girl. See? Same old Julie, washing down the
nasty stuff with more nasty stuff. I can take it; I'm *supposed*
to take it. Only now I couldn't get his damn zipper open.
Like a knowing smile, it gnashed its shiny teeth at me. If
you don't fix it, he'll really hate you. Oh God.

Frantic now, sure only that this was the penance I had to pay, or else . . . I began yanking desperately at the captive pinch of his expensive cavalry twill pants. "Oh, please!" I cried. "*Please!*"

"What the hell!" Timmy exploded suddenly, pulling away. Until then he'd been playing Statues, standing dazed, in the at-ease position, not knowing what the captain's orders were, if any, or whether this was a suicide mission, as rumored. He was probably drunk; he must have had at least five while I was looking, and more while I was conked out. And besides drunk, confused: how did she get down there, anyway? Fell or plunged to her doom, twenty feet into the courtyard below, clad only in . . . Foul play has not been eliminated as a possibility. He must have pushed her—he must have pushed!

Timmy finally freed his own zipper with one quick tug; now he stood there holding the metal slide. Should he pull it up or down? If down, did that make it all his responsibility? If up, did it mean that now he didn't want me to? Well, *did* he want me to? Poor Timmy, hoist on his own petard. I had to take the matter out of his hands. It was my penance, after all.

Like the zipper, his prick was at half mast, with the consistency of a vinyl garden hose or a tube of shampoo. *Pliable.* I plied it, thinking: Small, tapered. Never seen one that actually came to a point like that. More of a phallic symbol than a phallus. The Hebraic symbol for phallus is a phallustein. No, *stine.* Next year in Phallustine . . .

It was shaping up now. Richard likes it this way, tucking it into one side like a mump, tender when I touch it. I looked up; he liked it too.

Okay, but I wasn't dismissed yet. He wanted me to kneel slightly higher for more leverage. (When I was eight I'd talked the pediatrician out of using a tongue depressor to examine my sore throat. "Please, the wood makes me gag— see, I can open wide enough. *Ah.*" "Very good, but I still need to insert the stick—just for a minute now. There." "*Ahgh!*" "See, that wasn't so bad." Yes, it was. Yes, it is.

Now, ladies and gents, the contract demands that Julie the Sword Swallower perform the world-famous teething-ring trick. Forming a ring with her teeth, she must fit it carefully over the tip, thus, and proceed smoothly down to the very base. Notice how she does not bite down. Many males believe that the female has a natural biting instinct which must be curbed, like your dog. Hence the expression "man-eating bitch." The female must be taught how to eat it without taking the command literally—just as the male must learn that the female is harmless, even when aroused or frightened. She would not hurt a fly. Still, the male insists you can't be too careful; if the tamer doesn't keep cracking that whip, the lioness, though domesticated and raised in captivity, may still attack. Lassie the dog may have her day. The slave may rise, the meek may inherit, and the serving girl may not answer when the master rings. Did you ring, sir? Yes. Down on your knees, you sullen housewife. That's house*maid*, sir. Housemaid's knee. Are you forgetting your place? No, sir, I've got it—right down here. Down *there*. Down *on it.*

Time for our medicine now—here it comes. Let's see it all go down in one big gulp. No, you can't have water with it; I said you're a big girl now. Don't cry. I said *don't cry,* we'll hold you down on the bed and paint your throat with

Argyrol. Whatever happened to painting your throat with Argyrol?

Wait—he's taking it away. All gone. I called up to him, up over the dreary miles of shirtfront, a sterile snowy field with a neatly planted single row of buttons. "What?" I called.

"Seven o'clock," he said nervously, tucking and zipping. "Marian be home any minute. Come on, I'll take you home."

I got up, crinkly hair in my mouth. Ten years ago I would have pasted it in my memory book; seven years ago I would have swallowed it so he wouldn't feel rejected. I was all grown up now. Watch how easily I can get rid of it. But where? In the ashtray, like a calling card? Julie Messinger came to see you. Well, not exactly, but *Timmy* came while she was here, and she thought you'd like a little something to commemorate the event. I put the hair in my pocketbook.

"Hey, what about my ice cream?" I demanded in the elevator, blurting it right out in front of five or six fascinated other passengers. "I *need* it," I said. Two or three of them chuckled; I sounded just like their little Lisa.

Timmy flushed angrily. Now my presence in his building was clearly an embarrassment; did I have to engrave myself on their memories? (Isn't that Dr. Spector from 5-C? Yes, but the girl isn't—I'm *sure* his wife's a blonde. Yeah, didn't we see her leave last night with a *suitcase?* Hmmm.) He repaid me by staring sullenly at the ceiling until we got out, and then snarled, "All *right*, we'll stop someplace and get ice cream, all *right?*"

A very unpleasant person, basically. Not even civil. Nice would be asking too much, but civil, you'd think he could swing that . . . considering.

"*Evening*, Doctor!" the doorman shouted jovially from the

curb, already bucking for ten dollars next Christmas. Timmy had been hoping to hustle me out while he was busy whistling for cabs. "Goddamn," Timmy muttered. "Nosy bastard."

"Oh, goddamn yourself," I said. "I think I'll just go back in and wait for Marian. *And* I think I'll have dinner with you. I *was* invited, wasn't I?"

That shook him. "You *serious*?" he exclaimed. "What about the kids, what about—?"

"Yeah, what about," I said, smugly aware that I'd won something small but crucial. "It's okay, I'm not serious," I reassured him, in a tone that barely missed contempt. "I just don't much care for being smuggled around like Mandy Rice-Davies. Especially by you in your lousy apartment house, where I've been a respectable visitor probably two hundred times. I think you're a prick. And an idiot. And dammit, now I'm crying. I can't go home crying, even with ice cream."

Surprise. He said "I'm sorry" as if it mattered whether I believed him. So I did, which somehow made it worse.

"Don't, Julie. Oh Christ, don't. You're an absolutely sensational girl. Richard—I hope that dumb bastard really does appreciate you." (Oh, please make him shut up, *please*. Why don't they ever say the right thing for the right reason? Why do they always *patronize*? Don't patronize this company! Unfair! Why am I suddenly sensational—because I put his peepee in my mouth? I ate him—that's funny. God, how I ate him.)

We drove to an all-night superette that was only seven blocks out of our way. Better there than a deli; you can never get standard brands at a deli. You'd pay thirty cents more a quart and it would be some low-butterfat junk that allegedly reduces your chances of getting arteriosclerosis, if it doesn't turn gelatinous on the way home.

I'd never gone into a supermarket with a strange man before. Another Messinger first. There's something shockingly intimate about revealing your *Woman's Day* self to a relative stranger. I used to worry about hidden cameras researching my motivations at the frozen-food case. (Why is that lady buying Bird's Eye when White Rose is four cents off? It must be the picture—write that down!) Do you sleep in the nude is a cinch question compared to, say, do you squeeze the fresh produce even if there's a sign? Or would you sneak through the Express check-out with more than eight items? Just think what it tells you about a person.

Once I went to an A&P grand opening—free Hawaiian orchids and fluttering colored pennants and loaves of white bread for the first thousand customers—and the men loading the bags were front-office biggies in pin-stripe suits, just like for a Metro premiere. Even the customers came dressed up, without hair rollers, and some of them had made dates in advance to meet each other there. "Doris, look at these *pork* chops!" "Oh, they're gorgeous, but we had a roast loin last night at my mother's." "You think this chuck is fatty, Ethel? It looks fatty to me." "Hmm, yeah, it looks better in the 84th Street branch. Let's go see the fresh fruit."

Timmy and I were virtually alone at the superette. Who else would be in there at ten past seven on a Saturday night? Even the elderly singles crowd had cleared out with their sad weekend six-packs of beer and cat food. Timmy extracted one of the telescoped carts and started pushing it toward the dairy case. Annoyed, I called after him, "I don't need a cart for two lousy Dixie cups."

"You mean you're not going to find twenty other things while you're in here? Marian always does. I thought it was a classic female trait."

"It is, but I can't do it in front of people. Wait, I do need some pancake mix, though; tomorrow's Sunday, I forgot."

"Uh-huh," he said triumphantly. "Syrup?"

"Yeah, okay, syrup. But that's *all*." Why did I have to do that? It showed loss of dignity, lack of control, weakness, inability to resist the slightest temptation.

I couldn't seem to get the taste of Timmy out of my mouth. Do men ever taste it? Besides fags, I mean? I'd never asked one. "Did you ever—?" I began impulsively at the checkout counter, and then lost my nerve because of the clerk, a tall Negro with an Afro haircut and beads. (Laurie refuses to call them blacks; she thinks we should revive "colored gentlemen." I bet this one would love that.)

"Two twenty-seven," he announced. I reached for my wallet, but Timmy gave me a dirty look, so I let it go and demurely lowered my eyes while they completed the transaction.

"You want the stamps?" the clerk asked.

"I don't know," Timmy replied, turning to me. "You save stamps?"

I shook my head. The clerk flashed a knowing smile and reappraised me in the light of this new information. That bastard Timmy; couldn't manage a simple yes or no. A husband *knows* if the wife saves stamps. On the other hand, why should I care what the clerk thinks? Because I feel . . . conspicuous. I feel like the only one of my kind.

"Did I ever what?" he asked as we pushed through the magic door marked "Thank you! Come Again!" I felt the clerk's eyes on my exiting ass. "Did you ever taste . . . your own—when you come? Did you ever swallow it?"

"Why?" Amusement, titillation, wariness. What the hell was I up to now?

"I just wondered if men knew how they taste."

"Well, yeah, I did once."

"Your own?"

He shot me a funny look. Was I trying to find out if he ever had a homosexual experience? "Yes, my own." (Let there be no mistake about that.)

"Why?"

"Curious, I guess." He shrugged. "Scientific mind."

"And?"

"And what?"

"What did it taste like?"

"I don't know. Warm thick nothing." The boyish grin reappeared for the first time in hours. "How did I taste to you?"

"About like that. White of a soft-boiled egg that needs salt, or another minute on medium-low."

"Mmm. Is that, uh, different from other guys? I mean, girls all taste different, you know that? Smell different too."

"I don't have your highly educated palate," I said, defensively bitchy again. "You taste different from Richard, but I haven't sampled anybody else. Lately. The last flavor I remember distinctly was corn, eight years ago."

"Well, what about Richard?"

"What about let's change the subject now."

"You picked this one. I can't help it if I like it."

"Well, I don't any more. Anyway, we're almost home. Let's try to end it on a high keen note."

"What, end it? I sort of thought—"

"Well, just sort of don't, okay?" (Relax, will you! What can he do—start calling you up for dates? You're married, remember?)

The ice cream was a success. Nicky, Matthew and I had two scoops apiece; Darlene had three. I said they could stay up late and we played Snap and Animal Rummy and Crazy Eights and finally Circus Old Maid, in which every pair I drew seemed fraught with ironic symbolism—Sly Fox, Trained Seal, Pretty Kitty, Agile Acrobats, Bareback Rider! At ten o'clock I put them to bed and began reading to them.

"Mommy, what are you gonna do when we're asleep?" Nicky interrupted.

"Oh, just read in bed, I think. I'm in the middle of a mystery story."

"Is it scary?"

"A little."

"Monsters?"

"Not really. Just people."

"Bad guys?"

"Bad and good."

"Do the good guys win?"

"I don't know; I haven't finished."

"The good guys always win in stories."

"Not in grown-up stories."

"Why?"

"Because grownups aren't supposed to need a happy ending."

"Well, but do they?"

"Some do, because they're still little kids in some ways."

"Are you?"

"I guess so, yes."

"Then the good guys will win in your story?"

"Well, maybe. We'll see." How can you tell a kid there aren't any good guys in your story?

I locked myself in my room and took out Poor Richard's Almanack. How would I ever figure out what it all meant, who they all were? I sat there studying it until the letters blurred, trying to piece it all together—fragments of things I remembered, other things I couldn't possibly know. A date: Jan. 26: where was I then, what did he say that night when he left, what did I think, who could MS have been? Minnie, Mimi, Marnie, Moe? "2x: post, or; below." Two times posthumously? Orally? Below the Mason-Dixon Line? Marian Spector? Oh, no. Please, God, no.

At one-thirty A.M. I called Laurie, the only person in the world I could unreasonably expect to be wide awake and screwy enough to want to help. "Laurie," I said, "you're up, right? I need you."

"Don't tell me," she said. "You want to kidnap Richard out of there. Hold on; I better get a Coke."

"No," I said. "But get the Coke. It's harder than that."

The phone clattered, the refrigerator door slammed, and she was back, fortified. (*Fift*ified, Richard would say, prudently lining his vulnerable tummy with five glasses of milk before a cocktail party.)

"Okay," she said. "Tell Laurie."

"Well, you see," I said. "I seem to have this sex diary of Richard's, and you have to help me crack the code."

"What?" she said. "*What?*"

"You heard me," I said.

"That's funny, I thought I did too—I think."

"Well, so?"

"Jools, listen, why don't you hop in a cab or something and come over? I can't get out, but you can—Darlene's there, right?"

"Yes."

"So come on. Bob's in Washington till tomorrow. You could even sleep over. And listen, bring the, uh, thing with you. I promise not to cover it with Con-Tact."

I laughed and then of course I cried, carefully holding the receiver away from my mouth so the tears wouldn't fall in the little holes. I always worry about that: whether getting it wet in there can damage the wires and how would you explain to the operator. I was only trying to clean it, Operator, I hate a dirty mouthpiece. No, tears would probably just register as extra message units.

"Laurie, listen," I said. "Richard and Miranda Graham are having an affair and there's dozens of others, initials of people in this diary, and I think everybody is somebody I know—friends—and I can't figure out who, but I have to."

She gasped then, and I heard the Coke gurgling back into the bottle. "Oh God, Jools," she said.

"What, what is it?"

"I think . . . Listen, you've got to get right over here . . . I think I know something."

"I'm coming," I said. "Just don't fall asleep."

"I haven't fallen asleep since May eleventh," she said proudly.

W̶hen I got there Laurie was standing barefoot on the stoop in a billowy white cotton nightie. The Jonases live in a converted brownstone in what they call the urban renewal area, West 94th. So far nothing has been renewed except inside: better plumbing and higher rent. Outside, it's still pretty much plain urban, with bums sleeping on doorsteps like babies abandoned there more than thirty years ago and nobody ever opened the door to read the note pinned to their blanket: "Please care for Danny; I can't any more." She came floating down the steps, flagging my cab with her empty Coke bottle, and stuck her head through the window. "Before you even get out," she said, "I want you to know I've never even kissed him on the lips!"

The driver, Murray L. Mossbacher, got a laugh out of that, which almost made up for my not wanting to go to La Guardia. Somehow they're never happy after midnight unless you're going to the airport. "There aren't any LJ's in it," I assured Laurie. "You're in the clear."

We walked in through the kitchen, where the Coke empties lined the walls like standees at a hot-ticket musical. I sometimes think Laurie exaggerates for effect. It's bad enough when she goes to her friends' houses for dinner with two bottles in a paper bag because nobody can be trusted to have any.

"How do you know about Miranda?" she asked, getting right down to business.

"Informed sources," I said. "Cal Jaffe. Also she made a clean breast of it herself. So to speak. Also you'll find her listed prominently in this—wherever it says MGM, it does not refer to Metro Goldwyn Mayer." I handed her the diary, feeling oddly relieved, as if I'd just turned my case over to a competent attorney.

She studied it in silence for a while, and I amused myself by trying to pick out which items she had Con-Tacted most recently. There were so many patterns now, like a kaleidoscope or a Vuillard painting in which the people are only objects in print dresses sitting on print chairs against print walls—a lifeless jungle of lifelike forms, millions of prize-winning ikebana arrangements marching precisely across each other's inscrutable faces.

"Here, this is the one I know about—NW," Laurie exclaimed.

"Who? How?" I said.

"Nancy Wasserman. Remember Nancy Wasserman? Used to work with Bob at Lennen & Newell? You met her here a lot of times."

"Yes, vaguely, but not since . . . at least a year, right?"

"No, she was at my party in April—and also I think at Marcy Berns'. Anyway, I talked to her Wednesday—when everybody was going down to give blood for Richard, and to see you? And she said something—I thought it was strange, but she's such a nut I didn't even try to figure it out then—she said, 'I'm not going. I don't think Julie would want me there.' I couldn't think why the hell you wouldn't, why you'd even care, and anyway, it seemed to me you liked her, didn't you?"

"Yeah, I did—she's funny. I remember now—short brown hair and a good figure, but constantly dieting. She wanted prominent pelvic bones."

"That's right. Well, anyway, I thought it was peculiar what she said. And here she is: Feb. 27, NW 1x or."

"1x means one time, I think, and 'or' is oral. He's got all the positions listed, and you'll see 'or' more than anything else—which is logical, since he's very or-oriented."

"What's 'flag'? He's only got two 'flags' here."

"I'm not sure. I thought at first it was some kind of patriotic celebration, but now I think probably flagellation. I guess he tried it and didn't like it—or maybe the girl didn't, and he never found anybody else who'd let him. Or he left his whip at JF's house in 1966 and was afraid to go back. Who do you think all those J's are, anyway? They're not me—I don't think I'm even in it."

"Maybe that's a tribute. You're just not one for the books . . . wait, what's this 'post'? Seems to be a lot of it; all the J's do it and MGM too. Not post office? Richard's a little old for that."

"I thought posterior. And 'reg' would be regular. And the '2x' and '3x' business would mean either that they did it twice or that he came twice—see, some places it says '2x (she 3x),' which I figure means she came one more time."

"MGM seems to like 'or' pretty much."

"MGM thought she was pregnant this week, so she must have done a fair amount of 'reg'—"

"Hey, here's NW again, back by popular request. '2 to 5

P.M.' What day of the week was March 5, 1967? Look at Bob's five-year calendar over there on the desk."

I found it. "Tuesday. So?"

"So that checks. She had Tuesdays off in 1967."

"Laurie, have you got anything to drink besides Coke?"

"You mean like liquor?"

"No, like orange juice. I'm going through another orange-juice period."

"Julie, you know I wouldn't have anything citrus. I'm terrified of acid."

"At least it doesn't rot your teeth like Coke," I said self-righteously. She brought me some grape juice. "Are you still taking Dexamyl?" I asked.

"No, my doctor put me on some new yellow things. But I don't trust him; they smell like placebos and I don't feel the motor being raced."

"How do placebos smell?"

"Impotent. I don't blame my doctor, though; I was up to five Dexamyls a day. You start hallucinating, you know that?"

"Really? Did you?"

"Yes. A few weeks ago. I blacked out in a telephone booth at the Five and Ten. It was awful."

"God, how many did you take?"

"I don't remember—six, maybe seven."

"What was it like?"

"Dark, cramped, hot—like the usual phone booth. Didn't get my dime back, either."

"Oh, Laurie, honestly—the *hallucinating*, I mean."

"Yeah, that's what I meant too. And hollow voices droning in my ear long distance."

"No pictures?"

"A few line drawings. Hirshfeld faces with slanty eyes, like in the Sunday *Times* Drama Section. Paisley—lots of paisley . . . Anyway, I can still get Dexies on my cousin's prescription—you need?"

"I will in about a week. I've been up to four a day since . . . Laurie, what the *hell* am I going to do?"

I had snapped the mood like a dried wishbone; both of us were left with our broken ends, and neither had the top. Nobody gets her wish.

"God, Julie," she said, "What *can* you? There's no such thing as a sensible move, is there? Wait till he wakes up and then tell him—what, that you know everything and want a divorce?"

"That's funny—that's what I said to shock him out of the coma the first day he . . . the first time I saw him. And it was a joke! I didn't know *anything*."

"Well, but would you . . . divorce him?"

"I can't answer that, I don't even know. See, if you'd asked me two days ago, I'd have said no of course not, we're as happily married as there is—which maybe isn't very, but it's all anybody expects. Certainly all I ever did. So now it's two days later, and I'm sitting here with all this information indicating he's a whole other person! But *he* hasn't done anything for the past two days except be unconscious. Which means if . . . when he wakes up, he's exactly the same husband he always was, so why should I suddenly want to divorce him? I mean, he already *did* everything—and I accepted it!"

"But you *didn't* accept it; you didn't know."

"I accepted being married to him on his terms! I accepted

the marriage as happy! More or less. I assumed there *wasn't* any more; I settled. What's different now? There *still* isn't any more . . . or less. He's not planning to make me any happier or to take away what I had—as far as I know."

"He *cheated* you, though; there was more—could have been, if he hadn't withheld it."

"So what? Don't you see, he didn't force me to take half a loaf. That was all he had to offer, and I never thought of asking for seconds. I never asked in eight years. And nothing has *changed!*"

"Julie, do you remember that night last year when Richard called you from the office and said he was coming right home? And then he didn't get home for two hours?"

"Yes, I remember. I panicked, I thought he'd been mugged in the subway, and I called you. He *never* did anything like that."

"Remember I called the police? I'll never forget trying to convince that cop how well I knew Richard. I said, 'Listen, I *know* him. I know he's lying in a gutter somewhere, because if he told his wife he was coming right home, he was.' 'Lady,' he said to me. 'Lady, you know these people, you been best friends for years, right? You don't know nothin' more about 'em than I do. You don't know what goes on behind anybody's door! You go over and visit 'em, right? So what do you know after you go home? *Nothing*, is what. Lady, do yourself a favor—hang up and watch the *Tonight Show.*' And that was it—he wouldn't even take the name!"

"Laurie, you know what the worst thing is? It's that I don't hate him. At all. I don't even feel any kind of sustained anger. I mean, he's hanging there, waiting for some other judgment, and if . . . if it goes against him, I don't want it to be *my fault!* Maybe we'll never even get to discuss it! Who all the J's are—and whether the 'flag' really *is* for flagellation. Do you realize I might never *know*?"

"Yes," she said softly, and we both sat there a long time letting it sink in. When she looked up at me, her nice brown eyes were wet. My friend; she cared.

"You're really not angry," she reflected. "That's so strange. I think it's what I'd be most. I even think I'd *force* myself to be. What about Miranda—aren't you angry with her?"

"No, I *like* her. I'm sorry for her. She only admitted the whole thing because she felt left out. My part was bigger."

"Julie, you're not trying! She's not a nice girl—she treated you very badly!"

"Shameless hussy," I recited, nodding obediently. "Home wrecker, love thief."

"That's good—I think she's got it! Now, what about Cal Jaffe?"

"What about him? What did he do?"

"Well, he certainly didn't do you any good, telling you at a time like this. He's supposed to be protecting you! Why *did* he tell you, anyway?"

"I just think he was so hurt, he needed someone to kiss it and make it better."

"So he picked *you!* Boy, that's sick." She looked at me quickly, and asked, "Did you?"

I looked away, just as quickly. "I . . . I don't think it's possible." (What is called not responsive. But how *could* I tell her that? Any of what I'd been doing with any of them? Tell her and you lose your one sympathetic ear, that's all the good it will do.)

Laurie and her radar; she didn't push it. "Jools," she said instead, "do you think Richard wants a divorce?"

"Miranda says he does—that he wants to marry her. She was going to say yes this week, because of the pregnancy. But I'm not sure; I don't really believe her. Probably no wife ever does, though, not even when he's boarding the plane for Juárez. It's a defense; it makes it possible to live with being rejected. He's only fooling, he doesn't mean it, he's not really going, he's doing it to see how I react, he'll be back for dinner, I better start the potatoes. Then after he's gone, you call up the second string of excuses: he's impossible; he couldn't make it with any woman; he had the best chance with me and he blew it. Until he *does* make it with somebody else. At which point you quit talking and cry, because now everybody knows it *was* you all along."

"Do you know when it started—with Miranda?"

"A year ago, give or take."

"God. And he never made one mistake, one Freudian slip?"

"Oh, Laurie, for all I know he made hundreds; I just wasn't paying attention. Don't you understand—it never *occurred* to me!"

"But look at all the *time*," she said, waving the diary. "Weekends, nights, he was never *home!*"

"I know," I nodded stupidly. "The kids made him nervous; he needed to get away. It sounds nutty, but I wanted him to. I was *scared* to box him in with two screaming babies; he'd hate me." ("Why did you lie down in the driveway just because your sister told you to? You *knew* she wanted to ride over you with her bike!" I thought, If I let her, she'll be nice to me, and if I don't, she'll hate me. But now if they punish her, she'll hate me anyway. I won't even get any credit for letting her do it! "Please don't, *please* don't punish her!" "Isn't that child unbelievable?")

Laurie said, "The diary goes back seven *years*—before Nicky even. Almost since you were married! So you can't blame the screaming babies."

"Only myself, right?"

"No, I didn't mean that; I didn't even mean blame *him*. It's . . . what you have to see is, that's the way he had to play it. He never gave you a chance!"

"Hogamous, higamous."

"Huh?"

"Men are polygamous. Messinger's motto."

"Messinger's mistake," she retorted. "Phooey on that." And she went for another bottle.

"You're a chain-Coker," I said to her retreating blur of whiteness.

"Oh, *very* good," she said, pausing at the door. "Tell me, what's a witty girl like you doing in a mess like this?"

"Well, you see," I said, "that's what I came to ask you."

She laughed. "That's an indication of your judgment, right there."

"Yeah, I should have gone to my pastor. Or my faculty adviser."

"How about your family doctor?"

"I did that."

"Timmy?"

I nodded. "He knew all about it—Miranda, the diary, the whole thing."

"Who the hell told *him*?"

"Richard. He and Richard play together, see, like Nicky

and Matthew in the sandbox. They compare whose peepee is bigger, and who put it upside down in more places, and where and how and whose."

"God," she said, finally stunned. "God."

"Timmy taught Richard all the adultery he knows. Though Richard must have had an innate flair for it—you can teach the mechanics, but the gift, the *dedication*, that's something . . . Well, either you got it or you don't."

Laurie wasn't listening. "Does Timmy think Richard wants a divorce?" she asked.

"No, but that figures. Timmy's been sleeping around for years, and *he* doesn't. He likes things this way, where he can come home when he's through playing, and Marian keeps his lamb chops warm on the electric hot tray. I'm not Marian, though, and I don't think—at least, God, I *hope* that Richard isn't Timmy."

"You know damn well he isn't," she said heatedly. "Timmy's stupid and pompous and egotistical—and *stupid*. But for once he's right. Anyway, *I* can't see Richard leaving you, either."

"But what if you're wrong? What if he really loves her, and I'm going through this whole thing, this insane waiting-room game, for a husband I've already lost?"

(*"Well, I have lost you; and I lost you fairly;/In my own way, and with my full consent."*)

"But you're not! You haven't lost—you're his *wife!* And even if you do, even if he's really . . . lost, you're *still* the wife . . ."

(*"Say what you will, kings in a tumbrel rarely/Went to their deaths more proud than this one went."*)

"And besides, you still love him. You haven't even put up a fight!"

(*"If I had loved you less or played you slyly/ I might have held you for a summer more,/ But at the cost of words I value highly,/ And no such summer as the one before."*)

"So I should hang in there, by my very fingernails? And if, I mean *when*, he wakes up and says 'Miranda,' I should be standing right there to correct him?"

"You should be standing right there."

"With his box of Mallomars and all his pairs of socks rolled the way he likes. He even *calls* me his roommate. Oh God, I wish I were married."

"Jools, you know what? You need some sleep. You wanna sleep here?"

"No, I couldn't. But—my God, Laurie—it's after four *o'clock!* I'm really sorry."

She laughed. "Don't worry. If you hadn't come I'd have sat up and covered the baby's stroller, and I really like it just the way it is."

"Some things," I agreed, hugging her, "it doesn't help to cover up."

I could still see her on the steps when my cab reached the corner. Just standing there, caring.

Home and in bed, I lay forcing myself to think about the good parts. Come on, there must have been good parts. (In the end, when the specter of divorce is rushing at you, your entire love is supposed to flash before your doomed eyes.) Let's see, there was my first married birthday, when he sent me huge masses of anemones, wildly pink and red and purple velvet pinwheels, and the card said: "You are the most wonderful lioness I ever shot." That was nice. Every year after that, though, one bunch of exactly twelve anemones arrived, and not impulsively. The cards were written in haste; you could tell by the writing. A house cat is not a lioness, and you don't have to shoot it, just leave it a little milk in a saucer.

Well then, how about the night Nicky was born, and Richard sat heroic and smily in the labor room, holding my hand and making me laugh when it didn't hurt. And when it did, he tenderly massaged the small of my back, which we referred to in our private silly talk as the little of my back. And when he came into the delivery room, I opened my eyes and he said, "A boy child! You saved the Peacock Throne!" I was Farah Diba, Empress of Iran, and now I could stay married to the Shah, who otherwise would have had to repudiate me for producing only unworthy daughters. Now all Persia would rejoice, except of course for poor Soraya, the queen who was mustered out on an obstetrical discharge.

And it was nice how we used to make love on every new piece of furniture to welcome it. Tonight we break in the rug; tomorrow the table. I thought it was our own exclusive little family tradition until somebody else mentioned that *they* did that, and somebody *else* said, "You too?" Even on the satin sectional couch, whose sections kept coming apart so that we did too. But then no more outside the bedroom until the black leather swivel chair, of Cal Jaffe's blessed memory.

The happiness chair. Except that one night Richard walked

in and found Matthew sitting in it, in *his* chair, jabbing one
of its padded black arms with a broken Dinky car. Richard
erupted in one of his violent rages; I stood there shaking
with cold fright, and then felt that awful creeping paralytic
ache. He stopped abruptly, controlling himself until I'd
cleared the children out of the room. I always had to do that;
he wouldn't blow up in front of them, but then I'd have to
come back and take it, for whatever had happened, whoever's
crime it was, for however long he wanted to keep it up. It
was my fault, regardless. It became my fault that we were
all there, touching his things, breathing his air, crowding his
life. He'd slammed the bedroom door, shattering the new full-
length mirror attached to it on the inside. The crash sobered
him; suddenly his foul temper had gone public. The kids
would be on to him; Darlene; possibly even the Wyckoffs
next door. None of them was supposed to know how vicious
he could be. Richard Messinger? The cute and the funny, the
nice and the happy, the liked and the loved? Especially to
Nicky. Nicky was only allowed to see him in full costume
as Super-Daddums. That was what made Nicky interesting
to Richard; a small creature who would look up (*way* up,
mind you; Richard was not tall, but to *Nicky* . . .) and say
Da-da and mean God. He must never know that Clark Kent
changed in phone booths.

But Nicky and Matthew heard the mirror crash and came
running scared, bursting through the bedroom door:
"Mommy! Daddy! What happened?"

I made an after-you-Alphonse gesture to Richard and re-
treated to the john.

"*Nothing*, goddammit!" Richard shouted at them. "The

mirror just fell off the door. Now get the hell away from it—there may be splinters!"

"I know how it fell, Daddy—you slammed the door!" cried Nicky.

"I did not!"

"Then who did?" said Matthew.

"I said *get away!* Go to your room!" Goddamn little bastards!

"That was beautiful, the way you handled that," I said bravely from inside the john. "Never too soon to teach them."

"Oh, fuck off," he replied. "I'm going out."

"That's fine. It wouldn't feel like home otherwise," I said.

"What the hell do you expect! I haven't even got a goddamn chair to sit in without that little bastard fucking it up!"

"Oh, go on—go if you're going! *Please,* just leave me alone." See? I *told* him to.

I thought you were supposed to be remembering the good parts. You must be blocking those—you don't want to remember them. Why is that? Because then everything makes even less sense. It's much better this way; dye everything a darker tone to cover discoloration.

Mommy! Wake up! It's Grandma Carla long distance!"

"Mmf, no. I can't. *Please,* no. Go hang up, Nicky—say I'll

call her back. Later tomorrow sometime. Hmh, wait, never mind . . . might as well get it over with."

"Huh?"

"I said . . . Oh, Nicky, just go hang up in the kitchen . . . Hello, Mother. Yes, I'm very sleeping—I mean, I was trying to . . . No, not too much, I haven't been . . . Oh, *he's* fine—I mean, about the same . . . Not yet, no, but they think . . . What? You are? Today? (Oh, not today, not yet) . . . Oh . . . Yes, *sure* I do—I'm glad you'll be around . . . Mostly, yes, all day I just . . . usually go up and, well, just sort of . . . wait . . . Yes, people come. And go . . . All our friends, yes, family, some . . . Who? No, she hasn't . . . No, but they sent flowers, I think . . . Very nice of them, uhhuh, just as soon as . . . Yes, a nice note. Nina came, I think yesterday, or the day before. They all, the days, uh, very much alike. At a time like this . . . Right . . . Aunt who? No, I don't think so. You did? Well, I'm sure she will, then . . . Am I going there this morning? Sure, I go every—what time is your plane? . . . Oh, that's good. I mean, there's less traffic, the later it is . . . I usually stay there until—well, it depends . . . Anyway, you have the number—that phone booth number? And if I'm not, someone will know, or else here. Or . . . anyway, Darlene will . . . Yes . . . That's fine, Mother . . . *They're* fine, yes, both of them . . . I will, sure . . . Darlene what? Oh. Yeah, she certainly is. Couldn't possibly manage without one through all this . . . Mm, right . . . very lucky. Okay, Mother, I have to run now . . . Have a good flight . . ."

Eight goddamn thirty: two hours' sleep. I'm probably killing myself. That's funny—I'll die and he'll get up and marry Miranda and everyone will think how nice they had each other to comfort over the great loss of me. Besides, those two little tykes need a mother. And Miranda and Julie were such good friends—remember how she sat there, holding her hand? Oh, it's wonderful he found someone like that so soon.

Could you possibly shut up and go back to sleep? Okay, but I have to call the . . . "Hi, Miss—who . . . oh, Miss Detweiler? I didn't recognize you, ha, ha, this is . . . Yes, right, how is . . . ? Oh, *good*, yes, wonderful . . . I guess I always do sound, ha, ha, very relieved when you say that. Is Dr. Spector . . . ? Oh, fine. Well, I'll be up around then too in case anyone . . . Yes, okay, fine, thanks, Miss Det— hmm . . ."

My head sank slowly back into its niche in the pillow. Those two calls have cost me a whole day's adrenalin supply. Now, if you don't mind, I could maybe—Oh Jesus, I'm so tired. Tears again. Nerves. The poor shattered girl needs rest. How many days and nights? How many to go? Never mind; the human body is capable of withstanding—yes, but —a remarkable amount of corporal punishment. Re*mark*able. Yes, well, let's just see in this case, for instance, how exactly much that comes to—

"Mommy, Darlene wants—"

"Matthew, I'm sleeping! You know you can't come in when I'm—"

"But Nicky did!"

"But that was just— Oh God, what *is* it? Darlene wants what?"

"To know if we could have the blueberries. On our cereal. Could we?"

"C'mere, Matthew." He edged closer; I pulled him to me against the side of the bed and rubbed his small hard back under the candy-striped polo shirt that was really too small, but he liked it better than the new ones, so why not let him wear it one more summer. "Matthew," I said softly into the warm vulnerable curve of his neck, "I'm sorry."

"Why, Mommy?" I hadn't even meant for him to hear me.

"Oh, nothing—I guess just for being upset and yelling at you and Nicky such a lot."

He nodded, frowning. "Daddy called us rat-fink bastridges," he recalled.

"I know he did; sometimes grownups just—" I paused, sighing, and realized there wasn't any comfortable phrase to follow—"just lose their tempers, the way kids do, when *they're* upset. Like you and Nicky—"

"And say bad words, like Daddy—"

"Like *all* of us, I guess, but we have to try harder not to. *I* have to try harder; you remind me, all right?"

"Okay . . . Then could we?"

"Could you . . . oh, the blueberries?" He smiled, gap-toothed, irresistible, the runner-up in the Charming Child contest. (Not his fault, none of it; I wish—Oh, what good is *that*, but still I do. Matthew baby, I am so very sorry.) "Yes, baby. Tell Darlene I said okay."

"You come too?" He hesitated, wanting.

"Okay. In a minute." He hopped off, a small tender animal that one could soothe by merely stroking. Did he feel love in my hands? Somewhere in that anxious soft-haired head had I really fixed something? ("Make it go, Mommy. Make the dancing bear come back." "I can't, it's a TV program, it goes off when it's over, I don't control that." "Why, *why* can't you? You didn't even try. All those knobs, you know how. *Please*, Mommy.")

And what if *Daddy* doesn't come back? I took him to the hospital and I promised he'd be back next week, in the same time slot. Would they ever believe I spent all those days up there and still didn't know which knob? Would they look at me with the same disbelief, the same certainty that if I really cared about what they wanted, if I thought it was *important*, then I'd go fix Daddy so he'd come back?

I sighed and got up. That must be why they feed God to small children, along with television, slipping it into the cartoons the way they used to put cod liver oil in the orange juice. A bigger bully who, *in extremis*, can be blamed. I wanted to bring Daddy back but God wouldn't let me. Our Father Knows Best.

Not a good day. I could tell from one glance at the mirror. In fact, really bad. Dark circles—look at them. Dry flakiness at the hairline. Widow's pique? (My God, did you see Julie? She's aged ten years since Wednesday.) You are now leaving Shangri-La. No U-turns.

What's more, it was going to be Mother's Day at Mount Carmel. Father's Day for all the other kids; Mother's for me. Which meant that suddenly the place would look shabbier than usual, and there would be only worn spots on the carpeting as far as her eye could see. There would be no sheen on the few desks that were genuine mahogany; the magazines would be dog-eared, flowers wilted, gilt chipping off the mosaics. And how could I explain why I insisted on holding such an important function in this seedy place, especially now that it was clear that the quality of the medicine was as dubious as the ambience.

God, wait till she gets a whiff of that cafeteria. Wait till she meets our crack team of specialists! Well, maybe Mahler will impress her. She'd understand his kind of arrogance, if not Timmy's. And not Bleiweiss, either; poor soft fuzzy Bleiweiss was too special. Never mind; at least Richard had survived the week in their care, and his fantastic trellis of tubes and flowing liquid was undeniably a technological masterpiece.

Christ, how irrelevant it was to worry about what she would think of it all! But I knew I'd spend half the day with my teeth set, bracing for it, as if I'd mounted this entire production all by myself and now had to answer for the reviews. The matriarch de Medici was coming to examine this gigantic work on which I had lavished all my talent and strength. A huge fresco depicting the Massacre of the Innocents, with a cast of thousands. "Mmm, that's nice, dear," she would say, "but I'm afraid all the faces need to be turned a fraction of an inch to the left. How is it you didn't notice that?"

A rational person is someone who can think of parents as simply two older people whom one has known for many years.

Meanwhile, however, she was en route, and all I had was a tacky hospital in an impossible part of town, and these bunglers who had achieved no discernible progress in rousing my husband, whose condition couldn't even be satisfactorily explained, and on top of everything else I looked terrible. I couldn't even tell her I'd had my hair done Friday, because then what excuse did I have for how it looked now? I was thin, though, and that was something; I'd lost seven pounds since Wednesday. If only my clothes didn't all hang limp and unrelated to my body like strangers keeping their distance for fear of contamination. What the hell could I possibly wear that she wouldn't wish I hadn't, that she wouldn't *say* she wished I hadn't, in front of everybody. "What are you wearing *that* for? Don't you know that skirt needs fixing? Don't you look at yourself before you go out?" (You can't say, "Yes, Mother," because then how come you went out looking like that? On the other hand, you can't plead, "Gee, no, Mom," because then how come you go out without looking at yourself?) "Anyway, go somewhere and fix your *hair*, at least. And you need lipstick." "Mother, for God's sake, this is a *hospital*." "So what? Is there some rule that says you have to look disheveled in a hospital? Even patients fix their hair."

My mother would never understand that she and I belonged to different sects. I was one of the women destined to spend a lifetime carrying things home in lumpy brown paper bags that tear because the canned goods are on the bottom. She was one of those who simply do not carry packages, except perhaps a small hostess gift that looked so beautiful it was a shame to open it. For a small service charge, she moved through womanhood in clean eight-button gloves. (How had she mothered a beast of burden?)

Other essential differences: I stand with those whose small stains at the inner armholes sometimes refuse to come out in the wash. She doesn't even understand what that's from. I belong to the poor wretches who more than once have awakened from a sound sleep with the awful knowledge that their sanitary protection has expired, and that it is already too late; it's leaked onto the sheet, probably right through to the quilted mattress pad, maybe even the mattress itself. My mother, if she ever had the curse (as all mothers allegedly must), would never suffer it to leave its stain upon her Beautyrest.

One miserable day in the middle of my fifteenth ghastly year, she called me into her bedroom. "I want to talk to you," she announced nervously, tipping me off right away that what was coming was not good. She never *wanted* to talk to me.

It was the morning after one of my worst blind dates, a party at which I had necked with two different boys *and* passed out. She was in her steamy bathroom, seated before her kidney-shaped mirrored dressing table, naked except for a green satin-bordered bath towel tucked in a neat sarong around her waist. (That's another example; with me the end always comes undone.) "I understand," she began uncomfortably, addressing my watery reflection in her mirror (an indirect form of confrontation which both of us preferred), "that you let yourself . . . that you allow boys to . . . put their hands on you." She reached into the drawer for a tweezer and switched on the fluorescent magnifying mirror.

Oh God. Oh *Christ*. I felt my mouth drying, as if drained by a dental suction tube in preparation for the drill, and backed up mutely to sit on the john. Maybe the good toilet fairy would come and flush me away. Mother was plucking stray hairs; the tweezer flashed like a tiny two-pronged scepter. "Well?" she demanded, frowning harder into the mirror.

"Well, what?" I hedged.

"Is it true?" she snapped.

"Yeah, I guess so," I said, staring down at her feet. The bright polish, chipped at the edges, made her toes look like radishes. I said, "So I neck—everybody necks. What do you *think* goes on at those stupid parties—*political discussions?*"

She swiveled around suddenly so that she was actually looking at me; I had shocked her. "Don't be fresh!" she said trembling with embarrassed rage. "Your cousin Barbara goes to parties, she has constant dates, and I happen to know *she* doesn't allow boys to put their hands on her. Neither did your sister." (I took to studying her breasts for distraction. They were well shaped but not sexy—never used. "I had these made to order several years ago. They're like new. It pays to take care of things.")

"How can you hold yourself so cheaply?" she was saying. It had an odd Old Testament sound. She shuddered, truly repelled. I thought briefly of a hygiene teacher I'd had freshman year who used to warn us never to sit on a boy's lap without a folded newspaper in between. "Preferably a *tabloid*," she added meaningfully. But at least that was funny; besides, nobody had to think of an answer. Any minute now my mother would stop talking and wait for me to explain myself. I watched her mouth; cherry-red lipstick, carefully outlined, which never went over the edges. But it was too bright, as if she'd chosen it for an amusing centerpiece.

"Well?" she said again, leaning back and crossing her arms under her breasts, a businesslike pose which looked ludicrous, although perhaps she could have carried it off if she were dressed.

"Well, what?" I repeated, squirming on the chenille johnny-cover. (Listen, Mother, I neck better than I talk, and so do they. If you really want to know, I'd much rather have Bingo Friedlander fiddling with the hooks on my bra, timidly working around toward my boobs and blowing in my ear as he reverently approaches the nipples, than have to sit there wondering what I could possibly say that would make Bingo Friedlander call me for another date. Oh, never mind; you wouldn't understand.)

What would Mother say if I told her about Richard's diary? "Filthy and disgusting—but at least he had the decency not to bother you. At least he had respect for his wife. It's unfortunate, but men seem to need to go around pinching girls' behinds and having sex. It's silly nonsense, but thank God it wasn't serious. I'm sure Richard knew how lucky he was to be married to you. I knew you could have done better, but nobody can ever tell you anything. Maybe this will teach you to listen next time . . ."

As for *my* behavior of the last few days, clearly she'd see no excuse for that. "A *normal* young woman does not go around doing revolting things with men. Unless she's a queer. Abnormal, sick. Nymphomaniac's disease—that would be different. A normal woman couldn't care less what her husband does behind her back; she knows what's *important*. To have a valid, comfortable life. Attractive children. People's respect. She doesn't go around jeopardizing the wholesome, necessary things by acting like those terrible frustrated women one reads about in newspapers. Unless, as I say, there's something the *matter* with her—some peculiarity, or a mental disorder. Maybe I'm missing something (sniff), but I have never felt a need, not the slightest momentary impulse, to degrade myself for some disgusting physical urge. And I doubt very much if I've missed anything worthwhile!"

My father said he thought having babies would make Mother "more of a woman." They were divorced when I was two. His second wife, Fiona, was more cuddly, adored cook-

ing and hated both Europe and El Morocco. She always let
him pick their TV programs and didn't mind moving to St.
Petersburg, where he expected to make a killing in Florida
real estate. He was into golden-age housing developments,
and if he hadn't exactly made a killing, he was at least
eking out a long illness. We hadn't seen them since our wedding, but they always sent something interesting for Christmas. Last year it was a basket of realistic-looking rubber
pineapples; the year before, a subscription to the Exotic Con-
diment of the Month Club. "Affectionately, Fiona & Dad."

When I was eighteen and Nina was safely married, Mother
gamely tried one more husband, a suave-looking but oddly
docile Italian named Luis Ferrazi, who had an import-export
business, a pair of genuine silver sideburns and two midnight-
blue dinner jackets. She was very sensitive about people calling him Lou or Louie by mistake. They lasted four years, but
Luis thoughtfully died while they were still only having a
trial separation, which left Mother, la Sra. Ferrazi, a comfortable and socially secure *Town & Country*-style widow,
rather than a two-time loser.

There were no visitors at all
this Sunday morning. I kept wondering who could possibly
come that Mother would approve of. Miranda had a socially
prominent name, but she herself was neither social nor chic.
Audrey Lebow had a certain hard-sell charm, but her husband
sold insurance. Marian Spector would really try to be nice,

but that hair . . . The phone kept ringing, and I would run my fifty-yard dash alone, my footsteps echoing hollowly, no one cheering at the sidelines. Barnaby Halstead called just to say hello and that he was thinking of us in his Norwalk saltbox. Nina couldn't possibly get in; one of the kids had a summer cold; give Mother her love. Audrey would be there as soon as she got brunch over with. Arnie Buchalter had to inspect a serious violation of the Sanitary Code. Laurie checked in at eleven-thirty; if I needed her, she'd dump the baby next door with the *Newsweek* researcher and her computer-matched date, even though they'd both told the computer they hated babies. "No, don't, I'm all right," I said. "If I'm desperate, I'll call you back."

At noon Miranda called with a vanishing whispery voice, the negative of the Cheshire cat; all that was left was her disembodied sadness. Did I . . . would I want her to come . . . she'd like . . . to be with me. "Sure," I said, disgusted with myself for being pleased. To be with *me*, she'd said. Laurie would say I was nuts. But Mother is coming and one needs all the help one can get, I argued. Besides, what right did I have to say no? For all any of us knew, Miranda belonged there more than I did. "Cal called," she whispered. "He'd like to come too, if you . . ."

"Sure," I said again, automatically. At a time like this we should all stick together. Then I reacted: "Cal called you?"

"Yes." That was all; she let the simple fact speak for itself.

"Oh." Well, there you are. He too had forgiven her trespasses. Maybe their love was bigger than all of us. (Yessir, we've got a really big love here. Let's show these kids how our studio audience feels about a really big love.) "Sure," I said, yet again, "tell him sure."

On Sundays they served a special lunch in the cafeteria, and furthermore, this was Father's Day. There were printed napkins with little brown pipes and slippers on them, and D-A-D in gold letters standing up on the fudge squares. I wondered whether Richard's intravenous menu would reflect the holiday; essence of roast chicken with giblet gravy?

I went in to see him. Happy Father's Day, I thought, feeling tears dribbling into position on my face. I was so *sick* of crying; by now the whole process felt like recirculating water, gushing periodically through clever cast-bronze openings. Nicky had made me bring Daddy his Father's Day present, just in case he might wake up and need a pencil cup made out of a frozen orange-juice can sprayed red. Matthew hadn't quite finished his dinosaur picture. He hadn't quite finished the dinosaur picture for my Mother's Day present either, but he was *going* to.

Sunday is the day to call long-distance and tell them you're thinking of them. At twelve-thirty Bill and Jeannie Pollock called from Los Angeles; they'd just heard about Richard from Jeannie's mother, who played bridge with Audrey Lebow's mother, and they wanted to tell me how terrible they knew it must be and how sure they were it would be okay, and could they *do* anything? The last time I'd spoken to Jeannie Pollock, I asked her how Tony was. "You mean Curtis or Franciosa?" she replied. "I mean your two-year-old son, Tony Pollock!" I explained, suppressing a laugh that probably would have alienated us for keeps. It was appallingly evident that the Pollocks had gone Hollywood. Richard said thank God they'd missed knowing Larry of Arabia. This time I decided not to get personal.

Even my father called from St. Petersburg, sounding all

warm and ruddy. Goddamn shame about Richard; how was it going? I gave him the *Reader's Digest* condensed version, and he was confident everything would turn out fine. His Julie was such a strong, capable, level-headed girl that he knew she'd come through the way she always does. Call them if I needed anything; he and Fiona would be there. And don't forget to give their regards to Mother, and to kiss "the boys," whose names of course he knew, but actually wasn't *quite* sure of. They'd call again in a day or so.

Timmy wasn't expected till three P.M., but he'd been in touch this morning to say he was probably coming earlier. As Miss Farnsworth said, he couldn't seem to stay away from this case. "I tell you, he's something, Dr. Spector is," she said. "You sure are lucky," she added, shaking her dull brown curls at me in case I didn't appreciate. "I know," I assured her, nodding hard. "I hate to think what it would be like if we didn't have him."

"Oh, ssh!" she gasped; somehow I had touched her. She beckoned me closer, conspiratorially. "I think your husband's eyelid fluttered this morning. Just the tiniest movement. I'm not supposed to tell you, but . . ." She shrugged gallantly, having risked all.

I was so excited that I tugged at her arm like a child. "Tell me," I begged. "Please." She recovered her spray-starched nursey self at once. "I'm afraid I really *can't* say any more— I shouldn't have said that even. You'll have to . . . I'm sure Dr. Spector will talk to you after he's examined . . ." She wrenched free and fled.

I raced to the phone booth and spilled all my coins on the shelf. Screw the proper change; I had about $2.70 in various denominations, mostly quarters; I might as well shoot the whole wad. First I called everyone back who'd called me since yesterday—including Miranda, who sobbed. "Please don't *cry*," I said, feeling crazy. Then I called the people who were likely to get the biggest charge out of a fluttering eyelid: all the frat bros who had donated blood and whom I'd promised to keep posted, but hadn't; Aunt Addie; Danny Mack; Marcy Berns. Then I went to the cafeteria and changed a five-dollar bill and called some more: *Household* staff people; some of my relatives; Pamela Howell; the children's pediatrician; Darlene. And finally Isabel and Joel Krieger, the only genuinely God-fearing couple among our friends. Since Wednesday they had called every night to offer deep thoughts about why all this was happening, and what it *really* meant. Isabel was convinced from the start that some great mystical truth was being revealed to Richard, and that through him we should all be touched and forever changed. "I *know* he is going to come out of it," she would say, hushed and tremulous. "I think you do too, Julie. But the thing is, he's going to come out of it a *different* person, and we should be prepared for that."

Yesterday she had decided: Richard was destined to be a great artist, and this was a kind of catharsis to wash away the layers of mediocrity that had held him back until now. "*That's* what it means—a profound change in his whole creative thrust, I'll bet anything!" she exclaimed. "He's to be released; God is telling him to begin again, to wake up and be true to his talent."

"You see!" she screeched now, when I told her about the eyelid. "Joel, quick! Get on the extension! Richard's *eye*-lid moved! Oh, Julie, I am so . . . I can't even talk, I'm all goose pimples! It's like—like a birth, you'll see! A year from now you'll say to me, 'Isabel, you and Joel were the only ones who *knew!'*"

At the time she made a wild kind of persuasive case for God and His wondrous ways. I have always been reasonably comfortable about writing "Agnostic" where it says "Religious Preference," but in this kind of storm even Isabel's embarrassing old umbrella looked as if it might have been worth saving. I almost felt sorry that I'd given mine to the Salvation Army for a tax deduction. It would have been a godsend, so to speak.

For a minute there, listening to her, the whole absurd catastrophe had some grand point, some invisible thread that would pull all the ugly shapeless bits together into a lovely cosmic quilt. It wouldn't be just a mean, meaningless coincidence, a chemical trick to turn my limp little life into something bigger and harder. If it *mattered*, if it was *for* something, well, then at least it wasn't for nothing. Like an awfully sick joke that I didn't get, or like that dumbbell that Arlene Francis' maid used to keep her window propped open, until it accidentally fell onto 57th Street and Park Avenue one day, killing a well-dressed man who had just had a very good lunch at Le Pavillon.

I'd thought a lot about that when it happened. I imagined all his suits that were still at the cleaner's, and all the unsigned memos waiting on his desk. And I wondered if he'd paid his Pavillon check or just signed it, because then the restaurant would have to write a nice note to his widow and say how very sorry they were to bother her at a time like this, but . . .

I've never thought about plane-crash victims that way; one imagines that they've put their lives in some kind of order beforehand. At least it's possible that they've unplugged their refrigerators or left instructions for the mailman, or called people to say goodbye. Whereas the dumbbell victim had only fifteen minutes to spare between his fresh raspberries and his next appointment. And since it was such a beautiful day, he had decided to walk. I felt that if Richard should die before he waked, he would belong more with the dumbbell victim than on the "passengers killed" list. Or among a crowd of civilians killed in a bombing raid. Their sudden deaths never seemed grotesque or undignified. Was it because they were members of a group? Not really; I think it was more because there was always a motive, however bad it was. Somebody always started a war, so at least *he* knew it wasn't really such a beautiful day on 57th Street.

In a way, I suppose, I was wrong. Surgery, after all, is surgery; a malignant mole is not lunch at Le Pavillon. Except that in my case, in my blindly complacent, hopeless case, I thought it was.

Timmy breezed in at two and was not terribly impressed by the eyelid. The coma, he said, was still too deep for it to be significant. But didn't it mean *anything,* I pleaded? Maybe—that was as far as he would go. They had some tests coming back sometime this afternoon; we'd see. His vagueness hurt; I couldn't help feeling that it had more to do with me and him than with Richard. There you go again, I scolded myself angrily, but it didn't help.

Cal showed up alone, wearing a guilty expression. I wonder if he's done something to her, I thought darkly, and then realized how glad I was that she had stayed away after all. Either one of them alone I could handle—could even perversely welcome. Each in a way was an ally, a mutually injured party, a fellow victim—provided the other one wasn't there to confuse me as to who had done exactly what to whom. Oddly, I felt happy to see Cal now. Our sorry "affair" already seemed a remote and blurry small incident, an unidentified creature run over by a car in which I was riding. I could barely remember the bump, too soft to be rock, and then the squeal, but thank God I'd never really gotten a look at it. Anyway, it was killed instantly.

We drifted to the cafeteria without agreeing to; neither of us being hungry, we piled a few light dishes on one tray: lemon jello and grapefruit juice and iced coffee with straws to make circles with. We talked lightly too—easy topics like Richard's marvelous moving eyelid and the irony of Timmy's gross failure now to recognize his own success when it was fluttering under his nose.

But it didn't last long. Cal needed to get back to The Subject: Miranda; Miranda and Richard, the diary. "Have you got it with you?" he asked, with the husky urgency of someone with a slight drinking problem. As a matter of fact, I'd been carrying "it," folded in my bag, since last night. Meekly I brought it forth; it never occurred to me that I could have said no. With his mouth open, sweat-beaded head in his hands, he sat there studying it, cramming as if his final grade depended on it, looking up now and then only to cry out in sudden pain: "Jesus! I *remember* that Thursday! Can you beat that! Five to seven P.M.—and I came *home* at seven-thirty!"

"Cal," I said finally, feeling like a recent alumna who barely recalls what it was like, "for God's sake quit wallowing in it! What good is that?" Then it struck me: "Anyway, didn't you . . . aren't you and Miranda all kissed and made up?"

He laughed, fakely. "We had another little talk. I wanted to tell her about this; I had a feeling she didn't know." He flicked at the papers. "Just so she'd realize she had a listed number like all the other kids, that she could be looked up in the Yellow Pages."

"But why? Why did you have to?" I stared at him, trying to see if the wound was clotting or still raw under there. There were bright feverish spots on his cheeks and the rims of his ears. Calvin Jaffe strikes back; all retributions gratefully accepted. Well, at least one of us had—what was that stuff?— *spleen.* I had no idea what I would have done if I had any— certainly not vented it. My hot little airtight cubicle of a vengeful spirit was not properly vented for escaping spleen. Besides, revenge is something you have to know how to do. You dust your hands and say, "Well, I guess that's that," and saunter off whistling while the slitty-mouthed townspeople nod gravely and mutter, "About time, too!" I had no experience with that sort of feeling and I knew I'd be terrible at it; in fact, I'd probably spoil the whole thing by apologizing.

"What did she say?" I asked, cringing for Miranda.

"She wouldn't believe it! She said I was making it up! She was sorry I had to stoop to that sort of malicious mischief to get even. Like a spoiled kid, she said, telling lies about other kids who have something he wants. Goddamn stupid bitch! You know what?" His eyes brightened suddenly with unseemly delight. "I think when it finally penetrates—when she really gets hit by this goddamn diary—it'll be like he screwed her the worst of all!"

"Oh God," I said sadly into the warm watery grave that had once been my iced coffee, but Cal was back to memorizing important dates, conquests and double ententes cordiales. "It is not a phantasmagoria in which we live," I mumbled, "but a rationalizable cosmos."

"Huh?" he said, without looking up.

"Just something comforting from page one of my Geology 101 textbook. I got an *E* in Geology, probably as a direct result."

"Mmm," he said, not listening.

"Cal, I think that what you're doing is awful," I declared after careful deliberation. "I think you should be working on forgetting all this crap, not carving those damn initials in your brain. That's what I'd do; I'd like to forget it too, except I'm in no position to. Or at least *Richard's* in no position. But you could just knock it right off with Miranda, just like that. A bad scene, a good time to fade out. You could be lining up something else for next season." (Listen to me, would you just, a regular barrel of sage-old wisdom.) He ignored me; like most prophets, I did not make the honors list.

Pretty soon I figured out why he couldn't listen to me, though, why he *couldn't* just forget it, any more than I could. They were trading places, he and Richard. All this time they had been resenting each other by mistake. Richard had hated Cal for having such a wild, free sex life, and Cal had envied Richard for his warm smug harbor of a marriage. Now that everyone was exposed, though, poor Cal couldn't quite call it square. It was bad enough that Richard had turned out to be the big stud, but look where the bastard was! Infuriatingly out of target range, in the last of the great demilitarized zones. Just imagine the frustration of wanting to punch an acute hepatic failure in the nose.

Mother called from the airport to say she was calling from the airport. Also she was hot and crumpled and tired and going right home to take a quick bath, change and then come down. Unless maybe she could tempt me into coming up and having a quick bite with her? Someplace gay? I probably ought to get out of that atmosphere for a while.

Irritation can be clenched in your teeth like the leather strap they used to give soldiers to bite on while they cut out the shrapnel. In this case, I knew damn well I was annoyed because I *was* tempted. Someplace gay, in a clean raw-silk dress, shivering slightly in the conditioned air. "Mother," I said in the frosty tone of one who has suffered, to one who has just returned from vacation, "I can't possibly do that. I have to go home and see the children and get right back here." (I am responsible; you are ir—. I am sensitive and you are in—. I am wife and you are ex—.)

"Well, don't jump down my throat!" she retorted, returning my irritation. "I just suggested it! I thought it might be good for you to relax for an hour."

"Relax! Oh, Mother, honestly!" ("Honestly I don't *need* warm pants under my dress. *Nobody* wears wool bloomers over their underwear! How can I catch a cold there? You don't, and your girdle isn't even closed on the bottom. Honestly, I *want* to go to Stephen's party but I'm sick. Honestly, nobody sends Valentines, I don't care if Barbara got two hundred; nobody *I* know sent any. It's stupid. Mother, honestly, give me just one good reason why I can't shave my legs. You can see every single hair flattened down under my stockings. You shave *your* legs. Okay, then don't ask me why nobody ever calls me for a date, that's all.")

"Listen, Mother, would you like to stop and see the children, and eat with us?" Oh, no. God, please, I take it back, it's impossible. I'll have to find cloth napkins and butter plates, and she'll say all the worst possible things. How sick poor Daddy is and do they miss him terribly and are they being extra good while Mommy is so worried. I can't handle her; I'll collapse trying to make espresso for her and start having my long-overdue breakdown. "I don't know what came over her all of a sudden," she'll say, "the strain." They'll carry me up here and hook me up to all his hoses. His and hers hoses.

"I don't want to burden you," she was saying. "I'll just have my maid fix something for me, and see the children another time."

"Okay," I breathed.

I'm Mrs. Ferrazi, Mrs. Messinger's mother," she announced, bestowing a vague hostessy smile on every doctor and nurse whose path she crossed. "Yes, would you mind waiting in there?" they would say, not quite rudely brushing past her. It wasn't at all like Open School Week or Parents' Day in camp, where the staff falls all over the well-dressed mothers.

I was by turns sorry and embarrassed: I kept wishing there was something I could do to make her either less conspicuous or more entertained. She couldn't find a comfortable seat, and once seated, she was in everyone's way, stopping conversations simply by feigning interest. Nobody of consequence was there; in fact, the hair of everyone who showed up seemed to need combing. "Why are all your friends so . . . unkempt-looking?" she remarked at one point. I had no explanation. "It shows a lack of respect for you," she went on with a noise meant to show well-bred disgust. "Yeurgh." "Mmm," I said.

At another point she went in to see Richard, and returned immediately without any comment. I couldn't think of one either. A few minutes later she asked again whether I had *confidence* in these doctors. Oh, the utmost, I assured her, and offered Richard's fluttering eyelid by way of support for my judgment, although so far the tests had failed to justify the excitement. Like Timmy, my mother was unimpressed. "When do they expect some actual improvement?" she said, getting right to the point. "In his *condition,* I mean." I couldn't fault her for that, but as always I suddenly seemed to be defending myself again. "Mother, they don't know, I told you. A week, maybe longer. All they know for sure is that the liver always comes back." (I did a pretty fair Bleiweiss at that.) When I had finished, she sniffed, but dropped the interrogation.

Several aunts and uncles filtered in after dinner. They hadn't thought of coming before, but now that Mother was there, the atmosphere seemed to offer more for their age group. In fact, it seemed to have become her event. "Carla darling, you look marvelous; was Nassau gay? Did you see Donata? And the Freemans? Isn't that bracelet new? It's divine—did you get it there?"

"Hello, dear," they said to me, dutifully creasing their expressions into worried or sympathetic folds and scattering kissy noises in the air next to my cheek. Some of them brought exotic goodies like Perugina chocolates and candied ginger. Some put the boxes on a table; a few presented them directly to my mother. "I brought Julie some marzipan fruits I thought she might enjoy."

Mother had finally discovered a function she could perform with grace and style here: opening the packages and passing things, suggesting to Marcy that she "try these," or that the Howells "have another; go on; it doesn't look as if either of *you* need worry." "Julie, wouldn't you like to offer some to the nurses? You have so much in here!" she said, with only a trace of displeasure at the lapse in my manners right in front of the grownups. As I left, obediently bearing whatever she thought was appropriate for the help, I half-expected to hear her apologizing for me, "You'll have to excuse my daughter; she's a little upset about something."

When I returned from my rounds with the empties, it

seemed to be time to go. Audrey Lebow had politely shaken hands all around; most of the other younger people had escaped into the corridor, where at least they felt free to tell funny stories about relatives. Seeing me, they confessed they had to split; it was murder in there; couldn't I come too? No, I said, I'd better stick it out, but perhaps if they all left, the family would get the message. They nodded, blew kisses and took off like freed canaries.

Back in the waiting room, the older crowd was gathering itself too, murmuring about the hour, offering to drop each other off and deciding who could take Carla home. Looking straight at me they asked my mother if Julie was ready to leave too. "No," I answered boldly for myself, "Julie's staying a few minutes longer." I smiled to cut the audacity a little, and added that Dr. Spector would give me a lift; he lived practically next door. "Well, if you're sure," Aunt Helena said, looking uncertainly at my mother. "All right, dear," Mother said, smoothing my hair. This gesture always comes across as affection or maternal concern, but actually it has to do only with wanting my hair to be smoothed. "I don't like your looking so tired," she said on the way out.

"Mmm," I replied.

Timmy and I rode together in separate but equally oppressive silences, each counting on the other to come up with some relevant, safe subject before we got home.

"Richard," I said finally, despairing of anything else, "looked yellowish again tonight."

"Did he? Well, it doesn't mean anything. Depends where in the cycle he happens to be when you happen to be looking."

"Oh . . . And the eyelid also meant nothing, I gather."

He frowned. "Could have been a fluke. Or her imagination. None of the tests turned up any evidence that the coma's lightening. The corneals have been okay all along; I told you that."

"Yes, you did. I remember."

There followed another highly charged silence. We were nearly home.

"Let's talk about last night," he said suddenly. "I mean, we can't very well ignore it."

"Why can't we?"

"Because it marked an important change in our relationship. And because I'd like to take you to bed now."

I drew a painfully deep breath, since I had a long way to go before surfacing. "Timmy, listen," I began, plunging in fast, "I know you can't help it; I know you think I want that. I *admit* I opened the door, all right? But believe me, I don't. I never intended to start anything last night." (Was it only last night?) "I'm sorry about the whole thing. I mean, I'm not *sorry*" (watch it, don't hurt his feelings!), "I'm just sorry I started something I can't finish—didn't mean to finish. Don't want to . . ."

"Why the hell not?" He didn't sound angry, just puzzled.

(Well, first of all I don't like the shape of your peepee; it's funny-looking. Besides, you remind me of my husband —a couple of accountants figuring out sex returns. No pleasure trips without a business purpose.) "Look, Timmy," I said

finally, "I don't know what I feel about anything right now,
least of all, sex. Let's just say it's not my week; like Richard,
I'm not responding very well." (That's the right line; don't
let him think for a minute you're resisting his wonderfulness.
If you weren't so uptight, you'd be honored to take advantage of this sensational once-in-a-lifetime offer, which is
about as bona fide as anything else you could get within
thirty days.) Placating him, I despised myself for needing to,
and let him leave murmuring "Okay, sweets, then maybe
next week."

The last impetuous thing I did before falling asleep was
grope for ten minutes behind the pocketbooks on top of
the closet shelf in search of my diaphragm. Just to check—
in case? Its shiny plastic container (robin's-ovum blue) was
layered with sticky dust. The pliant golden rubber disc itself
crumbled apart instantly in my hand. I stared at the mute
mocking symbol, then laughed. Now, that *is* funny, you have
to admit. I couldn't, even if I wanted to. Thanks, Richard.
No, really, thanks a lot.


Monday was to be the first day
of a record three-day heat wave, the first of the season. Every
doorman would get to say "Hot enough for you?" approxi-
mately 280 times before it ended, and WNEW would gleefully rub it in that it was only the second hottest June 17th
since the Weather Bureau began keeping records.

When my mother called at seven forty-five, I had set a

modest record myself; four and a half hours' sleep, the longest since Wednesday. "Anything new?" she asked. (Richard's stock answer to that was "There's another dead horse in the bathtub," but it wasn't worth explaining to Mother.) "No," I said. "Nothing new."

"What are your plans for today?"

"Oh, I thought it might be nice to sit in that lovely waiting room for thirteen or fourteen hours," I said. "Why?"

Unfortunately she was paying attention. "Is that your idea of a smart answer?" she snapped. "I know you're irritable, but that doesn't excuse—"

"Okay," I mumbled quickly, "I'm sorry."

She herself wouldn't be able to get to the hospital until this afternoon sometime; she had an appointment to have her thighs waxed. (She had it done every June, before venturing into her modified bikini.) If I needed her, she'd be with Miss Lafarge at Elizabeth Arden. That sounded just about right.

Miranda was there ahead of me; I spotted the bare gleaming legs halfway down the hall. For the first time I felt a minute jealous twinge. What if something good or bad had happened—while she was alone here? Are you the wife? Presumably by now they all knew me, but what if there was a new resident on duty? What would she have said: "Well, not exactly"? Or, "I am the *prospective* bride"?

"Hi," I said nervously. Both of us were wearing sunglasses; we each took them off at precisely the same instant. Again I was startled at how alike we were. (They always marry the same person over again. Even Happy Rockefeller is beginning to look like Mary Todhunter Clark.)

"Hi," she echoed, also nervously. "I guess I'm early."

"That's all right," I said stupidly. (Of course it's all right; why wouldn't it be all right?) "Anything . . . anybody call?"

"No," she said, yawning. I had a fleeting suspicion that she'd spent the night there. "Timmy Spector stuck his head in about twenty minutes ago, but he said it wasn't important; he'll be back later."

I nodded and sat opposite her, trying to feel less like I was the visitor. Should I start reading my *New York Times?* Would she think I was rude, or that I was just trying to avoid something? Well, suppose I don't read? I'll have to say things then, and I can't think of any.

"Julie," she said softly, fixing me with her luminous X-ray eyes, "you don't have to talk to me. I just want to be here." Immediately I felt like the cruel-mouthed queen than whom Snow White was incontrovertibly fairer. "I'm glad you came," I lied; "this is the loneliest part of the day."

Actually, I had begun to like the quiet early mornings up there; they had a certain monastic elegance, like the least-interesting wing of a museum. Until Audrey and Marcy and the telephone and the nurses and other people's bulky visitors began filling the spaces with jarring lifelike sounds and motions, to which I had to grow slowly accustomed every day.

Miranda apologized for not coming yesterday. I waited a decent interval to be sure she didn't plan to explain (of course she didn't; she never does), and then said that it was all right; it wasn't as if she'd stuck me with tickets or anything.

She smiled and seemed to relax then, so I did too. The cafeteria wasn't open yet, and we decided to take a walk outside in search of a stray Bickford's or White Tower. After twenty minutes in the steamy grime of Union Square, having found nothing but newsstands selling *Kiss* and *Rat* and Hires Root Beer, we trudged back. Someone in heavy rust-colored wool was streaking past the waiting room; on a day like this, it could only be Bleiweiss. I raced after him, calling, "Dr. Bleiweiss?" and then paused in my tracks, already sorry. He turned slowly and peered at me foggily. "Julie Messinger," I prompted, smiling and wishing he'd just turn around again and keep going. "Yes," he agreed, rooted to his spot, twenty or thirty feet away. One of us ought to close the gap, I thought, and advanced uncertainly, as if the area might be mined. "Dr. Bleiweiss, could you . . . could I ask you . . . where do you think we, uh, stand now?"

He frowned. "I don't quite . . . know what you mean." The words were puffing out with obvious reluctance; maybe his mouth has rusted since last we spoke? His glasses were fogging up too. Why would he wear that hairy tweed in ninety-two-degree heat? Surely liver men can afford summer suits.

"How much longer," I said slowly and distinctly, "do you think before his—my husband's?—liver should, uh, begin to show some sign of regenera—starting to regenerate?"

"Ah, well, of course," he said, nodding and smiling. The exam was easier than he'd expected. "As we told you, there is . . . no way to pin this down. To predict it. Aha . . . wish there were . . . would make all our tasks so much simpler. But—"

"But you *did* say about a week. It's almost a full week . . . since you said that. Shouldn't there be some . . . shouldn't it have *started*?"

He didn't like that. "I beg your pardon," he said, and began mopping his pasty brow. "I made . . . no precise statement." Then he removed his rimless glasses and polished them with the same hanky. "Perhaps a week, I may have said. Perhaps longer." His eyes, tinier without the magnifying lenses, blinked rapidly, as if he were calculating the schedule again. "That would have been reasonable. And is still . . . quite . . . reasonable." He stopped, without winding down, like the end of a taped telephone message.

"Longer—maybe twice as long? Three times? Perhaps a month?" I persisted.

He had begun to back away. "Oh, probably not," he said, stuffing the soggy hanky into a pocket of damp tweed. "I would doubt a month. Would you excuse me now? I am somewhat pressed for time."

"Somewhat," I echoed. He took it for a goodbye and lumbered off.

An unstable person would be apt to begin crying now, I thought, successfully distracting myself by studying Bleiweiss' splayfooted Chaplinesque stride, which did not really belong under his bulgy shape. You can see I am not crying. Kennedys don't cry, Mooney's kid don't, big girls don't, queens and princesses . . .

Thanks to the unbearable heat, nobody wanted to stay long that day. The Naugahyde was sticky and the room felt like one of those portable saunas—a tiny torture-yourself

chamber designed to bring a sobering touch of Spartan misery
into your life. Audrey Lebow had to leave by eleven because
her kids needed tetanus boosters, and Joel Krieger called
Isabel to announce that his office was closing at noon so that
Con Ed shouldn't worry about the dangerous abuses of power.
I dozed off, plastered to the couch, and was awakened by the
sound of Arnie Buchalter's whiny apologetic voice. He was
forever apologizing, which made him even more of a nui-
sance. You couldn't help feeling guilty about wishing he
would go away. Danny Mack's wife, Paula, was silently cro-
cheting something, which was at least as mystifying as Bleiweiss' wearing tweed. Well, at least it was something sleeveless. What time is it, I asked—and where's Miranda? Her
absence startled me, as if she were an important key I mustn't
misplace. She had an audition, Arnie said, and would be back
around four.

The Howells stopped in very briefly to kiss goodbye; they
were off to London tonight for some business thing of Neil's
and I must wire them at the Dorchester, or they'd be frantic
worrying about us. I reassured them; after all, I pointed out,
we had Isabel Krieger's solemn word that God knows what
Timmy Spector is doing.

Arnie Buchalter left, apologizing, at three-fifteen. Paula
Mack was still clicking quietly in a corner, and a girl named
Doria Perkins, from *Household Magazine's* Patterns Department, had joined us. She delivered a two-minute speech
about what fun Richard was to work with and what a really
great person he was, unlike some others on that staff who
should remain nameless. She was very pretty, Doria Perkins;
oh God, I found myself thinking with a sickening lurch, DP,
DP? I think there was a DP in 1967 . . .

And then the siren went off, shrieking as if in a death throe of its own, from inside the Intensive Care Unit. I felt the fourteen-cent ball of cafeteria cottage cheese I had forced down for lunch; apparently someone had retrieved it and hauled it up to the back of my throat. "It's Richard," I said with certainty. "Oh, Julie, it can't be . . ." Paula began, with Doria repeating it like a musical round. They glanced at each other helplessly; Paula had dropped several stitches when the siren went off and couldn't decide now whether to pick them up. All of us sat rigidly, except for our eyes darting desperately back and forth, tennis spectators facing into the sun.

Finally I got up, dimly aware that I was whimpering. Fear, panic and the need to cry all smothered by the greater need to stifle it. Staggering into the hall, I saw the flock of white coats gathering, moving and fluttering like hens scuffling home to the barn in a storm. Then the swinging doors blurred into illusory stillness, except for the air they fanned and the squeal of hinges. I stood uncertainly in the traffic, letting myself be jostled across the threshold—just far enough to where I could see the fists, winding and swooping, the tight circle of white— around which bed, attacking whose poor chest? Richard? It was.

I backed toward the door, but I must have made some sound, because a nurse flew out of a corner, frowning. Then she was ushering me hence—out of sympathy or concern? "You're not allowed in here now," she was saying. "I know," I said, "I was just—"

She led me back to the waiting room, but I plucked at her sleeve. "How long . . . please, how long do they, will they, keep trying?"

"Three minutes," she said, not unkindly. "Possibly five. I doubt if he could take much more."

Over her shoulder I spotted Timmy. Just in time; if you hurry, you'll barely miss it. I turned to the waiting-room window to avoid looking at Paula Mack and Doria. DP. Displaced Person. They were both DPs, obviously aghast at being caught here at this moment. My God, how terrible to be either of them. "I'm sorry," I started to say, but that was insane. Facing the window, I dug my nails into my palms to draw sacrificial blood. I ground them in, making little comma-shaped dents that hurt, but not nearly enough. As the nurse had said in the labor room, "Don't tell us about *those* little contractions; they won't get you *any*where."

After a few minutes I heard Timmy's voice behind me. "Julie," he said, sounding very unboyish, almost paternal. The voice of doom. I turned slowly, catching a vague fluttering hand gesture from Paula. "Would you like us to go?" Doria said hoarsely. "I don't know," I said, and propelled myself toward Timmy's spectral form. I couldn't look at his face, and the whiteness of his jacket came and went and undulated, like broken moonlight on water. The ringing in my ears stopped—but no, that was the siren. Someone had shut off the siren. He was dead.

"I'm sorry, Julie," Timmy said, engulfing me. His coat was hard and stiff and crackled like dry wood. "I know," I said, muffled against him. "Thank you. I'm sorry you lost." One of those would be all right; one of them would certainly cover it.

He was leading me somewhere. The rest of the staff, like volunteer firemen, were going back to their posts, fists uncurled, whispering, intense, pausing to light up.

I only started to cry when I saw where we were: that same little secret broom closet where he'd taken me to sign the Consent for Operation form. "Why in here?" I sobbed at him. "What more is there to sign?"

"Nothing, Julie, sweet, nothing, just sit down. I thought you'd want . . . to be somewhere for a minute without people around."

I nodded, meaning that he sounded sensible and well thought out. Meaning I understood what he said.

There was a sharp knock on the door. I jumped, and he said, "Yes?" "See you a moment, Doctor?" "Okay," he said. "Julie, stay put; I'll be right back." I nodded again. He left a cigarette burning in a glass ashtray; I watched it carefully; there wasn't anything else to do. Do they always take people in here to tell them the husband is dead? I wondered. If so, they should fix it up more. Paneling—pecky cypress, even if it's plywood, like a suburban rabbi's study. And the examining table is wrong, unless it's there in case someone faints. But then why not a hide-a-bed examining table? Simmons must make one; opens right up, even a doctor could do it.

Timmy was back. "Anyone," he said, ". . . is there anyone you want me to call?"

That was a strange question, to which there must be an answer. But whom would I want? Laurie couldn't leave the baby. Miranda then? Miranda, because . . . "Cal Jaffe. And Miranda, I guess."

"Miranda's here," he said. "I'll go call Jaffe." He left again.

Carefully, neatly, slowly, I ground out Timmy's cigarette. Then I got up, checked to see that I'd stopped crying and walked out into the hall. Miranda, very pale, wordlessly handed me my sunglasses. "Thank you," I whispered. They were just what I wanted; she knew that; hers were already in place; she was shielded for the same battle. Arms linked, we reentered the waiting room and sat down. Doria and Paula were gone, leaving notes. ("Dr. Spector thought it would be better if there were fewer people around. He *told* us to go.")

When Cal arrived, Timmy said he would drive us all to my house and see to it that I went to bed. It didn't occur to me until later that nobody but Timmy spoke at all.

The corridor was flat and clear, like a voided intestinal tract after a final awful upheaval. Not even a nurse was visible for miles; it was as if they had gone into hiding following a crime. Did they ever say goodbye, I wondered, or only when they could add something cheery: take care, now; glad to have been of service. Passing the glass-walled telephone, whose number I had already forgotten, I thought how strange it was that I would not be back tonight or tomorrow. Like graduating? No; more like being expelled, never to attend class reunions.

Cal had collected the candy; we left the flowers for Miss Detweiler.


D addy died this afternoon."

"Our Daddy?" Trusting round eyes. He wouldn't do that, not our Daddy. Our Daddy who art in . . .

"Yes, baby, ours."

"Does Matthew know?" (Had we all conspired to spirit Daddy away?)

"Not yet. I guess we should tell him together. I told you first because you're older." When you're six, you can take it. I hugged him hard, as if that would make one of us hurt less.

"But, Mommy?"

"What?"

"How do they know? Did they listen to his heart with the stratoscope? Like Dr. Tom's?"

"Stethoscope . . . Yes, it stopped beating."

"Did they know it was going to? Did you know?"

"No, of course not. Nobody knew. Go get Matthew now, Nicky. Please." (Because I am going to break down otherwise, and one must not do that. They take their cues from what you do. His small precise intelligence, though; the clarity of his disbelief . . .)

Matthew came in, bearing the dinosaur picture; he had finished it after all. Oh God . . .

"Matthew, Daddy died." Nicky, the Messinger bearing ill tidings. They used to execute the courier, so as to discredit his report.

Matthew looked at me for the denial. Instead I nodded confirmation, swallowing again. "Nicky's fooling, isn't he?" He was going to force *me* to say it.

"I am not," Nicky declared. "Mommy just *told* me—didn't you?"

"Yes, I did. It's true, Matthew. Daddy died this afternoon." Now what? What comes after that?

"Then where is he?" Show us the unliving proof.

Carefully, and without ribbons, I said, "His body is still in the hospital. But he . . . it isn't Daddy any more. Daddy doesn't exist any more."

Matthew nodded gravely. "Like the goldfish." (We had just lost two.)

"Yes," I said. "Yes."

"You threw them away."

It was clear where we would go from here, and I couldn't. "The dinosaur picture is beautiful. I'm glad you finished; would you like to frame it? I think Daddy would have liked that."

"A real frame? Not one out of paper?"

God, it was so easy to distract them. "I think so; it's really very good. What do you think, Nicky?" There was no answer; the finger was tight in his mouth. One down. "Nicky?" (Please let me help.) "I think Daddy would want you to use the pencil cup you made—maybe just for special pencils. Colored ones—for really special pictures." (Oh God, let him smile one time. He did, and took the finger out.)

"He would? *New* colored pencils?"

I nodded, grinning inanely. "Why don't you both . . ." (Do what, besides take your small terrors away so I can acknowledge my own?) "go ask Darlene for a snack? Just milk and one cookie—no Kool-Pops!" I called as they raced away, released, like Doria Perkins and Paula Mack. Strangers and small children are excused. Not admitted unless accompanied by a responsible adult. That would be me, right?

When I was six, a young uncle of mine died suddenly. The news came by telephone while Mother, Nina and I were having dinner. Uncle George was a bachelor, nobody's daddy. I remember bursting into a fit of uncontrollable giggles at the house-of-horrors sound of it: "Uncle George is dead."

Mother was shocked by my reaction, and I was banished to
my room without dessert. "She's too young to understand,"
I heard the cook saying. "That's absolutely no excuse," my
mother replied angrily. "It's a matter of respect; she's not too
young for that." Respect for Uncle George? For death? For
him for being dead? I never asked, and no one ever explained.
Later my sister informed me through the bathroom door that
I had missed lemon meringue pie and that the cause of Uncle
George's death had been heart: "He died of heart." I went
to sleep imagining Uncle George's Daedalus wings springing
through shoulder slits in a dark-blue business suit. As he
soared sunward, his striped tie streamed behind him like
Smilin' Jack's white silk flier's muffler.

But he was only an uncle. And my Daddy had already
flown.

I called my mother, since I
had to start someplace. "Oh God, no," she said. I waited.
"Oh my *God*, no." Still I waited. "I was just getting ready
to go down there! I'm all dressed! I sent you some fresh flowers for that dismal little room! Oh my God, *Julie*, are you all
right?"

"Yes."

"Is anyone there with you?"

"Yes. Dr. Spector . . . and some friends. Brought me home.
They're here." I was dispensing words in neat thin ribbons.

"What about arrangements? Julie, don't you think I should

call Uncle Walter and ask him to make the arrangements?"

"No!" I said, alarmed. *"Don't.* I mean, go ahead and call —call *all* the uncles. But please, no arrangements! I mean, we'll take care of it. I'll do . . . whatever needs . . . arranging." And I hung up before she could explain why this was not the way things are done.

Next I called Laurie because I wasn't ready for the "Oh Gods" of Richard's Aunt Addie or any of those cousins. "Help," I pleaded softly when she answered. "He's dead." For once she was stunned silent; I even thought she might have fainted or something, though the receiver hadn't dropped. "Laurie?" I asked, my throat closing up like the shell of an injured clam. "Y-yes, Jools," she said finally. Her voice sounded more ragged than mine. "You all right?" "Just peachy," I said, beginning to cry.

"Okay, Messinger," she said, snapping right back. "Just tell Laurie. Everything."

"I don't know what to do," I said. "I mean, what am I *supposed* to do? I'm not there any more, I'm home."

"First off, you don't have to do anything you don't want to. Who's with you?"

"Well, you won't like it . . . Miranda, Cal and Timmy Spector."

"Oh Jesus . . . In your *house? All* of them? Oh, Julie."

"Well, they brought me home," I explained. I didn't bother adding that I had requested their presence.

"You want Laurie to come and tell them all to go away now?"

I laughed, picturing her shooing them out with an old-fashioned twig broom. "No," I said, groping for some reason that wouldn't sound deranged. "I feel better having them around. They sort of belong."

"All right," she said, because she did understand, bless her square little Cokehead. "But after this is over, *no more*. Promise? Do I hear a promise?"

"Yes, Mother," I said, thinking, But it will never *be* over; this aircraft will just go on plummeting, and never, never land. That will be my life sentence. Life is the only sentence which doesn't end with a period.

O<small>nce</small> again Timmy Spector took over the management of the case. He called relatives, answered calls from relatives, fielded questions from Marcy Berns, Audrey Lebow and Barnaby Halstead, and told the whole world he had ordered me to rest. He and Cal composed an announcement for the *Times*, and Cal telephoned someone he knew on the obituary desk. "Richard Messinger, art director of *Household Magazine* and illustrator of many best-selling children's books, died of . . . died yesterday in Mount Carmel Hospital. He was thirty-nine . . . Cause of death? Uh, could you call back on that? It's sort of complicated."

Miranda and I went out for a walk with Nicky and Matthew, and stopped at Lamston's for the frame and the colored pencils. Miranda hardly spoke, though she smiled whenever one of the children said something poignant or funny, which was often. There was something perversely comforting about the simplicity of their terrible questions, the easiness with which they demanded straight answers. "Will we be poor now, Mommy?" "No, we'll be all right." "Will we get another Daddy?" ("Will we get another gold-fish?") "I don't know; maybe." "Do you want us to get an-other Daddy?" "I guess so, someday." But where can you get one? Who would you get—Mr. Jaffe?" "I don't know who—" Miranda smiled—"probably not Mr. Jaffe."

Back at the house Timmy and Cal were grappling with the grown-up questions that didn't matter at all. Funeral services? Rabbi? Burial arrangements? "I don't want any of those," I told them evenly. "Just whatever the City of New York re-quires in the event of death."

"But that's the point; the city *requires* a funeral—unless you're destitute."

I was not prepared for that. "I thought Jessica Mitford ex-posed that!" I protested.

"She did, but she didn't change it," Cal said. "All the or-dinances are designed with your friendly funeral directors in mind—not to mention the cemeteries and coffin makers and gravestone cutters. That's the way it is."

"Well, it's disgusting; can't I just *say* I'm destitute?"

"You'd have to prove it."

"Oh Christ," I said, beginning to dissolve again. "You mean I actually have to get some chicken-fat rabbi to say 'beloved' fifty times? And they can make me get Richard pumped up with silicones and tinted pink? There's an actual law that says he can't go without being wrapped as a gift? And I have to sit there surrounded by gladioli, watching Aunt Addie cry? It's obscene—and I won't. That's all, I *won't*. He . . . he . . . A nice neat cremation and put the ashes in . . . in the sculpture garden at the Museum of Modern Art! At the feet of one of those huge Maillol stone nudes—that would be fine. In fact, that's just *exactly* where! They won't mind—we're associate members, and I've never even had lunch in the members' dining room!"

"Is she serious?" Timmy said to Cal.

"Yes, she is!" I said, convinced I was on to a good thing. "He *said* he wanted to end up in a great art museum, even if they didn't appreciate him in his lifetime. That qualifies as an expressed wish of the deceased."

"Well," Timmy said doubtfully, "I guess we could try . . . Julie, can I talk to you inside for a minute?"

I couldn't imagine what was coming: permission to conduct the service? We went into the bedroom and shut the door. "How do you feel," he said, "about . . . an autopsy?"

"You mean generally, or in this case?"

"In this case, obviously." He frowned.

"Why does it matter how I feel?" I hedged.

"Because I'd like to order one, with your permission."

"Why, for God's sake? You know damn well what he died of!"

"Julie, don't start getting upset again. You've been so great . . ."

"I know; you've said that before."

"But you are; you're amazing. And this is important; it's something you should do; it could help a lot of people."

"Such as you and Gideon Mahler? If it showed—"

He winced, and then decided to ignore it. "Such as other surgery patients who might be hurt the way Richard was . . . by getting that anesthetic."

"Well, if that's really it, what do you need an autopsy for?

Why can't they just throw the stuff away? They don't *have* to poison other people with it!"

He sighed; I was being difficult again, and he was tired. "Bleiweiss and I—"

"Bleiweiss! That bastard! Did you tell him the liver didn't come back?"

"Bleiweiss and I—"

"What did he say when you told him?"

Defeated, he answered me, "He said it was a rotten goddamn shame; it had looked so hopeful until the kidneys went. And the damn virus . . ."

"Oh, yes, the virus. That must have been it. Because the liver *always*—"

"Anyway, Bleiweiss and I want to present Richard's . . . this case . . . to document, to help us prove the dangers of this stuff. There's really a big dispute over it, because the anesthesiologists love it. Every hospital in New York uses it routinely; it's a cinch to administer, nonflammable, doesn't need any special care in storage. And a case like this is so rare that nobody's been able to document . . . to give them a good solid reason *not* to use it."

"Richard would be the good solid reason?"

He nodded.

"And you'd be a hero after all. Lose a battle, win a war. Over Richard's . . . over—" I stopped myself abruptly. "All right, Timmy. Go ahead and do your autopsy."

He whipped out the authorization form, which he had just happened not to forget when we left the hospital. Or maybe he never traveled without one. *Semper Paratus.*

I signed. "Will that be all now?"

"This is a good thing you did, Julie." He patted the breast

pocket where he'd put it, looking reverent, as if the flag were passing. "It'll do a lot of good."

"That's a real comfort," I said. "Now please can I stop?"

He leaned over and kissed me gently. "Try to get some rest. I'll call you later." I didn't ask where he was going; it had to be Mount Carmel, to arrange for Richard's last (first? only?) contribution to society. I locked the door behind him and lay down to sob quietly in the pillow on my side of the bed.

All night strange relatives and relative strangers seeped through our living room, trailing sighs and smoke and praise for the dead. Platitudes du jour. Every time the doorbell rang, Matthew streaked out to greet the company, announcing brightly to the stricken faces: "Our Daddy died today and now we have to get a new one!" Nothing he had ever said produced such audience response; it was heady stuff. I made no attempt to discourage him, not even by explaining that all those people already knew about Daddy— that, in fact, knowing about Daddy was why they were here drinking coffee and asking each other what else was new.

Aunt Addie brought homemade sponge cake, presumably leavened with tears. ("I didn't know what to do, so I baked.") Everyone else, who didn't know what to do, ate.

Surprisingly, it was Barney Halstead who persuaded me that there should be a funeral service after all. Not for the Aunt Addies, he explained quickly, reading my unpleasant thoughts, but for the people who had come to the hospital last week in such astonishing numbers. People who knew Richard, who would miss him. Who respected his talent, or laughed at his jokes, or somewhere had brushed against him and come away feeling warm. A chance to say goodbye, or thank you, was all any of those people wanted. Most of them, including Barney himself, he confessed, seldom felt like saying goodbye to anyone, but this time it was almost a physical need.

I had never seen Barnaby Halstead make a whole speech without his pipe until now; this alone was impressive enough to persuade me. Then there was the guilt he aroused: how rotten and selfish of me to deny all those Richard-warmed souls a gesture of farewell. "He was," said Barney, "a loved man."

I capitulated. A small service, then—but no coffin, no gladioli. Barney offered to arrange it all; it was the least, he insisted. Well, better he than Uncle Walter. But what about the speech? If there was a service, the family would insist on a rabbi. All right, Barney said, he'd get a rabbi. He knew an inoffensive one, young and bright, who had written a piece for *Household's* big religion series: "Have Faith in Your Home." Oh God. "Did it begin 'Thou shalt have no other *Household* gods before me'?" I said. Barney did not smile. "So shall I call him—Dr. Dave Solomon—or not?" "All right, Chief," I said. At which he did smile. "Good girl. He'll probably want to talk to you tomorrow. They do that, in cases where they don't know the, uh . . ."

"Beloved," I said.

The *Times* obituary desk called to confirm the death and fill in a few details. "Could we get a cause on that now?"

We had been trying, off and on, to work that out. Died after a short illness? But he wasn't even *sick*, I pointed out. Died of complications following surgery? No, that meant hemorrhaging or gangrene.

"Well, what did they put on the death certificate?" Cal asked. "Acute hepatic necrosis," Timmy said. Well, that's impossible; you never saw anything like that in the *Times*. Probably it isn't fit to print.

How about just "died following surgery"? They certainly can't fault that for accuracy, as far as it goes—except it only tells when, not why. Still, it was the best we could do, so that's what Cal told the *Times*. "What kind of surgery?" the reporter asked. "What kind of surgery?" Cal repeated, for my benefit.

"Minor," I said, "tell him minor. He just got a little bit malignant, but he kept his nodes clean. Oh Christ, tell him the whole damn thing! Tell him the whole crazy thing and let him rewrite it so it sounds plausible!"

I wondered how long the obituary would be. Richard cared intensely about that: the number of inches, and how prominent. Like the size and shape of one's penis, it was a measure of the man. Six inches with a two-line head was respectable; less than that, you were—well, less than that. And no fair if the space was filled up with a long list of survivors, or a description of the suspicious circumstances surrounding your death. Just the achievements, just the record, just a straight accounting of what you managed to do in the time allotted, and whether it was worth doing well, and whether you had.

The autopsy was performed (a once-in-a-lifetime performance) at eight o'clock on Tuesday morning. Timmy raced down right afterward—some two and a half hours later—to tell me all about it. I had sent the children to school, braving my mother's horrified disapproval, on the off-chance that it might help them believe that life hadn't stopped since yesterday. I had also taken the phone off the hook (for the same reason?), hidden it under the pillow, and walked to the corner for *The New York Times*. I hadn't quite opened it to the obituary page when Timmy rang the doorbell.

"You wouldn't believe how many people showed up," he exploded halfway through the door. "Even the off-duty girls from Intensive Care came and stood outside, waiting for the results. They were praying we'd find some evidence of metastasis."

At first I wasn't sure I'd heard him right; then I began trembling, stricken by posthumous panic. "Why," I asked, deliberately low and calm, "why would they pray for that?"

"Well, obviously," he said, settling into Richard's leather chair, "if there were cancer cells in him somewhere, if the melanoma had spread, then his death would make sense to them. In a way they'd even feel it was better—"

I cut him off quickly, hating what he was about to say. "But you *knew*—I thought you knew there was no metastasis. Days ago, when the lab report, on the lymph nodes—"

"Well, yeah," he said, flushing. He had unexpectedly painted us into a corner. "Yeah, that's true, the nodes *were* clean. But there's . . . see, there's no way to check the blood. It also . . . melanoma can also spread through the bloodstream."

I tried to let this news just wash over the surface; what difference did it make now, after all? But I couldn't seem to stop shaking. My teeth almost chattering, I had to pursue it. "Then the lymph . . . removing the lymph nodes, the whole thing, was no guarantee of *anything*? Clean or dirty, it was sort of beside the point? Because if it could spread through the blood, and if it had, then that was that, regardless. Only, you never even mentioned that. You never *suggested*—"

"Julie, what would have been the *point* of mentioning it? Come on, for Chrissake, be fair. There's no way of knowing for sure—ever. All you can do is what you can do, and hope you've stopped what can be stopped, and let the patient hope."

"But I don't see the point of what you did! What *difference* did it make if the damn nodes were clean!"

"Only that if they were, it was much less likely that the melanoma had metastasized. And if we'd found a few cells in there, catching them this early would keep it from going further. It's like shutting off one of two possible leaks—it's fifty percent better than nothing."

"Not quite," I said bitterly. "Zero percent, as it turns out."

"Well . . ." He inhaled, shifted in the chair and started over. "Anyway . . . There was nothing . . . he was totally clean. Blood, everything—not a trace. He would have lived a normal life."

"Too bad for the nurses," I said.

"Yeah," he agreed, thinking I meant it. "You know Farnsworth and Wachtel were both crying? I never thought I'd see that."

"Crying," I repeated, "because he was clean."

"Well, as I said, because there was no good reason for his dying."

"Funny," I said, "I already knew that."

"No, you didn't," he said. "As a matter of fact, we all only just found out."

Could that be satisfaction? Pride? Not possible. On the other hand, it must be nice for him to see how right he was all along. "I guess you found what you wanted, what you *expected*, though?" I ventured.

He brightened, then caught himself and said soberly, "The liver was just about totally gone. Less than two percent left. *Exactly* the way we figured it. Bleiweiss—he was there, of course—"

"—of course—"

"—Bleiweiss and I are going to present the report at the next full-staff meeting. We thought . . . it may be possible to get some real attention finally. I mean, to wake them up to the dangers of this goddamn anesthetic. Most of the biggest anesthesiologists here have been refusing for ten years to acknowledge any risk of liver damage. We may even invite one or two from Mt. Sinai to the meeting, so that—"

"Congratulations," I said, needing desperately to shut him

up. Tasting sourness, I had been trying to breathe deeply and swallow it down.

"Julie, are you okay?" he said, suddenly aware that I wasn't.

I got up slowly, so as not to jostle the stuff in my throat. "Oh, yes," I said, edging carefully toward the john in the hall. "Just fine. Got a clean bill of health on my late husband . . . Clean bill . . . came to a little more than we figured on, but certainly . . . probably . . . worth it in the long . . . run." And then I was over the toilet bowl again. Since I hadn't eaten anything, I had nothing to offer, so I just stood, leaning against it, heaving dryly and reflecting that there must be some good reason why Timmy Spector always made me sick. Like Miss Farnsworth and Miss Wachtel, I'd feel better if there was a good reason.

The obit was much longer and more impressive than I expected; they even ran his picture—the one with the dignified near-smile that *Household* had sent out three years ago when Barney promoted him to art director. His hair was shorter then. They mentioned all his children's books, and called *Melancholy Melinda* one of the most appealing and durable comic heroines in recent children's literature. They also had much more information than Cal had given them: all his previous magazine jobs; a one-man show of drawings and photographs he'd had six years ago; even his army service: "He served as a corporal during the Korean conflict." Reading it, I had a sudden sensation

that it was all a mistake; either it wasn't Richard who had
died, or else I hadn't been married to him. Yet there was my
name: "He leaves his wife, the former Julie Wallman, two
sons, Nicholas and Matthew."

"He leaves his wife." That's what he does, yes, sir; they
certainly got that part right. One way or another, he leaves
his wife. Having left my bed and board, I am no longer responsible for his debts. For his death.

T he instant I replaced the
telephone, it rang. David Solomon, the rabbi, who had been
trying to reach me all morning, wondered if it would be con-
venient for me to see him briefly at three this afternoon.
Could I ask some good friends to join us, I asked; I thought
they'd be helpful. "Fine, fine," Dr. Solomon said. He had, of
course, read the very fine obituary in the *Times*, he added,
and what he'd be needing was not so much additional information as a more "intimate" portrait of the man, of the
artist as a husband and father. (Of the artist as beloved.) I
promised to try, although increasingly I felt less like a well-
informed source.

I invited Cal and Miranda to come help me draw an intimate portrait of Richard, suitable for rabbi's ears (antennae
for holyvision?). Then I spent two hours wandering around
the apartment in Darlene's sluggish wake. She was more or
less dusting and weeping; I was timidly exploring Richard's
legacies. I didn't even know how to work the hi-fi; he had

never let me touch it. There were reference books on erotic sexual practices in primitive cultures, both overdue at the Webster Branch of the New York Public Library. Volume two of the three-volume boxed biography of Freud was missing—who could he have lent it to? There was partly exposed film in three of his cameras; there were odd-shaped keys to unknown locks; there was, in every drawer and coat pocket, on every table surface, in the hamper, on the closet floor, some piece of unfinishable business, some unexplained and now forever inexplicable fragment of the living Richard. What should I do with the new fifty-dollar Italian shoes, worn twice? The old ones could go to the Volunteers of America, but no barefoot Volunteer would even appreciate handsewn Gucci slip-ons.

Everything in the bedroom smelled of him: anti-bacterial soap and athlete's foot powder. Even the kitchen bore traces on the shelves: boxes of Mallomars and Wheaties which nobody else ever ate. Cuff links. What do you do with cuff links? And contact lenses? At least in a divorce you divide things up; he empties the drawers as well as your life. A place for everything and everything in his place or yours. But no place for a corporal's uniform whose owner hasn't worn it since 1953?

Suddenly I understood all those eccentric old widows living for fifty years with their late husband's things left exactly as he liked them: the folded striped pajamas on the bed and his worn tobacco pouch still filled with sweetly rotting Prince Albert. It wasn't morbid sentiment or senility at all; it was just too much trouble to clear it all away. Close the doors and leave all the dispossessions. *Things* have squatter's rights; why else do we call them *belongings?*

You don't have to do anything you don't want, Laurie had said. But the new mother involuntarily expels the afterbirth; a widow has no choice either: the afterdeath must go. How to de-create a person out of everyday items found in the home? Step one: throw out all suitcases full of the drawings he saved for thirty years. Two: empty that file cabinet drawer of Donna Sue Birnbaum's well-preserved bust. Three: discard his exhaustive collection of 78 rpms which would probably ruin the stereo even if I could operate it. But, please, how will I get the film out of those cameras? How do I know I even want the pictures developed?

Maybe Nicky and Matthew would eat the Mallomars.

Dr. Solomon reminded me of someone—Bleiweiss? That was it. Slimmer and handsomer, though; and he had a well-tailored summer suit, though perhaps a man of the cloth ought not to wear one called seersucker. But it was definitely a Bleiweiss face, pale, soft, foggy-lensed, and there was the same pathetic urgency about his life's work. Even the work had a certain sameness: two logies —theo and hepato, both concerned with observing mysterious processes, natural and/or super-, over which neither of them exercised any significant control. If faith should falter, Solomon would watch over it, knowing that it would either regenerate or die. He presided, a high-salaried junior vice-god in charge of nodding expertly, because with his training, it is understood, he understands.

"Now then," he began in his predictable melodic whine. We had all assembled, and the congregation was seated. He folded his neat hands, the nails buffed; if you looked closely you could see traces of pink buffing powder. "Can you tell me a little about Mr. Messingill?"

"Messinger," I said. "Mess-in-ger."

He checked a small spiral notebook. "Ah, yes." (I *knew* I was right.)

"Well, you know, he had an, uh, artist's view of things, of his world. He thought it should fit some ideal—and that if he tried, if he kept trying, perhaps he could make it fit." (Perhaps that was even true; perhaps he could have; perhaps he died trying.) ". . . And he was funny—genuinely funny. Subtle humor, but sharp too." (Like the cruelty; you knew it stung, but not why.) ". . . He was—as Barnaby Halstead put it yesterday—a loved man. Probably more than he knew." (Did that include my love—did mine count?)

"And what else? Well, he . . ." (He had these problems, Doctor. Rabbi. He had *sexual* problems. He lied. He cheated on his roommate. He was only faintly amused by the first baby —and not even that by the second. He hung onto all the wrong things—for dear life. Ah, Rabbi, there was method in his sadness. He kept everything that mattered. That was the matter. He kept what mattered to him. To himself. Except what I gave him. He was . . . a good guy or a bad guy. A loved man. He was . . . I didn't see him too clearly. It was dark, and it all happened so fast. And when I woke up he was gone.)

"Did he have any, ah, hobbies?" Dr. Solomon asked, looking around for possible clues. (Well, he did go in for peepage —you know, looking across the street with powerful binoculars. Do you mean things like that? And he enjoyed carnal knowledge of, in addition to some of the people you see here, a number of others who could not be with us today.)

"His music," Miranda offered softly, moist-eyed behind her fashionable violet sunglasses. I experienced another uncomfortable shiver of envy: they shared music.

"Music," Solomon said, nodding and jotting in his notebook.

"Jazz," I said, indicating that I knew him too.

"Your children are quite young?" he inquired.

"Five and six," I said. He was looking around again. "They're in school," I explained. He frowned slightly and jotted again. Their ages, or the shameful fact that their mother sent them to school the day after their father died, in defiance of all Jewish tradition, including the Reformed? "I thought it would be better for them," I went on apologetically, "to have life go on as normally as possible." (Actually, I'd thought it would be better not to have them perform as shooting-gallery targets for poor-dearing second cousins, clucking great aunts and rabbis who might ask if they believed in the everlasting.)

Dr. Solomon nodded again, Solomonly weighing whether to let me off with a suspended sentence. "Your husband must have been very proud of them? I see a picture there on the desk—very handsome boys."

"Yes-he-was-very-proud-of-them," I recited.

Cal cleared his throat and said, "If I may, Dr. Solomon, I knew Richard very well, I'd like to tell you how I felt about him—how most of his friends felt."

"Please," Dr. Solomon said, poising his ballpoint over the book. Between notes, he made tiny preliminary circles in the air, as if waiting for landing instructions.

"He took such delight in life," Cal said. "People enjoyed hearing him laugh."

"Just a moment," the rabbi said, writing rapidly. "That is . . . you express it very well—" He was having trouble with the pen, probably because his hand kept perspiring on the page. Cal and I smiled over his damp curly head; Miranda was too moist-eyed to notice.

"Ready?" Cal asked politely when the rabbi had stopped writing.

"Yes, yes," he said, wiping the page with the same perspiring hand.

"Well," Cal continued, "he was probably the youngest boy of his age and responsibilities I ever met."

The rabbi began writing furiously, but then stopped. "I'm sorry?" he said. "I don't think I quite . . . caught your meaning."

"He seemed fantastically *young*," Cal said, more carefully.

"He had a youthfulness that belied his years and achievements?" said the rabbi.

"Something like that, yeah," said Cal.

It went on for about another half-hour. Miranda remained almost totally silent after her musical contribution. I was only slightly more cooperative, monotoning monosyllables to questions directly addressed to me. We must have been extremely happy? (Yes.) His artistic flair must have been a profound influence on our lives? (Very deep.) We must have derived great joy from our lovely home? (Yes.) Were you members of any synagogue? (No.) I see . . . But in a sense your husband must have been a deeply religious man? (Not really.) Surely you see that his great love of beauty, his joy of living, were expressions of faith in the living God? (I see, yes.)

Thanks to Cal, Solomon seemed delighted with it all. He filled almost the entire notebook, except for the damp spots, and expressed his heartfelt sympathy all around. It was an honor and a privilege; he felt a very real sense of what a fine man Mr. Messingill must have been. "Messinger," I said. He looked it up again and apologized.

Miranda had to go too, she murmured, and they caught the same elevator.

"Do you do this sort of thing often?" I asked Cal when they'd gone.

"No," he said. "This will be the only time."

"You were great," I said, "and I'm grateful."

"I meant most of it," he said. "Believe it or not, I meant it."

"I know," I said quietly.

Cal had a favor to ask, before he forgot. If I could . . . if I didn't mind, he'd like to borrow the last few pages of Richard's diary—just the pages with handwritten inserts and marginal scribbles, covering the last six or eight months, up to the last . . . the last weekend. I guessed why he wanted it; Miranda still refused to believe it existed. But I was too tired, too drained, to talk about it any more, or to try to persuade him how irrelevant and silly it all seemed now. "I threw it out," I said simply. "I'm sorry." Then he asked if I'd like to have dinner with him; I definitely should not have to hang around this apartment, if it was going to be like last night. He was right, of course, but having dinner with him seemed wrong, I thought. On the other hand? No.

After he left, the Spectors called and asked if I'd like to have dinner at their house. The fact was, I no longer believed in dinner. Whatever else I might ever do in flagrant disrespect of Richard's memory, I considered the taking of hot food unthinkable. "Why don't you drop over here later, though, if you feel like it?" I said. I'd said that into the phone some thirty times that afternoon, trusting that enough of the bearable people who'd said maybe would outnumber the unbearables who'd said yes.

Although the cast was essentially the same, the production was different each time now—the timing, the dialogue, even the movements. There was no eating tonight, and less smoking. People said strange things, obviously meant to be profound, about their new consciousness of being alive, and how unusual that was at our age. If there were jokes, they were furtive or accidental; some of them occasionally laughed, but the sound actually hurt several ears, or so it seemed from the way people in the vicinity winced or shrank back. I have no clear idea of who was there besides Cal, Laurie, my mother and sister and father, who had flown up from Florida (Fiona was coming tomorrow), and the Spectors. There were perhaps a dozen others. Miranda did not come or call; Cal offered no explanation, and I didn't ask for one.

The next morning was hot and sunny. It should have rained for Richard's funeral, I thought. He would have felt more at home with rain.

The service was to begin at ten. At eight-fifteen my mother telephoned to ask whether I was planning to bring the children to the chapel, and whether I had something appropriate to wear on my head. I didn't think so, in both cases.

"I certainly hope you're not planning to send them to *school* again," she said, making the word "school" sound vaguely like concentration camp.

"No," I said, controlling myself, "they both know it's a special day to think about Daddy, to remember him and say goodbye . . . privately. Which is what I would have liked to do myself."

"I think," she said, ignoring this, "that it would be far more appropriate to have them attend the funeral. It is the only way to expose them to the *importance* of the event."

"The importance is the least important part!" I cried, forgetting the importance of keeping calm with her. "What matters is what they remember, and what they feel—not the Solomon version of what appeared in yesterday's *New York Times*, with colorful details provided by me and my friends!"

"Well," she said infuriatingly, "you have all the answers, as usual. Nobody can tell you anything!"

"Not right now, I guess," I said, throwing myself on the mercy of the court. Sometimes I despise my desperate cheek-turning worst of all.

"Well," she said, somewhat mollified, "have you got anything appropriate to wear?"

"Sackcloth culottes?" I said, again defying the natural human instinct for self-preservation. Why do I *do* that?

She was furious, of course. "Another one of your smart answers! There is just no *point* in my talking to you!" (Well, that was certainly true.) "I simply don't understand you at all." (That too.)

"I'm sorry, Mother, really," I surrendered wearily. "I have

a dark-blue sleeveless dress; I think it will do. I'll see you there, all right?"

"Sleeveless?" she was saying doubtfully as I hung up.

The mail came while I was getting dressed. In it were seven envelopes containing laminated clippings of Richard's obituary, with the Lord's Prayer printed on the back. "We know you will want to treasure this keepsake," said each of the accompanying form letters. "Please send $1 by return mail. If for some reason you do not wish to keep this beautiful memento, you must return it within five days." They bore postmarks from seven different places; it must be a hotly competitive field.

The bill from the anesthesiologists had arrived the day before. It came to $100: very reasonable. They'd sent it Saturday, so they really had no way to prevent its coming on the actual day he died. Timmy had brought back the suitcase last night. Everything was there, including the unopened gift set of *That Man!* cologne, which Barney Halstead automatically sent to any hospitalized male employe above the level of assistant editor. Another communication in the morning mail was a letter from a well-known real estate firm specializing in the sale of cooperative apartments. It was addressed to "Estate of Richard Messinger," and they were taking the liberty . . . In case I was contemplating placing the apartment owned by the late Mr. Messinger on the market at this time, they would appreciate . . .

$\mathrm{T}$immy and Marian drove me to the funeral home. It was a five-story elevatored premises, air-cooled and so lushly carpeted that the footprints made on entering would surely still be imbedded there on departure. At first I thought the walls were carpeted too, but it was only some spongy soundproofing material that matched the floor. As a result you couldn't hear anything; even the elevator stole up and down like a huge, polite intruder. Its golden gate rolled silently open at every stop, revealing a silver-headed male zombie in a thick (soundproof?) black suit with a white carnation indicating he belonged there. "Good mourning," he said. "Name, please?"

"Messinger," we mumbled.

"This way, please." (Fourth floor: sporting goods, unpainted furniture, gourmet cookware, Messingers . . .) There was considerable nodding and bowing, which looked properly dignified and formal, but oddly incomplete without smiles. I understood why, finally: the attendants all looked like apostate wedding caterers.

The "chapel" was a two-room arrangement: a small reception salon where "the immediate family" was to gather and compose itself, and a largish auditorium for those expressing more distant grief. I was delivered into the family room, and the Spectors were instructed to join the others. The family room was filled with white pompons in white baskets and all the relatives who at last felt obliged. So far, at least, Barney had kept his word: there were no gladioli. My father and Fiona were there: lovely blond Fiona with a new fluffy hairdo under her perky half-veil dotted with occasional black-velvet beauty marks. My mother looked sensational in a crisp black linen suit that did not have a single wrinkle. Had she remained standing in the taxi? Jet buttons picked up the dustless two-hundred-dollar gleam of her baby-lizard pumps and handbag. Not a crack, not a smudge; she had traveled across New York sealed under a spotless glass bell. Don't think I don't notice; I notice.

I said polite hellos, and accepted kisses or near-kisses, whichever was being served. Remember to say a thank-you for each so-sorry. Then I sneaked cautiously toward the wailing wall between the rooms, to peek at the hushed crowd of outsiders, where my friends must be. The lighting in there was churchly, the pews polished, the place jammed. There was a platform banked with dozens more flower baskets, mostly yellow and white, with a few patches of blue iris. Still no glads; that was nice.

Then I saw the box: long, shiny-handled, evil, barbaric. I didn't order that I don't ever want I won't have any no please don't COFFIN.

Oh, no. Oh, please, no. I turned around, helpless, devastated, and began sobbing and choking "No, no, no."

But there was nobody in that family room who could possibly understand. "Coffin," I sputtered, ". . . promised me no coffin . . ." I was crying harder than I'd ever cried, pounding my useless outraged fists against somebody's jacket. I have never felt so alone. Everyone was Greek-chorusing sympathetic cooing idiocies: ". . . natural for her to break down . . ." "Poor Julie finally letting go . . ." ". . . so brave . . ."

". . . it had to come out." ". . . much better for her to let it out this way . . ."

"Bastards," I was howling muffledly into a Dacron jacket. "Bastards, the bastards. *Promised* me no coffin." Breach of promise; jilted at the funeral pyre. Listen, the editor of a leading ladies' magazine promised me. Well, but perhaps his brother-in-law makes coffins. An exceptionally fine coffin, leakproof and durable; lasts up to three times longer. And the commission only comes to . . . Besides, they positively will not handle arrangements for uncrated individuals. Everybody travels first class. Every body. But that's—wait, there *isn't* any body. There was an autopsy . . . my God, it's an empty box. It's a fake. A prop! . . . Unless—no, they couldn't do *that*, please, no; not even in New York could they require a thing like that. All former persons must be wholly present and accounted for, in proper containers, regardless of condition when last seen. Violators will be liable to the ultimate corporal punishment.

But Timmy had told me the remains would go straight to the crematorium after the autopsy. Timmy told me; Barney promised me. The remains: a beautiful word. All that remains. However, we remain, as ever, very truly yours.

"Would you lead your daughter inside now, please? Dr. Solomon is ready to begin," said the undertaker to my father. To my father? But yes, of course the bride is always escorted by her father. And so I walked in there solemnly on his arm. Doesn't Julie make a lovely widow? Doesn't she look radiantly unhappy? Aren't we glad we talked her into having a big funeral after all? It's something a girl always remembers.

It was a packed house, hundreds more than had been arranged for; there was an overflow in the hall, and extra folding chairs were hastily unfolding in the now-vacant family room. God, there are a lot of girls here. I wonder how many were . . . listed. The first three rows were reserved for immediate family, those who by reasons of blood or marriage had earned the right to shed tears practically on the platform, anointing both Dr. Solomon and his flower-strewn empty box.

In five hundred words or less, or more, in Calvin Jaffe's words and mine, Solomon did then draw an intimate portrait of this man, this Richard husband, artist father, lover and leaver of life. The smell of the flowers drifted relentlessly through the room, like too much scented air freshener. I thought, Richard would have sneezed and rubbed his eyes. There would be an unbearable histamine itch in the back of his throat, and afterward he would need two hay-fever pills. Oh, where is Laurie? Where did they put Cal? Why can't I just turn my head to find one pair of friendly eyes? Why may I not hold one hand that knew us or him or me? Because the first three rows are for the immediate family, that's why.

The service was neither short nor long. I forced myself to tune out completely after the first Messingill. Solomon caught it without checking his notes, though; I'll give him that. "Didn't the rabbi speak beautifully?" I heard Aunt Addie sob to Cousin Leonard as the family trooped out, satisfied as after a Thanksgiving dinner. "You'd swear he knew him all his life." "And never met him once; amazing," Aunt Helena chimed in. (Yes, indeed. The definitive biography of what's-his-name-again, as told to Rabbi Dave. Sidewalk artist captures lifelikeness in five deft brush-strokes.) "Called him Messingill once or twice; otherwise he handled it just right," said my father.

"Lovely flowers—really beautiful, those irises. Who sent those?" asked my mother. "Julie, darling, did you see the arrangement I ordered, the big yellow one over there? I thought yellow for a change. All that white is so . . . dead-looking." She frowned and then smiled, reconciled to her involuntary quip.

"Yellow was lovely for a change, yes, Mother," I said obediently, as in the responsive reading. She smoothed my hair.

Outside the blistering sun waited; people were spilling into it, blinking and gasping at the attack. There were many faces I knew or should or might have known—or maybe not. All the hospital ones and more: from the army, from the book publishers, from the magazine, from college, from high school, from somewhere, anywhere, elsewhere, nowhere. Miranda was not there. The Pollocks had flown in from L.A.; the Howells had flown back from London. Stacks of shocked and saddened telegrams had flown or were flying in from wherever the shocked and saddened others were when they heard. Doria Perkins (DP?) was there, but I didn't see Nancy Wasserman (NW). The streaming faces jarred me, and I could only cry again because no one, *no one*, spoke. Suddenly I was hurling myself against one and then another, like a salt-blind swimmer caught by too swift and strong an undertow. Helplessly reaching for a hand or face to touch—something to hold or recognize—but then I lost it or they moved or I did. I wasn't drowning, just suffocating; the crushing waves were only heat and longing. At least wash over me, at least carry me out a little way. Wait, don't go. Help! I *need*. Was I trying to draw love or air? I only touched the streaming faces and skimmed the spray of outstretched hands, as if one of them might revive or restore some ragged fragment of me. "What can I say, Julie?" Barnaby Halstead was saying above a low pounding noise that may have been the dull echo of my voice. "He was a loved man, and he died."


The Museum of Modern Art regretted that it could not grant permission for Richard's ashes to be placed in the sculpture garden. One of the directors confided to Barney, who had tried to change their minds, that they feared it would set a precedent. First thing you know, every artist they'd ever overlooked would want to be buried there.

The Greenvale Crematorium sent a Certificate of Cremation, Re: Cremation number 201,649 (Richard Messinger), accompanied by a notice: "Dear Madam: Six months' storage of cremated remains is payable in advance at the rate of $2 per month. Payment of $12 is therefore requested. If payment is not received within ten (10) days, cremated remains of No. 201,649 (Richard Messinger) will be shipped to you, collect, via parcel post. Note: Scattering of ashes is expressly forbidden by New York State law. An illustrated brochure showing our complete selection of magnificent bronze memorial urns and niches is enclosed for your consideration."

Bills were also submitted by Drs. Mahler, Bleiweiss, Tompkins and one for fifteen dollars from a Dr. Harvey L.

Wiseman. I finally recalled that Dr. Wiseman was the elderly neurologist who had diagnosed Richard's coma as unmistakably the result of a brain tumor.

The summer is over now. We waited it out, spent or passed it somewhere, weathered it, survived it or lost it. Perhaps there really was no such summer. In any case, I see that somehow the closets have been emptied and the joint checking account closed.

Miranda Graham and Cal Jaffe are together again, I hear, though not from them. I haven't heard from them at all. Surprisingly, I am not surprised. Laurie says that's very healthy. (A sense of perspective is something you develop when all your other senses have taken leave of you; it's nature's way of compensating for your loss.)

Timmy Spector apparently wrestled with his conscience awhile, but finally sent a bill for $350, which he assured me Blue Cross would cover. They did. He also sent a copy of the August A.M.A. *Journal*, which contains a report on *Diagnosis and Management of Acute Hepatic Necrosis Caused by Anesthetic in a 39-Year-Old Male*, by Ralph G. Bleiweiss, M.D., and Timothy P. Spector, M.D. Other than that I haven't heard from the Spectors either.

I gave Nancy Wasserman's phone number to Arnie Buchalter.

I can eat dinner now. I've been going out some—no one special. Nicky and Matthew, not to mention my mother, have begun to complain that I'm not really *trying* to find a new Daddy. I will, I promise. We do need one. And Richard, I begin to think, Richard and I remain—friends. After all. Not that I forgive him—in fact, the one merciful thing is, we've both been spared that. But I keep wanting to say *something* to him—something like I ran into some old friend of his who's lost more hair than he has. Or that Matthew is suddenly growing a sense of humor like his. And I catch myself wondering whether he'd make a face over this dessert, or the bill for these shoes, and how would he look in sideburns.

For his sake I glare at strange men in their late thirties, just because there are so many of them. Why are you still here, for instance? I demand silently of them. You're just as bad a husband, worse probably, and nowhere near as lovable.

What it is, I guess, is that I don't really miss *him*; I miss something that must have been *us*. Because we *were* something, in spite of each other, weren't we? Ah, Richard, I'm sorry we didn't get to grow up together. Anyway, anyway, we have—how does the phrase go?—we have parted amicably.

Oh, and we got a new goldfish today. That's a start.

ABOUT THE AUTHOR

LOIS GOULD, *a former magazine editor and nonfiction writer,
is the wife of a New York psychiatrist. They have two
children and live in a Manhattan brownstone. This is her
first novel.*